Praise for *Nucleation*

"A superb, smart debut! Love this woman who has to fight her way back to the top using her intelligence and expertise. The confident, sharp details made me feel I was there, in Helen's head, at each step of her remarkable journey. I can't wait to read more from Unger, a welcome new voice in science fiction."
—Lissa Price, author of the Starters series

"Science fiction fans will be captivated by Unger's smart, plausible vision of the future of space travel, especially the elegant solution of utilizing quantum entanglement to communicate across light years."
—*Publishers Weekly*

"Forget your wide-eyed explorers, your prime directives, your philosophical debates. Forget all of Humanity nobly uniting in the face of the Unknown; our response to First Contact is far more likely to consist of mutual backstabbing in pursuit of the upper hand. *Nucleation* starts a clever journey down that less-traveled road, and passes through some fascinating territory en route."
—Peter Watts, author of *The Freeze-Frame Revolution*

"Author Kimberly Unger has created an absolutely inspiring main character who demonstrates how believing in one's conviction and own intuition will always lead to truth. *Nucleation* is an immersive tale that has blockbuster scale and emotional story-telling you won't soon forget."
—Terry Matalas, showrunner, *Star Trek: Picard*

"VERDICT: Unger's (*The Gophers of High Charity*) video game credits are well matched to this space adventure. Dialog among rivals, teammates, and machine interfaces keeps the story moving quickly. Recommended for fans of technothrillers and those who

appreciate a strong lead character navigating readers through the technical bits."
—*Library Journal*

"This smart, gripping debut weaves technology, embodiment, and corporate espionage into a tense vision of the future that readers won't be able to put down."
—Jacqueline Koyanagi, author of *Ascension*

"In technology we so often look to science fiction for inspiration. Kimberly Unger is the rare author with a foot in both worlds and it shows as she gives a thrilling glimpse into the future with *Nucleation*."
—Andrew Bosworth, Vice President of Augmented and Virtual Reality, Facebook

"*Nucleation* delivers top-notch suspense, deftly weaving together industrial espionage and first contact in a futuristic world that is all too plausible. Unger brings to her world a special sensibility for human psychology that gives realism to futuristic nanotech and corporate politics alike."
—Juliette Wade, author of *Mazes of Power*

"Unger weaves real-world insights about virtual reality, technology, and art into a space opera packed with high adventure and dastardly intrigue."
—Eliot Peper, author of *Veil* and *Breach*

"A near-future, tech-driven thriller marked by grounded characters, wondrous discovery, and a compelling mystery at its core."
—Joseph Mallozzi, Executive Producer, *Dark Matter*, *Stargate's SG-1*, *Atlantis*, *Universe*

"An inventive, exciting page turner that mixes mystery, bleeding edge technological speculation, and the promise of a potential sequel. If

Grisham was a better wordsmith and chose to write hard sf thrillers, it would look a lot like Kimberly Unger's gripping *Nucleation*."
—Charles Gannon, author of the Caine Riordan series

"*Contact*'s Ellie Arroway. "Story of Your Life""s Louise Banks. *The Last Astronaut*'s Sally Jansen. Add Helen Vectorovich to the ranks of great science fiction featuring remarkable, driven women serving as humanity's first contact with an alien race. With *Nucleation*, Kimberly Unger offers a richly detailed, thought-provoking peek into our not-so distant future and a mind-blowing means of taking us to the stars, but are we prepared for what awaits us out there?"
—Dayton Ward, author of *Star Trek: Kirk Fu Manual*

"Unger moves the reader from one vivid scene to the next, skillfully weaving in context and background . . . The verdict: A spectacular debut novel, at once thoughtful and exciting, packed with innovative ideas and plot twists."
—Deborah J. Ross, author of *Collaborators*

"*Nucleation* is a cool twist on the New Space Opera. Full of great ideas and combining elements of cyberpunk and space opera, it's a fun ride from start to finish."
—Karl Schroeder, author of *Stealing Worlds*

"Taut and snappy, *Nucleation* is solid science fiction with a whole lot of heart."
—Cat Rambo, author of *Carpe Glitter*

"As a lifelong fan of science fiction, I've read it all. But it's always a surprise to be captivated by a new work and for her first novel, Unger's *Nucleation* delivers a rich world-building experience on top of a narrative that grabs at you and satisfies that urge for something fresh. I'm so looking forward to more from this author."
—Kate Edwards, Executive Director of The Global Game Jam

NUCLEATION
KIMBERLY UNGER

KIMBERLY UNGER

NUCLEATION

TACHYON
SAN FRANCISCO

Nucleation
Copyright © 2020 by Kimberly Unger

Interior and cover design by Elizabeth Story

Tachyon Publications LLC
1459 18th Street #139
San Francisco, CA 94107
415.285.5615
www.tachyonpublications.com
tachyon@tachyonpublications.com

Series Editor: Jacob Weisman
Editor: Jaymee Goh

Print ISBN 13: 978-1-61696-338-5
Digital ISBN: 978-1-61696-339-2

Printed in the United States by Versa Press, Inc.

First Edition: 2020

10 9 8 7 6 5 4 3 2 1

for Chuck and Mary

00110011

CHAPTER ONE

THE GOLFBALL was reaching the end of its line drive—the hole in one an orbit around an orphan star. No planets depended on that burning ball of resources for life. Nothing would suffer when it launched its payload and started consuming every asteroid within reach. The starship-sized jumpgate would take a year to complete, after which the job of stripping Otlyan23's asteroid ring of every valuable asset could begin in earnest.

"Mark local time 24:48:16." The NAV's voice wasn't in Helen's ear, precisely. She didn't have ears out here. Different bodies took time to get used to, and ears were a luxury item. The vibrations of sound shivered along the walls of the Golfball's interior and filtered through receivers placed along her spine. "Station live. Station live. Station live."

"Live and well, Ted. Operator Helen Vectorovich, personal identifier T4T4-957." She responded automatically, rattling the words and numbers off without thinking. Helen was only the first shift on this year-long project and every shift started this way, every mission, every time. She refocused her vision as Ted worked to unlock the capsule controls from his station in the Fishbowl, a billion miles away. The lights around Helen brightened, moving from hibernation blue to heartbeat yellow. System after system came to life after two years of silent spinning through the black of deep space. From Helen's perspective through the eyes of the waldo, the room opened up like a cathedral, lights and buckypanels rising around her to a point just over her head. In real-world terms, the whole space was the size of a basketball, but from inside the waldo it was oh, so much bigger than that.

"Okay, Helen, let's start running the system checks." In the corner of her vision, a list of tasks popped up, bright enough to be seen, but not so bright that it obscured Helen's view.

"Starting with hull integrity." Helen confirmed from memory, rather than consulting the checklist, and was brought up short.

"No, wait." Ted's voice rang sharply in her head. "Stick to the new protocol, Helen, personal systems first. If your waldo goes out, this all goes sideways." The mission checklist filled the right side of her vision, blurring out that side of the room.

"And if the Golfball goes out?" she asked, even though she already knew the answer he'd give. The checklist slid out of view and was replaced by another, much more intimate list.

"We'll have you in there to fix it."

"Good thing this *waldo* works in a vacuum then." Glib replies were part of the job. Confident chatter was a great defense, not just against the butterflies in your stomach, but against the analysts who would go over your comm chatter line by line if anything went wrong. Helen and Ted both had been through that wringer before; the Ferguson's Asteroid Incident had made both their careers, but it had also made them much more careful.

Helen turned her attention back to the waldo's systems. This robot body wasn't humanoid so much as arachnoid: eight legs folded up around a glittering central core of processing power and memory shards. Helen carefully unfolded each pair of legs, noting the fine grey dust that arose from them, and sketched her motions in the air. A quick refocus of the lenses showed her the thousands of tiny corpses, left-behind fragments of the nano-robotic *eenies* that had assembled the ship and its instrumentation out of interplanetary dust. She grabbed a few still images from the waldo's memory and sent them through the quantum Feed to Ted's screens.

"Ted, do you see all this dust?"

"Stay focused, Helen. We need you checked out as quickly as possible."

"Yeah, but check out the pics. Everything should have been used up in construction, I shouldn't be seeing these eenie shells all over the place." Everything, from the ship, to the waldo, on down to the idiot lights had been built up from a thumb-sized packet of eenies shot through a wormhole the size of a quarter. It was a hugely efficient way to establish a presence around a far-flung system, but it took a long time to build out.

"Everything in order, this is all on record, remember? We'll look at them when we get to checking out the ship. Protocol, protocol, protocol."

The waldo couldn't scowl, but Helen tried it anyway. Waldo Operators like herself were, in a word, interchangeable, as long as there were protocols, lists of instructions to follow. No one pilot got too comfortable with one kind of waldo because you never knew where they were going to put you next.

"Fine." Helen ran through the checklist, meticulously testing each joint, each actuator, every fiber in the robot body she was remote-piloting. The automatic checks had been run well before she'd been entangled. These first tests were all about her ability to control the body down to the fingertips. Ninety percent of her jobs were like this, following the list, endless lists that could just as easily be run by an AI, if you asked most people.

Leg eight felt sluggish; Helen felt it before the computer gave her the heads-up. Less than a millisecond slower than its siblings to respond, it took her a little extra focus to get it to match pace with its twin. "Ted, are you getting this? Leg eight?"

"Affirmative. Still inside the workable parameters."

"Yes, but it still should be a *perfect* match. This whole rig is professionally built, not extruded by some kids' crappy apartment printer. It's not supposed to have that kind of slippage."

There was a pause before her NAV replied. Entangled communication meant no lag-time, which meant that Ted was considering, or maybe consulting with someone before he replied. "Helen, are you telling me you cannot work within these tolerances?"

"No, I'm handing you the opportunity to wring a mea-culpa payment out of whatever contractor slipped a decimal point." Smart-ass was the only response that played well. Too many complaints got you written up. Keep the NAVs laughing and they might not take every comment seriously enough to notate. Piss a NAV off and you'd hang yourself with the rope they'd given you.

Except Ted. She'd been partnered with Ted long enough to know he wasn't about to write her up for being particular. Helen handled the hardware, Ted handled the management. Between the two of them they'd managed to stay one of Far Reaches' top operations teams for the past year. *A position that makes high-profile gigs like running the Golfball much easier to get assigned to.*

Ted's snort reverberated in her head. "Good luck collecting on that . . . it's all code by committee these days, you know that."

"Team-based engineering provides better results," she quoted, tossing a line from one of their training manuals back at him. In the years since they'd arrived at Far Reaches, they'd found their rhythm working within a structured system, but Ted's rebellious streak was always looking for an opportunity to complain. Three years before, the Ferguson's Asteroid Incident had made them an inseparable team, which meant covering for each other's personality quirks. Ted handled the people, Helen handled the hardware.

"Committees aren't teams, Helen. In fact, they're the opposite of teams." She could hear his voice change, the words spoken so the rest of the team back at Flight Ops could hear him.

Ted never could resist an audience.

The items on the task list turned green one by one as Helen worked her way down the line.

"Are you seeing the bad sensor on memory shard three?" he asked.

"Yep." Helen stretched out an arm and popped a claw-tipped manipulator out to give the shard in question a tap. The numbers on her screen changed, running up and down as the offender shifted in the socket. "It's just loose, hold on."

"Loose?"

"I'm deploying point-one-one picoliters of mix M37 at the base to re-seat the shard." Helen rattled off the specifics so Ted could add them to the mission report. The blue gel, loaded with specialized eenies, filled the empty gaps in the socket and started to harden immediately. "Can you run the diagnostic?"

The eenies were too small to hold their own programming. They would pick up on the instructions Ted broadcast through the NAV computer and repair the chip's base to match the specs. As long as he sent the right programming streaming over the air, everything would go smoothly.

"It's not supposed to be loose, Helen."

"Congratulations, that makes two, count 'em, *two* mea-culpas on one job. Company record is five, Ted, are we going for the record on this trip?" Helen was settling into the waldo properly now; dispensing the repair mites had been as simple as drumming a fingertip on a dashboard. It was telling, the things that Ted worried about. As long as she'd known him, his focus had been on the people, the reports, what to say and how to say it—he was the medium between the managers and the waldo-jockeys like Helen.

The memory shard came back online, joining the twenty others now jostling for her attention. Helen put them out of her mind for now, focusing on getting the checklist out of the way so they could get on with the fun stuff.

"Are you seeing the readings from array two?"

"Array two? Ted, we've still got to finish this bit here."

"I'm breaking protocol." Something in his tone of voice shifted, a note of panic that shouldn't have been there. "NAV override one-five-five."

Helen felt the locks release and her waldo was free, unrestricted. It was amazing. It was totally off book. She didn't dare move a finger, or a claw. "Ted, what's up?"

"Remember how we were just talking about how you could fix the Golfball?"

Oh shit.

"You're going to have to fix the Golfball."

"Oh sh—" She cut the words off before they could be recorded. "Okay. How bad?"

"Bad. Bad enough where I just put in a call to Ivester and XE-RMo, so let's get on this. I want something to tell them when he logs in."

"Okay, what broke and where do I start?" Helen waited for Ted to throw the appropriate checklist into her line of sight. She counted to two . . . then three . . .

Nothing?

"Ted? Do we have a protocol? There is a plan for this, right?" She could feel her heart rate quicken. A billion miles away, trapped in her coffin, her palms began to sweat.

"Working on it." Two or three lists popped up as Ted cycled through, one after the other, all with names like "Catastrophic Hull Failure" and "Venting Acidic Atmosphere Breaches."

"Ted, can we run something with 'Catastrophic' in the title? It'll make me sound more like a badass." It was meant to be funny, to take the edge off her own worry. What was supposed to be a high-end, high-priced milk run was starting to turn into the kind of situation that could end with her driving moles for the remainder of her career. Ted wasn't listening and the joke fell flat.

The lists settled down and Helen was faced with a number. No title, no designations, just a number, 9523. After each step was listed a single word. *Evaluate.* It was a slow list. Test and assess, test and assess. It wasn't Ted's usual efficient task-making. It was a list full of fear.

"This is it?" She didn't *need* to ask, but she did, just to be on record. Even when they were crèche-kids, Ted never operated from a point of fear. That caution alone told her things were coming off the rails.

"So far. See where it says '*Evaluate*'? Those are our riff-points. That's where we get to make stuff up if we need to. Just make sure you verbally justify each and every decision before you take action so we have it all documented." They were moving into unfamiliar territory now. A small part, a very small part, of Helen's brain wished they could just go back to following the original boring checklist.

"Roger that. First on the list, checking hull integrity."

This time around, Ted didn't interrupt. Helen opened a connection from her waldo to the bank of glittering shards that comprised the Golfball's processing core. It was much like watching a video. She could see the data coming in, but at this level she couldn't interact with it: that was all on Ted. The waldo and the Golfball were isolated from one another, two completely separate entities, down to the eenies that built them. Any connection between them had to be made manually.

"Ted, are you seeing this?" The numbers never lied; it was Helen's most and least favorite thing about them.

"Affirmative."

"It's like the hull never got finished."

"Just the facts please, we don't do theories."

"I'm the one running the waldo, I *get* to theorize. Especially since I'm going to be making the repairs." The visualization of the outside of the Golfball appeared in her line of sight. "The reason you're not getting any data from sectors two through six is there are no sectors two through six." She spun the image, noting where the green lines crossed into red as numbers came and went.

"What? Why?" That note of panic was back, more than a note, an aria of panic that Ted's voice wasn't qualified to sing.

"There's no signal coming back, no power going in. It's gotta be something simple. Maybe the eenies just didn't get initialized properly?"

In the corner of her vision she could see the mirror image of Ted's console displayed in outline. Ports opened and closed as he dug deeper into the Golfball's programming than Helen was allowed to go. Helen did her own digging, accessing the layout of the Golfball to see if she could get a better read on the outer hull.

The hissing sound broke her concentration.

"Ted, are you *whistling*?"

"Am I what?"

"Shut up a second, I hear something." It was a high-pitched sound, tickling the same place in her brain that a dentist's drill did, making the muscles along her spine twitch. She checked to see if any of the sensors inside the capsule were picking it up.

"I hear it too, but it's not in the capsule. It's in the entanglement Feed somehow." Ted's voice was hard to make out through the sound.

"In the Feed?" The Feed was quantum, less than a pinprick of matter that allowed her body back home to control the waldo from a distance measured in years rather than miles. It was an intimate, two-way connection, one molecule to one molecule. Whatever that *sound* was, it couldn't be in the Feed.

The sound hit a higher pitch, she could hear it, but not *hear* it, like it was being applied directly to the space inside her skull.

"Ted, can you stop it? Find out where it's coming from?" Her right eye went blind as the sound twisted in her skull like a knife. Curling up to defend against it was no help. The waldo body had no soft bits to muffle the noise, if it was a noise. Helen hung in the center of the Golfball, legs curled up like a spider playing dead.

"Ted?" She ground his name out. Her other eye, the one still receiving input, had stopped making sense, the lines and colors jumping like an old CRT screen that had encountered a magnet.

Something responded. Something low and shattered and horrible. The piece of her mind that wasn't scrabbling for a way out insisted it was Ted's voice. She wanted to scream, to push back against the sound with her own, primal roar. *Fight or flight*, a small voice said in her head. She gritted her teeth, willed herself to differentiate between where the sound stopped and her own thoughts began. *Always fight.*

Without warning, the sound stopped. The emptiness that followed hurt almost as badly.

Helen forced herself to focus, adjusted the lenses, unfolded her legs, and reached out. Data continued to flow in, uninterrupted, sketching lines and symbols in the space behind her eyes.

"What. The. Hell." She was trembling, the involuntary twitches translating to the waldo in a thousand tiny adjustments. Just in case he hadn't heard her the first time, she roared the words, "WHAT THE HELL, TED!"

She started tearing apart the data, sucking it out of the Golfball and searching for the source of the sound. Protocols be damned, something was really wrong.

"Vectorovich."

"Piss off, Ted."

"Vectorovich, respond please." It took her a moment to figure out that it wasn't Ted's voice coming down the line.

"Where's Ted?" She barked the question, ignoring the consequences of snapping at management. Ted had already told her Ivester had been called in; for some reason they had pulled him off the line and Ivester was taking over, that had to be it.

That thought brought her up short.

The entanglement that linked her body to the waldo was no less complicated than the one that also tied in Ted to the Golfball as her Navigator. Unlinking him should have taken an hour or more. Whoever it was had to be using the emergency channel. There was always a backup ready, but then she should be in contact with them both at once.

"Your NAV had to be taken offline for the short-term." The sentence followed another of those long, considering pauses she was coming to hate. "What is your current status?"

Helen wanted to laugh, the kind that made the other person step back a pace.

"Current status is indeterminate, sir." Helen didn't stop pulling apart the data, but all she could find were errored-out figures and bad connections. Everything the Golfball could throw at her was popping up into her line of sight and there were still no answers. She continued talking, more of an information dump than a conversation, speaking out loud so the recorders would pick it up and add it to the mission logs. "We brought the Golfball live, but are getting no readings at all from sensors two through six. Ted and I had just started trying to determine what was responsible for the dead areas when we got some kind of horrendous feedback."

"Feedback?"

"I'm not sure how else to describe it." She held back, reminding herself that whoever this guy was, he'd just walked into the middle of their situation. "Something, I think it was a sound, started up. The last thing Ted said about it was that it was in the Feed. I experienced visual impairment and physical discomfort for the duration. You'll have to ask Ted what he got on his end." The more clinical phrasing played better on the recordings, never mind that her heart was racing and she felt as though tiny insects were crawling over every inch of skin. The one that panics first . . . It was like a high-stakes game of chicken when a mission went bad. Somebody was going to go down for the mistakes, even if she managed to pull the mission back out of the bin. If she started freaking out now, there would be no saving her. As long as she stayed cool and collected, Ted could handle management in the aftermath.

"Affirmative. That follows with the records as we are seeing them."

The crawling feeling on her skin was getting worse, harder to ignore. She popped out a diamond-tipped claw and scratched at the itch, leaving visible furrows in the carbon fibers of the waldo's limb.

"Have you checked the integrity of the payload yet?"

The Golfball's payload had long since fallen off Helen's list of things to check up on. If they'd managed to finish up on the protocols, she would have gotten to it in proper order, but now . . . Well, now she had more important things to worry about.

"No, sir." She contemplated throwing Ted onto the rails, dropping the blame into his square. It wouldn't make any difference;

there was going to be more than enough trouble to go around unless they could rescue the mission. The thought was distracting. She scratched, felt the fingertip break through the skin. When she turned her attention to the damage, she was struck again by the presence of way too much dust. The waldo's itchy leg appeared to be oh-so-gently sublimating, dissolving into powder.

What the hell . . .

She ignored the voice in her ear and refocused her attention on the waldo, shunting all the data off to the side. She had missed it on the first pass. *The corpses.* All those microscopic eenie shells that gathered like dust on the panels and joints. Ted hadn't thought they were important. Helen opened the video recorder and pulled her focus in tight, zooming in to examine them, dumping copies of the video to the waldo's memory. Maybe one in a thousand of them showed some sign of movement. Like hermit crabs, the dead shells had been occupied by something else? Something that was busily deconstructing every surface it touched.

"Sir, we might have a bigger problem."

"With all due respect, Operator Vectorovich, the biggest problem right now is—" There was backchatter, Helen could hear it. However Ivester was linked in to the Feed, it wasn't a secure connection. "Can you confirm the data you sent over earlier?"

"Confirmed. The whole damn cabin is covered in dust. I'm continuing to keep a record."

More backchatter. The voices faded into the background as she stayed in close focus, watching the tiny forms grind and chew. She'd thought the eenies had failed to finish building the capsule, but the opposite was true. They'd been stopped by a microscopic army. An alien army that was doing exactly what the Earth-built eenies were programmed to do. They were breaking the Golfball back down into stardust, back into components that could be used to build anything, as long as you could transmit the right program. She'd come online not into an experiment on the edge of failure, she'd walked into a battleground too small to see.

"Vectorovich, can you confirm the payload?"

"The payload?" She refocused on the voice from a billion miles away. "I'll have to open a two-way link with the Golfball to do that. Protocols require—"

"Vectorovich, we have lost all capability to access the Golfball's systems. Whatever killed Theodore Westlake managed to lock us out."

Wait. Killed? She must not have heard correctly because that was impossible. The itch was back, coupled with a sour taste that didn't belong.

"You have to deploy the payload, do you understand?"

The payload, of course, the payload. The whole point of this mission. Everything else was expendable, the Golfball, the waldo, everything in service for the greater good. Everything to deliver a block of eenies the size of her head, big enough to build the mother of all power stations.

"Confirmed." She didn't have to refocus to see them now; the tiny alien eenies were swarming, covering the lenses like overlapping scales. The itch was almost too much. She could feel them now, FEEL THEM as they nibbled and bit. She continued to pull data, now focusing on dumping as much information as she possibly could down the line to the NAV station. They attacked her joints, the soft spots where the dust could get in between the cracks. Leg eight went first. Helen had to laugh at that, they had first gone for the weakest member, a mindset she could understand. She opened the direct link to the Golfball, ignoring the warnings that clustered around the edges of her vision. *Deploy the payload, then break the link to the waldo*—she would snap back to her own body and spend the next six months fighting with the psychiatrist, no problem.

"Deploying payload." She felt the crack and shiver through the legs of the waldo as the payload was launched from the Golfball's cargo space. No rockets, no jetfuel, just the clever application of inertia and physics.

"Confirmed, we are receiving telemetry."

"Permission to return?" she asked, debating whether or not she should just hit the button and eject, even without their sanction.

"Granted."

Helen breathed a sigh of relief. The itch, the gnawing disassembly of the waldo was all background noise now. She could ditch out, go back to her own body and let the union lawyers sort out the mess. After this tour, even the moles seemed like a dream gig for the next couple of years.

"Confirmed. Operator Helen Vectorovich, disembarking. Entanglement disengaged in three . . . two . . . one . . ." Helen focused her vision on the Golfball's main panel, entered in her personal identifier, and keyed the release.

The view blinked once, twice. The connection pulled her back, the long slow slide back into her own body, more than a billion miles away. She could hear voices, a cacophony filling the void of the quantum feed in a language that had no reference.

CHAPTER TWO

GETTING ABRUPTLY CUT OFF from the waldo was like waking up with a hangover. The nasty kind that followed booze, ice cream, and parasols with little flowers on them.

Ow, what the hell? The reaction headache didn't wait for Helen to take a breath. The pain was immediate, eyeball-deep, and made worse by a nerve-deep twang that came out of nowhere. She'd been dumped right back into her own still paralyzed and disoriented body. Pain and panic closed in, chasing her down the billion miles from deep space to the inside of her own head. The bubble of the coffin was always dark, to help ease the transition from waldo to self, but today the warm and soothing black felt alien and isolating.

Helen was trapped in an immovable body with a voice that failed to reach her lips.

Slow down. The idea came to her from long experience rather than rational thought. Helen tried to take comfort in the checkboxes she knew were being ticked off, one by one, toward her release. The coffin started dripping drugs into her bloodsteam to counter the backlash from her barely controlled return.

One breath.

Two breaths.

The outer corners of her vision were framed with the soothing blue lines and icons of Insight, Far Reaches' communications system.

Little lights and readouts winked green and blue as the screens inside the coffin came to life. Normally it was a bit disappointing to come back to earth. Today it was a relief.

Helen still couldn't move, but the panic started to recede. This was familiar. This was safe.

Protocol, protocol, protocol.

"Helen, are you awake in there?" Against the black a hawkish face appeared, the golden brown skin and silver hair in sharp relief against the darkness inside the coffin. Dr. Lillian Hofstaeder, the company doctor, worried about the wrong side of the emergency as always. She was smiling gently. Never a good sign. Helen was fairly sure the woman practiced that smile in the mirror. Doc was perpetually worried, perpetually insincere. In Helen's opinion she was all too eager to sideline an operator at the first hint of trouble.

Hofstaeder's just another box to be checked off.

Something is out of order here. Where the hell is Ted? There were holes in her recollection, pieces missing. They'd come back, they always did after a bad drop-out. The checklists demanded immediate human contact after a bad ejection, actual contact. Face to face through a screen didn't cut it. In the time they'd been working together, Ted's had been the first face she'd seen every time something went wrong. It gave a tangible connection back to the real world; it helped fill in the holes in their conversations. Instead Helen's first friendly face was through the Insight, off protocol, all wrong.

"Yes." Helen responded curtly. The neoprene supersuit that restrained her, kept her from banging around inside the coffin, didn't stop her from talking. This wasn't her first bad mission. Operating a waldo by remote across a billion miles of space had occasional problems, but even within the bounds of really bad trips, this was turning out to be a doozy.

Normally they yanked you out of the pod as quickly as possible and dragged you off to the medical bay.

Normally they popped the top and got you back to seeing real light, breathing real air, before they did anything else.

Normally they stuck to the goddamn checklist.

Helen was being held in limbo and nobody was telling her why.

"Doc, why are we off protocol?" The words left her lips as quickly as she could call them to mind.

"Relax, Helen, we will have you out of there in a couple of minutes."

Helen recognized that tone of voice. It meant you were being "handled." It meant something had gone wrong and they were scrambling to come up with an explanation. She shifted her attention to getting stiff fingers moving across the keypads inside the coffin. Hofstaeder might not be willing to give her details, but something in the coffin's computer might.

"We are pulling your connection pod entirely. Dr. Ivester cut all the media Feeds, so the reporters started mobbing the Mortuary to try and get a story." Helen caught Hofstaeder's grimace. Doc might not take overt issue with the operators' grim nicknames, but she hated using them herself. It didn't fit with her strangely rosy mindset.

That's going to cause a mess. She'd managed to launch the payload, this she knew with certainty. Other memories were blurred, slipping away as she tried to grab on to them. Between the emergency disentangle and whatever recovery drugs Doc was giving her through the coffin, Helen's memories were starting to stutter.

So what made them cut the media Feed? It was an extreme step. Establishing contact with the Golfball had been a well-publicized event. Far Reaches hired the best operators and navigators to run their offworld exploration exploits and Ivester loved to show that aspect off whenever possible. Ted had enjoyed it of course, shaking hands and chatting with every warm body in the room. A media blackout was against Ivester's "transparency" policy. He showed off their mistakes so the wins would glow brighter. *So what did I miss while I was out there?*

The coffin's computer was a dead end, its network access cut off. Undaunted, Helen continued to poke around in the coffin's subsystems, driven by a need to do something.

"I don't know who decided what, but everything went dark," Dr.

Hofstaeder's voice continued blithely. "They're taking you straight to medical to get checked out, so relax and enjoy the trip." As Doc said the word "relax," Helen felt so much better. A flood of warmth and smiles started between her shoulder blades and crept forward.

"Can you at least shut down the supersuit so I can wiggle my toes?" A crawling sensation started in her feet and calves, prickling like little needles. The needles and the smiles disagreed, coming together somewhere in the middle and making her decidedly uncomfortable.

"Not until we can open the lid. If it makes you feel any better, Ivester's pulled the entire team. Everyone's sequestered in the third-floor conference room. XERMo will be on hand to oversee the next steps and Ivester will be addressing the group shortly."

That can't be good. XERMo was the government oversight team; they stayed invisible most of the time. Far Reaches made sure they were brought in on every major incident. *And a major incident is not what we needed today.*

"Can you pass a message to Ted, have him get me a link in so I can see the meeting?" Helen stayed focused on Hofstaeder's voice by main force of will, staring into the black in front of her face.

Wait. When did I lose the video? The soothing lines and whorls of the Insight were still painted on the screens that hung in front of her face. At some point Hofstaeder's angular face had vanished. Helen couldn't remember when that had happened.

"I'll make sure you get a copy of the recording later." Hofstaeder was a little too quick to answer, a little too eager to agree, voice pitched a little too high.

The whisper started in the trailing edge of Hofstaeder's reassurances. In the dark of the coffin, an echo of the scream that had chased her back up the rabbit hole struggled to come to the fore. Helen closed her eyes and focused on that memory. She tried to pick out words, phrases, anything to tie it down to an actual language. It gave her something else to do, some other place to hold her focus until she could get loose.

"Helen, are you all right in there?"

Helen opened her eyes again, irritated, train of memory interrupted.

"I'm fine, Doc. Wake me when we get there."

"And how are you feeling?"

It was the kind of idle chatter you used to hold focus to keep a patient from going into shock. What was worse, Helen should have felt some sort of concern, some brief spark of panic. Nothing. *Everything's fine.* It calcified the idea that she was being manipulated, handled. Helen couldn't stir up the impulse to be angry, but she could tick off those boxes. She knew what she should be doing, even if she didn't have the drive to make it happen, not yet.

"Doc, what aren't you telling me?" Helen rooted around in her own head, looking to reconnect with that moment of panic, the memory of whispers that made so little sense.

"I told you, they're moving the coffin to keep you out of the spotlight. The press swarmed the Mortuary."

"No, that's not it." Helen found the feeling she was looking for, the memory of panic, and let it rise. The fear helped counter whatever chemical Hofstaeder was dripping into her system. *Now there's an idea.* Helen ran her fingers across the keypad again. The screen woke up and began giving her information. All operators had top-level access to the chemical drip from the coffin. Hofstaeder could override it, but it still belonged to Helen, she had the final say. *She's been keeping me distracted.* The list of drugs paraded across her line of sight, names she was intimately familiar with. One name in particular left her cold.

"Doc, what are you loading me up with? They won't let me back into a coffin for weeks after this." The offender was an anti-psychotic, the silver bullet if an operator snapped and lost the link between reality and the inside of a waldo. It was not, should not, be applicable here.

"It's standard procedure after a bad drop-out," Hofstaeder explained.

The excuse was weak, spoken for the mission recordings, and

Hofstaeder knew it. Helen could hear the lie in her voice. Every operator knew the names and effects of every damn drug on their own personal biology. Custom cocktails were standard for the higher-end operators and Helen was no exception. That Doc would be using the big guns on her meant something had gone very, very wrong. The little spark of panic flared up and Helen directed it right at her current problem.

"Bullshit." Helen ground the word out between clenched teeth, not bothering to keep her opinions to herself this time. *Someone needs me quiet and compliant.* She might not be able to move her body, but any operator was far from defenseless. The difference was that Helen had no compunctions about twisting the coffin computers to her own devices. Those little flickers of terror and panic were bringing her back to herself, making it easier to resist, easier to tackle the problem at hand. An adult lifetime spent operating every type of waldo, every type of remote system meant Helen knew, in great detail, exactly what the coffins were capable of. She knew better than Hofstaeder exactly how to fight back from inside the machine.

"Wait, Helen."

Helen ignored the doctor, continued to hack the coffin's computer from within. She changed the drug mix, taking out the worst offenders and countering what Doc had given her. A drip of stimulant, a kiss of dopamine by-product, and everything came into focus. Her decisions belonged to her again.

"Talk fast, Doc."

Hofstaeder was bargaining now; she knew what Helen was up to. "Give us five more minutes. Once they get you to the medical wing, we can get you properly checked out."

Helen had tracked down the subroutine that kept most of her body paralyzed within the supersuit. She examined it, checking the up and downstream connections before making any adjustments. On the outside of the coffin, it would take less than five keystrokes to set her free. From inside the code, it required her changing just one variable.

"Helen, we are trying to get you into isolation before . . ."

"Before what, Doc? And stop screwing with the recovery drugs, I've revoked your access."

"Helen."

Helen released the body lock and keyed in the exit sequence to open the coffin lid. The lights inside the coffin started to glow, giving her a better sense of the edges, the tightness of the space.

"I didn't snap, Hofstaeder, there's no reason to isolate me, the only reason I'm not walking around already is because you're keeping me in here. So what the hell else is going on?" Now that Helen had regained control, she felt compelled to move, to push forward into the light.

"I can't give you all the details, Helen, I don't have them."

"Then I'll have to go ask myself. You said Ivester isolated everyone on the third floor?" The lid on the coffin rotated out of the way and Helen got the impression of a tight warehouse room that went straight up into the black.

"Sorry, ma'am."

A hand came down from the dim-lit space outside the pod and slapped Helen on the forehead. She had enough time to register a Far Reaches insignia and a flash of bright white before she was stunned back into the dark.

CHAPTER THREE

THE ALIEN WHISPERS RECEDED. Stripped into broken phrases and impressions, they disintegrated in the light as Helen opened her eyes.

"She's back!"

Helen winced at the shout and turned her head to find the source. Someone had unlocked the supersuit while she'd been unconscious. The tiny pops from the various tubes coming free made her shiver. She wiggled her toes. The numbness that usually came with a long-term tour hadn't had time to settle in. It took her a moment to remember that her trip to the Golfball had been cut short. She was back early, and for the worst possible reason.

"Keller, she's up!" the tech on station repeated, not taking his eyes off the controls. Helen sat up, drawing her knees to her chest, rolling the tightness out of her shoulders. The coffins were gel-lined, built for work shifts of eight hours or more. This time Helen felt sore all over, like she'd been banging around the inside of a tin can.

The recovery rooms at Far Reaches were designed with transition in mind. Eenie-maintained walls of duct tape grey, floor of thick, soundless blue carpet, and lights that never reached more than half their possible intensity. The transition from a day- or week-long wholly in-your-head experience back to the squishy heft of the real world wasn't always a smooth one. It could take a few hours to make all those connections feel real again.

The imposition of other people into your personal space was part of the process. In the early days of the program, operators had retreated, becoming isolated from their peers, their families. In extreme cases, they might be unwilling to connect with the world around them at all, save through the same kind of waldo system that had gotten them into trouble to begin with. There were still a few of them out there, operating long-haul asteroid miners, only coming out of their self-imposed stasis to maintain the meat that housed their minds.

In quieter moments, Helen herself felt the pull constantly, the siren-like call to plug back in as soon as possible, to return to the waldo. For most operators, it was a constant, unspoken battle. Manic bouts of physicality, tattoos, sex parties, extreme sports, all to push off thoughts of blessed isolation for just one more shift. True to an operator's isolationist mindset, Helen was already regretting waking up from this mission.

When Ingat Keller showed up, his expression was somewhere between panic and annoyance.

"Just what the hell happened up there?" Keller was a slight man. Normally his skin had a warmth that matched his demeanor, but something had drained all the bright right out of him. Even the garishly patterned shirt that made him stand out in a crowd seemed oddly diminished, colors washed out.

"Something ate the Golfball!" Helen answered without forethought. Keller ran flight operations, and unlike Hofstaeder, had been an operator himself. Inside the hyper-competitive environment that Far Reaches encouraged, having Keller in your corner was something not to take lightly. You didn't hide shit from Keller. Helen swallowed twice, trying to clear the gravel from her voice. Keller cracked the twist-top off a water bottle and passed it over. Helen accepted it gracefully.

"You've got about a minute before Ivester and the rest of management get down here, so talk fast."

"We didn't have time to figure out the specifics, but Keller . . . Something ATE the goddamned Golfball," Helen explained tersely. She gripped the edge of the coffin with her free hand, feeling the line of the rubber seal press into her palm. The underlying drive, the need to get out there and do something, to act, was still inexplicably there. Like she'd forgotten to close the door behind her and a hurricane was coming.

"You got the payload deployed, right?" Keller was all business, standing stiffly, carefully back from the coffin. This was not going to be a conversation, everything was being recorded. His tone told Helen to hold her flood of statements and questions, told her to be careful. *Something's wrong, something's up.*

"Yes, the payload launched," she admitted. The lights in the room came up; she could feel the shift in the air as the outer doors opened in anticipation of visitors. He should know that, why doesn't he know that?

Keller visibly relaxed, "Okay, maybe this isn't as bad as it might be." He rubbed his hands together and paced a few steps back and forth, footfalls muffled by the carpet. He was making her nervous. Keller's agitation, his body language, the fact that he was avoiding looking her in the eye, all spelled out disaster.

"Keller, where the hell is Ted?" Helen spoke the words before the question had formed in her mind.

"He's in ICU, they shifted him to County Medical." Keller kept pacing, still not looking at her. All the drugs in the world couldn't counteract the chill that crawled up Helen's spine.

"ICU? Keller, what happened to Ted? How the hell does a NAV end up in ICU?" The words came out in a rush. A NAV didn't have the full-body hardware to link into a waldo. They didn't take the physical or psychological risks that came along with total immersion. They ran everything from the command center, not so affectionately called the Fishbowl. NAVs kept all those connections at arm's length except the quantum entanglement Feed itself.

Helen's feeling of urgency was replaced by a hole, a sick empty space, like she'd checked off a box and had nothing new to replace it with.

Whatever had happened to Ted, she was sure she only had part of the story, but she couldn't get around those holes in her memory.

Keller bit his lower lip. "Look, we get through the debrief and we can work through all the details."

"That bad?"

The sick feeling in her stomach turned to acid. She imagined it chewing away at her insides.

"I'm not gonna lie, it's bad. But it's in the hands of the medical team now. We need to focus on what happened out there and how we keep you two from taking the hit for it." Keller jerked his thumb towards the sound of expensive leather shoes rattling down the stairwell. "Hofstaeder's on hold for the moment. You need to focus on explaining just what happened out at Otlyan23 as best you can without pissing anyone off."

Helen took a deep breath and swung her legs out over the edge of the coffin. Damned if she was going to be caught sitting down. She needed to be on her feet to face the fallout.

"Operator Vectorovich." Dr. Ivester came through the door first. Close on his heels were the pair of XERMo reps that had been in attendance when the Golfball had gone live.

The eXoplanet Exploration and Resource Management oversight team had practically moved in as mission-time had approached. You couldn't work with the kind of equipment Far Reaches shot into space without XERMo's sign-off. Helen had met the government agents before the launch. They had been there in the background for the photo op, lots of handshaking in the place of real interaction. The look on the Ivester's face said the speeches for both the good mission outcome and the bad had been scrapped.

"Dr. Ivester," Helen returned evenly.

"I didn't expect you awake so soon." Ivester stopped abruptly, looked her up and down, ending his assessment at her eyes. He was a head taller than both she and Keller, skin a shade lighter than

Helen's and hair in that early state of grey that said, "Fuck it, I'm distinguished now." The room light reflected off glasses with heavy, translucent frames. They allowed him to carry his computer screens with him at all times.

"Let's be civilized. Get out of your supersuit and meet us in Conference Three for the debrief. Make sure Keller gets your hard drives and speak to no one else until you are debriefed, do you understand?"

Helen nodded. "Understood."

Ivester breezed out, the XERMo guys following without a sound. The CTO had that effect; he set a course and dragged everyone else along in his wake.

Helen didn't take the time for a sigh of relief. She threw Keller a woeful glance, got a shrug in reply, and continued her walk across the carpet to the locker room.

Her brain was still trying to process, trying to set the order of events straight. Everything that came back down the link between her and the waldo was recorded. All the data from her heart rate to the feeling of the waldo joints disintegrating should have been stored somewhere. Not only for future analysis by the techs, but as a "cover your ass" in case something went wrong. Far Reaches' impeccable information gathering was one of the reasons they'd been able to stay ahead of their competitors. Her job during a debrief would be to put it all in context. Between the context and the data, she and Ted should be exonerated.

Helen continued to try to figure out what she'd missed. What was behind the feeling that she needed to turn around and get back out to the Golfball right NOW.

Which is stupid. And impossible, Helen reminded herself. Protocol demanded an operator be kept out of the coffins after a bad drop-out. She wouldn't be able to run so much as a training mission after this until she had Hofstaeder's checkmark.

Probably shouldn't have pissed Doc off.

The neoprene supersuit peeled off, releasing the layer of conductive gel it had held close to her skin. The shower was hot, the towels were dry, and the clothes she had in her locker had not yet picked up that vague pong of warm sweat socks. It helped her feel more human, a little less close to the machine. Not completely, but a little.

Helen exited the Mortuary with her hair still wet and headed for the mission rooms. The sound of her shoes on carpet was overridden by everyday noise. The interstellar mining duties of Far Reaches continued around her. With over a hundred paired OPs and NAVs, and even more support personnel, the bread-and-butter operations dwarfed Line Drive by comparison. The heart and soul of the company continued to putter on around her as if the world hadn't changed one bit.

Maybe it hasn't. Helen had done her job, fulfilled the mission requirements. The payload had been released into its near-final orbit, even as the Golfball had begun to fail around her. Despite all those successes, all those boxes being checked off, there was no getting around the fact that Ted was now in the ICU. That was going to have to be explained and dealt with.

He'll be fine, she told herself. *Ted's in the best hands.* THAT was the one thing she could be sure of in all this mess.

Helen almost stopped short at the sight of two armed XERMo agents flanking the door to the conference room. Everyone knew that a chunk of Line Drive's funding came from government backers, but she was surprised to see their reps out in uniform. They'd taken up position outside the room where pizza and dry cupcakes had commemorated successful first contact with the Golfball just hours before.

They didn't stop her, didn't even look at her as she approached the door and tapped the handle. The NFC chip embedded in her wrist exchanged a word with the lock and the doors swung open in response.

Inside, every member on the Golfball mission support team had self-segregated into little protective groups. Helen paused and took a read of the room before focusing on Dr. Ivester and the XERMo liaison, Dr. Frederic Tate, having some kind of discussion. Tate was already too far into his sentence to stop talking but Ivester waved Helen into an empty seat. She wasn't the only OP in the room. Mira and Bright, the team slated to take the second shift, looked surprised to see her but made space for her at their table. Both were wearing pre-mission sweatsuits in Far Reaches blue. Mira had her thick yellow hair pinned up at the back and Bright had long ago opted for a buzzcut to keep his frizzy black mane under control. It had looked exactly the same every day for the two years Helen had known him.

"What the hell happened?" Bright whispered, careful not to take his eyes off the speakers at the podium. The factionalism was palpable, every team broken up, like to like. Everyone would be looking to be sure their piece of the project didn't catch the blame.

Helen shook her head and drew her fingertips across her lips in a zipping motion to signify that she wasn't allowed to say.

"Shit," Mira whispered. The team exchanged worried glances.

Tate finished whatever conversation he was having with Ivester and stepped back, conceding the podium to the CTO.

"Ladies and gentlemen, I know you are all deeply concerned." Ivester was not the tallest person at the front of the room, but when he was speaking it didn't seem to matter. He had a reputation as someone utterly unable to recognize the potential for failure. Tate was scowling in the background, but Ivester was speaking to his own people. He had their trust.

"I want you to know that, so far, the mission to build a jumpgate out at Otlyan23 is proceeding on schedule . . . ish." Ivester grinned at the bastardization of the last word. "But we have encountered an unexpected variable. Since you were all on task when the Golfball went live, you're already in the know. Or most of you are." He hesitated, gaze lingering on Helen for a moment. "You're all going to be pulled off the primary thread of Line Drive to help take care of this new variable. We need a smaller, more agile team to research what happened today. You're going to have to be able to move quickly and make decisions with limited data."

The chattering started, whispers and questions among the different groups. The boundaries of the protective factions dissolved as team members fist-bumped and high-fived across the gaps.

This is being spun as an honor, now we're all "elites," working to save the day. The thought came unbidden. Without Ted within arm's reach, Helen found herself doing double duty, focusing on reading the room, reading the reactions of the assembled OPs and NAVs. Helen had been an OP long enough to understand management spin. Such things almost always ended in a contract being terminated.

"Regrettably . . ." Dr. Ivester had to raise his voice to let the other shoe drop. "Being part of this new team means sequestrations."

That . . . that's an unprecedented step. Far Reaches had the right to sequester a team. It was in everyone's employment contracts, it wasn't that unusual a move. Everyone would be given temporary housing on the Far Reaches campus to limit the opportunity for leakage either to press or corporate rivals. But as far as Helen knew it had never been dropped on a team this way. There was usually a warning, a run-up. You usually knew a sequestration period was coming weeks in advance.

The room fell silent but when the chattering started up again it was more excited than upset. For the singles or those without extended families, like Helen and Ted, it was less of a hardship. For those who lived off campus it could be a strain. But an on-campus stay meant bonus pay and lots of little perks, like maid service and real coffee, for the duration.

Ivester held his hands up and the room quieted, although a little more slowly this time. Helen didn't take her eyes off the podium. Tate was looking antsy, the "someone's about to get fired" kind of antsy.

"I want to commend you all for what appears to be a very successful mission in the face of . . . well, unexpected difficulties. The uncertainty of working in deep space always seems to bring out the best in our people."

Applause.

"Second, you all will be happy to know that Theodore is in ICU and is being cared for by Launch City's finest. We will provide your team with updates on his condition as we know more."

Helen felt relieved at the confirmation. Mira nudged her with an elbow and gave her a thumbs-up.

The reactions from the collected Far Reaches personnel told Helen that they'd begun receiving their instructions. She fished in her pocket for her own communication pad, the screen lighting up at her touch. Insight icons blossomed all across the bottom edge of the glass.

"Information is being sent to your team leads," Ivester continued. "All communications regarding this matter are to take place over your secured team chats on Insight only. Don't write anything down, don't even ask a question out loud once you leave this room. Your families have been notified using the secure key-phrase you gave us when you signed up."

There was an audible groan from the back of the room and a smile pulled at the corner of Ivester's mouth. "For those of you who have been lax in keeping your personal information up to date, HR wants to have a word with you."

The roomful of laughter helped to relieve the tension.

Helen's own communication pad was trying to get her attention. While Ivester kept talking, she shifted her focus to the alert icon that glowed red.

"You've all been moved to basement level III. Please collect your teams and get any gear you need from your workstations. Remember, no conversation regarding these actions outside of the team comms."

Helen popped the icon with a fingertip and scanned the first few lines. Her instructions were different, very different. She'd been moved to the no-fly list, pending review. *Of course.* Her screen flickered and across the top a line of text appeared, "ACCESS RE-STRICTED." She barely had time to read the words before her access went offline, leaving her with a useless brick in her hands. She took a moment, pretending to read the screen, hoping Mira and Bright wouldn't notice she'd been cut off. When they moved to stand, she placed the tablet, face down, on the table. Losing access to company communications didn't speak well for what was coming next. She didn't need the rumor mill to get going.

"Operator Vectorovich."

She looked up to find Ivester staring at her from across the room. The chatter of the various Line Drive sub-groups breaking up and heading out dimmed for a minute. Ivester gestured to the tablet on the table in front of her. Bright gave her a friendly pat on the shoulder as he and Mira got up to leave.

Helen flipped the pad back over and Ivester's next words printed themselves out across the screen in her hand, Insight to Insight.

"We need you for a full debrief. Right now."

CHAPTER FOUR

HELEN DROPPED the whiteboard marker onto the table. With her Insight still severely limited, she had no access to any mission resources. No photos, no data, only her own memory. Every minute, every minute she stayed in the grip of the mood-kicking drugs meant more time recovering. Every minute spent in debrief meant another minute she had to put off finding out how Ted was doing. The only tool she had was focus and she used that to set both those problems aside for the moment. If she couldn't deal with the fallout, she was never getting back out to a waldo. And if she couldn't get back out there, she'd never figure out what happened.

The double bind grated, lurking under the surface, but it had its place on the checklist she kept in her head. She'd deal with those issues when she got there.

And your drawing skills are trapped back in fifth-year art class, she thought sourly, pulling her attention back to the wall covered in doodles and arrows.

The full twelve square feet of the presentation wall was covered in whiteboard panels linked to Far Reaches' computing system. It would record everything she'd laid down. Every list, every sketch, would be chewed up and translated into a digital form. The analysis team could pore over it at their leisure later.

Ivester and three other engineering leads sat in judgment at the back of the conference room. The space was one of the bigger, theater-style ones, the kind with tiers of seats so everyone in the room got a good view. Helen felt more like she was on trial than conducting a debrief.

Every part of the surface had been covered in details, the clean panels sliding down to within arm's reach. Helen flogged her memory, working around the holes and stutters until it dissolved into incomprehensible noises and a tremble in her hands. Helen edited that last part out by simply dropping her arms to her side and giving a shrug meant to conceal her unease. A bit of post-mission nerves was not out of the ordinary, she'd dealt with it before.

"That's not one of ours," Ivester pointed out. It was a "gotcha" moment, his tone gave it away. Helen turned to regard the sketch. One of the weird eenies she'd seen through the waldo's electron lens, re-translated through her shitty drawing skills. She'd been trying to give an overview of the shapes and forms of the empty shells. Each shape meant a different kind of eenie with a different kind of job. She wasn't sure how he could tell from the ink on the wall, but he'd picked up on something.

"You mean a mutation?" The XERMo engineer, tall and dark-skinned with somber blue hair and an air of perpetual suspicion, got to her feet and trotted down the stairs for closer look.

That one's Finch. Helen recalled the engineer's name with effort. Working without access to Insight meant she had to pay a little extra attention to match faces and names, using a muscle she'd not needed for a while.

"Maybe." Ivester stared, cold grey eyes unblinking, eyebrows drawn down into a line behind the glasses. "Something's wrong there, it doesn't fit any of our key design elements."

"A competing design? You think we might be looking at sabotage? Someone else's tech got on board your Golfball?" Finch selected a black marker and redrew the outlines, making the weird hexagonal shape easier to understand.

"There are high-res snaps coming down the pipe," Helen pointed out. "You can get a better idea from those."

"Unfortunately, no," Ivester said. "Since you hit the eject button, all the data coming back has been corrupted, out of sync. We've given it over to James to fix, but it may take some time to sort it all out. Time we can't afford to lose, hence the 'Helen Vectorovich Variety Show.'" He gestured at the braindump covering the walls.

Helen nodded. James was Far Reaches' artificial intelligence, the "big gun" insofar as data analysis was concerned. Without Insight, she couldn't look through any of her own personal files to see if they'd been corrupted as well.

"Memory," Dr. Finch, still peering at Helen's notes, said offhandedly, "tells us what's important. It tells us where to look, where not to waste our time looking. You're an operator, that gives you a different perception than we have, a different focus. You shouldn't have even bothered with the eenies until you got to that point on the checklist. That suggests what you saw was so far out of line with your unconscious expectations that you broke protocol to run the electron micrograph." She gestured broadly at the multi-legged stick figures and seashells now outlined in black marker.

"There wasn't really a protocol to break at that point," Helen protested weakly.

"I think this is worth a deeper look, Nate," Finch said over her shoulder to Ivester. "If Animus or Beyond Blue managed to sneak a couple of their eenies into the delivery, that would explain a lot of things. It also makes it much less likely that you've got an eenie overrun situation." Finch turned her attention back to the assortment of engineers at the table.

There were maybe a dozen companies competing with Far Reaches. Animus had a long history of industrial espionage, but Beyond Blue was a genuine contender. The rival firm preferred to sell themselves on bleeding-edge discovery rather than reliability.

"I don't see it," Ivester countered. "Animus uses a different constant. Everything is built on top of a base-ten design standard. If

Operator Vectorovich is even vaguely correct, then we're looking at a base-three or maybe a seven."

The specifics went over Helen's head, but she understood the "constant" referred to the way the eenies could build off one another to create larger structures. It suggested the eenies she'd seen were something the engineers hadn't seen before. It suggested she might not have been wrong about the Golfball being "eaten" as opposed to failing to initialize. She felt a glimmer of relief through the stillness of Doc's drug cocktail.

"Why the hell would anybody use a base-seven?" Finch didn't quite sneer, but it was clear she thought the idea silly. "That's just adding extra work. No offense to your drawing skills, Ms. Vectorovich, but what you're seeing, Nate, is probably due to the medium, not to the source."

"But . . ." Ivester stopped himself from rolling over the other engineer's objections. "Okay, fine, I agree that we need to drill down on this as our starting point."

Helen's glimmer of hope got stronger. Sabotage meant that she was off the hook. Exigent circumstances. She had already known the mission problems were well out of her control, but having this, having some concrete proof would make a difference in how everything could play out. It was just one more babystep back to her coffin and from there, back out into space. *Ted's going to be thrilled to hear that.*

"If one of our competitors sabotaged Line Drive, that's actionable. We can go after them and negotiate for forgiveness on the milestones with Tate until we can get this fixed."

As Dr. Finch rejoined the engineers at the rear table, the conversation coalesced among them. Helen found herself on the outside, apparently forgotten. She found a more comfortable position, butt on the edge of the desk, feet braced against the railing. She desperately wanted to sit down and close her eyes for just a second, but she didn't want the higher ups to catch her at it. Normally you didn't pull an operator out of recovery right after a mission exit, but whatever put Ted in the ICU had broken a great number of "normalies." Helen settled herself to wait for things to calm back down. Once the emergency measures were over, she could get a handle on what she needed to be doing to get back into the mission rotation. *Let the big dogs sort out the whats and whys*, she advised herself.

"Why didn't the security eenies catch this?"

Ivester still wasn't convinced they'd found a solution; Helen could read it in his expression. She wasn't sure why not, why he wasn't jumping at the ready-made solution that Finch had latched on to. It wasn't like he already knew the answer, but something wasn't adding up for him.

"Maybe that's why it's built on base-seven." Finch shrugged. "Something we haven't seen before, might not know to look for."

"Okay, take point on figuring out where that eenie came from. Get everything you can from the mission downloads. Start with Helen's observations. Dave . . ." Ivester turned to the younger, yellow-haired engineer to his right. "I want you to go over every bit of the mission development chain. Identify every point where a foreign eenie could be introduced; I want to know how those could have made it into our payload."

"Can you let my team loop in with Dave?" Finch asked. "I want all the images as we get them un-fucked." Finch held up her Insight, framing Helen's sketches in the screen, snapping pictures.

"Done. When we get what we can from the datastream, you're first on the list. In the meantime, I have to start the rest of the team prepping for the second run."

Helen had been watching the professional banter of the scientists and nearly missed Ivester's mention of a second run. On the other side of Doc's chemical cocktail, something stirred in Helen's memory. A sense of dread that didn't quite strike home, not yet.

"After you figure out what happened to Ted, right?" Helen asked the room. It was an effort to raise her voice to get them to remember she was present, but it had to be done.

"A second run is already on the books. We've got to recapture that asset," Finch pointed out tartly. "Right now there's nothing to show this wasn't an accident."

"Which team is going on the second run?" Knowing who was going mattered. She had to remind herself it mattered. More side effects from Doc's cocktail.

"We want a fresh set of eyes, so Mira and Bright are next up, based on your pre-mission assessment," Ivester said. Helen had worked with Keller to develop the pilot rotation and, no argument, Mira and Bright were a good team. Following the original mission rotation schedule, she'd be back up again in a week. If they treated this like a one-off, then the mission would continue, uninterrupted. She just had to get through the checklist of "mandatory operator recovery items" in time.

"We're moving you onto the planning and analysis team for now," Finch added.

"In all fairness, Dr. Finch, I'm usually the one who executes the protocols, not the one who makes them up," Helen said. It wasn't quite a protest. She wasn't sure she had the energy left for a full-blown protest. Helen gripped the edge of the desk, letting it bite into her palms. The quick stab of discomfort lifted some of the weight from her eyelids.

"Time to expand your skill set, then," Ivester said. Helen heard the ping from her Insight. She fished the tablet out of her pocket for a look; the edges of the screen framed anew in orange and blue fairy lights. Her access was restored. *Not fired yet.*

"You're back on the system, Operator Vectorovich," Finch said. "You'll be getting access to the mission reports over the next hour or so. Please review them before tomorrow's meeting. We'll need you to accept the terms of the new NDA before you can leave the room, of course."

Helen's Insight flickered and a new list appeared, each entry marked with the skull and crossbones icon that in IT-speak meant classified. A new set of terms and conditions floated at the top, commensurate with her temporary position and paygrade.

Helen settled herself into it to read the documents before she signed.

CHAPTER FIVE

HELEN HAD SPENT TIME in dozens of recovery rooms over the course of her career as an operator. This room was doctor's-office small with a couple of useful things like comfortable chairs and a table. The upper half of the walls were coated in non-reflective black to better showcase any information that needed to be projected. Dr. Hofstaeder gave Helen the courtesy of knocking. It gave Helen just enough time to sign off a call with Keller before Doc entered.

"Was that Keller?" the older, hatchet-faced woman asked without really listening for the answer. She called up Helen's medical files, using her Insight to throw them onto the wall for Helen to see. "I swear that man treats you operators like children. It's not my goal to keep you out of the coffins, but if I don't bring the hammer down, you all will end up in the ground for real." Hofstaeder settled into the room's other chair with a snort as she accessed the medical servers.

Helen chose diplomatic silence. Trying to justify the lengths that operators would go to stay on rotation was pointless. It was like trying to explain why swallows did barrel rolls or dogs chased cars. The words just never managed to live up to the observed reality.

"Well," the doctor focused on something on the Insight screen in her palm, the light from her screen painting blue lines against warm brown skin, "you've managed to both piss off and impress our CTO within the space of a few hours. I'm not sure if you're bucking for promotion or trying to get fired."

Quick motions of her fingertips sent information Helen couldn't see out to the edges of the doctor's Insight tablet. She charged ahead, not waiting for Helen's response. "That was a panic attack you experienced right after returning to your own body, yes? Rather than trusting us and waiting to finish out the exit procedures, you hacked your own coffin and escaped. Well, nearly escaped." Satisfied with the arrangement of information, Hofstaeder sat back in her chair. She finally turned her attention to her patient, rather than her patient's data. "Classic near-trauma test results, but you still managed to act, which is suggestive."

"Suggestive of what?" Helen asked suspiciously. As much as she wanted to relax and trust Hofstaeder to fix things, Doc held the final say on her being declared mission-ready.

"Of a course of treatment. There's a reason here to take you out of circulation for the near future. I am sure you will object. Either way, you will need a course of treatment to help manage the fallout; PTSD is easy to end up with in your line of work. I'm going to tweak that prescription and see what the minimum dose might be. The question now is—"

"How quickly can we get this fixed so I can get back into rotation?" Helen finished the sentence the way she wanted it finished.

The interface between operator and waldo meant mental health was just as important as physical health, if not more. Per every company policy, this was maintained through scheduled downtime, forced breaks that every operator complained insincerely about even as they enjoyed walks on the beach and time with family or friends.

Being taken out of rotation post-mission was different. It meant you were an expensive risk. It told the other OPs that you'd screwed up, that you were a potential liability. For a senior operator like Helen, it meant the younger OPs were going to start campaigning for her spot in the rotation. In a competitive workplace like Flight Ops, it meant keeping her job was about to get harder.

Helen knew she had not screwed this up.

She needed to get back out there before the sharks started circling. The feeling of urgency crept in, pressuring Helen to go, to run to the Mortuary and get back out there. To go do something, to find something. She clenched and unclenched her fingers, willing herself to be still.

"Hmmph." Hofstaeder's gaze changed focus, looking from the medical display towards her patient. "This isn't your first time being pulled off the line. You had an incident three years ago while you were still working for Animus, before you came to Far Reaches. Heroic action, if I recall, supporting a live mining team on Ferguson's Asteroid?"

Helen winced. "I drive a waldo, Dr. Hofstaeder, I was never in any actual danger."

"The catastrophic biofeedback from your waldo caused you to crack your own ribs. Only one member of the mining team was lost. Animus was known for using shitty tech. There's no way you didn't know what you were risking." Hofstaeder's gaze returned to the information on her Insight. "I presume that's why you took a lateral move to Far Reaches rather than jump for Distant Sun's more lucrative offer?"

The line of questioning was getting uncomfortable. The Ferguson's Asteroid Incident had been a huge boost to her career, but it had followed her, haunting her like a ghost. Helen stood her ground. She'd answered questions like these more than once. She knew the answers that would shut people up.

"Distant Sun uses the same discount tech as Animus," Helen replied shortly and carefully. As an OP, your profile followed you. It was yet another one of the thousand "cover your ass" tactics that went along with the stresses of being an operator. The saving grace, if there was one, was that only medical personnel had access.

"So you knew exactly what you were doing." Doc cut through the bullshit. "My concern, you see, Operator Vectorovich, is that now we have two incidents on your record. I am concerned that your post-mission . . . shall we call it an anxiety attack, until we have a formal diagnosis? That this was a result of not only the most recent issue, but it has touched on some unresolved issues from the first? You are getting a stacking effect, as it were, which means we may have not seen the end of your erratic behavior."

"I completed all the required therapies at Animus at the time. I passed my quarterly evaluation less than a month ago." Helen wasn't sure where this was going, but she felt like she was being set up for something.

If Far Reaches used this "anxiety attack" as an excuse to keep her out of the coffin, her time as an operator could be over.

"Yes, that is interesting." Hofstaeder closed the Insight, the screen going dark before she slid it into the pocket of her coat. "The question, at this moment, Ms. Vectorovich, is what is it that you want?"

"I beg your pardon?" Helen had expected condescension, a lecture on trusting Hofstaeder's skill and experience. She hadn't expected this.

"You have an opportunity here," Hofstaeder sniffed. "Ivester has asked that you be placed on the analysis team until you complete your therapy. He wants to keep you involved, one way or the other, and Keller is backing his play. With so few operators on this project, I am being pressured to get you back into a coffin right away and damn the consequences."

Hofstaeder leaned back in her chair, hands folded primly on her lap, and continued. "My concern, however, is with the health and well-being of my patients. Something even the Almighty Ivester treads lightly around. We have just gone down in the annals as the first, and I certainly hope the last, company to ever lose a NAV on a live mission. With your history, a case could be made to take you out of rotation entirely, move you over to project planning and analysis on a full-time basis."

Helen was taken aback. She was used to arm's-length professionalism from Hofstaeder, not frank honesty. It took a moment to wrap her head around what it meant. "You're . . . you're offering me an exemption?"

The exemption was the mental health clause in her contract, in everybody's contracts. It gave you an out if you cracked, if you disassociated while on a mission and lost track of where the human ended and the waldo began. It was in deadly earnest—a bad psych evaluation was the number one reason an operator got locked out of running a waldo for any reputable firm. It was close to the worst of all possible endings, as far as Helen was concerned.

Hofstaeder smiled, showing the bare minimum of teeth between lips painted a shade too orange. "A bit simplistic, but yes. Look, I know Ivester. If you do not set a limit on what he can take, he will ask for everything you have and then be surprised when you can't keep up. Once I give my sign-off, he will have you back in that coffin and talking to that waldo again just as quickly as the computers can be re-calibrated." Hofstaeder sighed. "But I also know operators. And I know that, as soon as I give the all-clear, you will jump right back in with a smile and without so much as a second thought. So, I am compelled to ask you, Helena Vectorovich, what, exactly, is it that you want?"

Helen resisted the urge to retort at her full name being laid out, like she was a rookie caught using mission-time for daydreaming. The pause in the conversation was made longer by Hofstaeder's unblinking gaze. It was a strange question, coming from someone Helen had always regarded an opponent rather than an ally. Helen took her time, trying to give a real answer to what seemed like a real question.

"I want to get back out there." Helen cast about in her own head, trying to find the root of that urgency. "I want . . . I need to figure out what went wrong; why Ted's the one in ICU and not me. The NAV chair is supposed to be the safe spot, the risks are supposed to fall to the operator. It doesn't make sense."

Hofstaeder sighed. "Yes, but you can do that from the relative safety of an analyst's chair. Why go back? I mean, why actually waldo back out there? What's calling you back?"

Helen considered, for just a moment, telling Hofstaeder about the tiny alien mites, the thousands upon thousands of empty husks worn by thousands of tiny enemies. Then she made the connection. She was in here because of what she'd said on mission. She'd told Ivester over the line and then Keller when she returned that something had "eaten the Golfball."

No wonder they're keeping you under wraps. Until those images are brought in, until someone can confirm what you saw out there, you need to keep it to yourself. The offer of an exemption was on the table, but for now it was voluntary. One slip-up on Helen's part and it might not stay that way.

Helen backpedaled inside her own head, sought a simpler answer. She'd misread Hofstaeder's intent, trusted a touch too much. She could go over the conversation later with Ted and figure out what she'd missed. For now she had to course-correct, get the conversation back on the rails.

"Look, Doc. We tripped something out at Otlyan23. I don't know what it was, but if I can get back into the coffin, walk back through the scene, I know I'm going to be able to figure it out. There are cameras not working, holes in the coverage, missing pieces, but I was there. I saw everything firsthand, know every step we took from our first connection to my dumping out. I'm the best one for that job."

"Even though it might kill another NAV?"

That thought set Helen back a bit. Doc was talking about the unthinkable. Whatever had happened to Ted, that had to be a one-in-a-million convergence, an accident. *Right?*

But if Doc was right, another living NAV might face the same risks if they moved too quickly.

"An AI NAV is always possible," Helen began, already working up the scenario on the fly. "I've worked with them before, no one else needs to . . ." She trailed off as Hofstaeder's words finally made sense.

Wait.

KILL another NAV?

The chattering, whispering memories started to creep back in. Helen cast her mind back to the waldo, to the conversation with Ivester after Ted had been pulled offline. Ivester had said the same at first. Keller had said otherwise when she'd climbed out of the coffin. Ivester had said something different to the mission team. They had kept her out of the loop and it had taken her too long to put it together. The news blew right through the last of the emotional stabilizers Hofstaeder had given her in the coffin and left her soul unprotected.

"Y-you . . . just said kill," Helen stammered.

Hofstaeder blanched, held up a hand to forestall her. "What I meant was—"

"Ivester said the same thing . . . now you. You haven't told *anyone* yet."

Helen was only barely listening. The world tilted a bit and she felt the crawling on her skin again, nibbling and scurrying. She was back in the waldo listening to Ted's ruined voice over the comms. She kept trying to fast forward to the moment when Ivester signed on, to hear what he'd said. The urge to take action, to get back to the coffins and get back out to the Golfball, to get back out and fix this was becoming unbearable.

Deep breaths.

Helen fought back, deliberately turning her attention back to Hofstaeder, back to the lie that Ted was alive and safely ensconced in the ICU at City General.

"Helen?"

"I'm fine, Doc." Helen sat a little straighter, forced herself to smile against the despair and look Hofstaeder in the eye. "Truth, please."

Hofstaeder met her gaze solidly. Helen knew she wasn't fooling anybody. She was far from fine, but the doc allowed her the illusion for the moment. The consideration mattered, made it a little easier for Helen to hold it together.

"Theodore passed away at two a.m. this morning. His family elected to take him off of life support in accordance with their beliefs. I'm sorry."

"Why didn't you . . ." Helen kept her voice steady with an effort of will, forcing the sound in her memories back down. ". . . tell me? Why didn't you tell anybody?"

Hofstaeder shook her head slowly. "Moving parts. At first it was because we didn't want to panic the rest of the Line Drive team, especially since we first hoped Ted might be able to recover. While that was going on, we were trying to get as much information as we could. You had to be debriefed while the incident was still fresh in your memory. After you disentangled, the Feed was useless." She folded and refolded her long, thin fingers together. "Simply put, too many things moving too fast. I know that sounds cold. We got Ted off the Feed as soon as he started seizing and got him to the ICU in record time. Unfortunately, the damage to his nervous system had already been done."

Helen took one deep breath.

Then a second.

Intellectually, she knew that honesty was better. She would need to get her head around the brand new hole in her world. Helen could count her close friends on the fingers of one hand. Ted had been her NAV at Animus and they'd made the jump to Far Reaches together. Never lovers, more like twins, they'd been crèche-mates as kids and found each other again at Animus. They were better as a team; they filled in for each other's flaws. *It's not right. It's not FAIR.*

In the back of her mind, however, accompanied by chatters and deep-space cold, was a resentment that she couldn't hold on to the lie a little bit longer.

"When are you going to inform the rest of the Line Drive team?" Helen asked quietly, trying to keep the surge of emotions in check.

"That's really not my call, but I know it's going to be soon." Hofstaeder's concern was evident, but Helen didn't trust it, now knowing what they'd kept from her.

She suddenly felt very tired and very alone.

"I'll authorize the therapies you need to get back into the coffin," the older woman continued, "but be warned. I'm keeping you out until I'm sure you're ready."

"Can I be alone for a bit, please?" Helen was losing the battle and she knew it, she closed her eyes, tried to find something to hold on to.

Hofstaeder took a breath, as if about to deliver some kind of useless platitude, then changed her mind. "Of course. You can stay in here as long as you need to."

Need to. Not want to.

What Helen really wanted was to get out. To go somewhere, even back to the fifteen-by-fifteen box of concrete and glass she called home and just . . . not be part of the world, a part of the mission any longer.

But none of that would give her any answers.

Helen managed to hold it together until Hofstaeder closed the door behind her. Then the tears started to fall.

CHAPTER SIX

THERE WERE ONLY a half dozen remote operation companies in Launch City, a fact that made it nigh-impossible to silo all the personnel. Documents were signed and discretion was expected. The indiscreet were offloaded to other, less sensitive areas of the industry. The family of OPs and NAVs was small enough that a death like Ted's touched them all.

Far Reaches had closed out Wade's, buying out the entire multi-level restaurant for the night. It provided a sort of air gap between those paying their respects and those looking to feed a media machine that was already predicting Far Reaches' demise. The downstairs room was quiet and dimly lit, the path to the stairs outlined by small, flickering lights. Helen had come dressed in her only good suit and fancy shoes. Climbing the stairs in the dimness took some care.

Ted's actual funeral had been private, family only, a distinction for which Helen did not qualify under Ted's mother's strict adherence to Homesteader cultural code. Helen was consigned to attend the company-sponsored wake instead. She sat somewhere between offended and relieved. She wasn't sure she'd have been able to hold it together if she'd had to face his family.

The upstairs room was filled with OPs and NAVs. Ted's memorial brought out pros not only from Far Reaches. but from competitors as well. The event had been opened to any registered OP or NAV. She recognized people from Animus and Beyond Blue, Distant Sun and Kitterhammer in the crowd. Every person in the room was someone Ted had connected with. The space was somberly lit, the usual sparkle and gloss toned down, visible only in the shadows. The life was just waiting to come roaring back in once the mourners departed.

HR had churned through Ted's personnel files and contacted friends and family to put together a carousel of images displayed on the wall. As his current OP, Helen had been asked to add her thoughts to the video eulogies that played out between the images from Ted's life. She'd come up with a half dozen ways to pay tribute. Her original plan had been recording from the Mortuary or that really shitty VietFusion restaurant that he dragged everyone to. Some place where Ted was recognized on sight. Each attempt made her a bit more miserable and anxious than the last. She'd finally recorded her thoughts in the privacy of her flat the night before, and handed them off to be included. They hadn't shown up on the wall display yet and Helen wasn't entirely sure how she would feel when they did. She took another sip of her well-garnished soda water and singled out Ray, Ted's youngest brother. Already painfully honest, and now well on his way to a hangover, Ray had cornered the last person Helen wanted to meet up with.

Catherine Beauchamp was nearly a head shorter than Helen, and had ensured she drew everyone's attention with a pouf of aqua-blue hair that argued with the olive undertones of her skin. She had been hired when BrightWinds had gone bankrupt and their assets snapped up by Far Reaches. The younger OP's romantic relationship with Ted had been under the radar. Helen wagered only she and one or two others had known, and the whole thing had ended badly. Helen didn't know all the details. As close as she and Ted had been, romantic entanglements were always off limits. She knew that Beauchamp had blacklisted him as a NAV, she would not work him with under any circumstances, and Ted had returned the favor.

It can't have been that bad a breakup if she's here to say goodbye.

Ray was gesturing his way through the story of Ted's attempt to launch a series of model rockets from the top of the town Crèche, pantomiming with broad gestures that threatened to split the seams of his only dress shirt. Helen smiled. The motivations changed every time, but the outcome always involved a very contrite Ted helping build indoor playgrounds for the Crèche kids in the neighboring towns. As Ted's close friend, she knew the truth of the story. Ted's strict family unit had handed down the community service as a punishment. Ted always said it was the best punishment he'd been forced to endure.

A quick read on Ray's limited audience of Beauchamp and *still-stranded-at-Animus* Migos showed the kind of polite expression used to conceal boredom.

If she can't handle Ray, it's no wonder she and Ted didn't last. Meeting that family must have been an eye-opener for Beauchamp.

"Helen!" Ray enveloped her in a boozy bear hug, which Helen returned with equal enthusiasm. Ray was Ted's family touchstone, the sibling who'd stayed close when Ted had left the family compound. "Helen, this whole thing fucking sucks."

Helen hugged him a little bit harder. "I'm so sorry, Ray. How's your mom doing?"

"As well as can be expected. She always hoped he'd come back to the family businesses. I think she's as sorry about the death of that idea as she is about Teddy himself."

Helen grimaced. Ted had always joked that his people skills were due to navigating the pitfalls of his tightly wound family. Ray had, by all Helen's observances, gone the absolute opposite route and thrown himself into the role of black sheep with gusto.

"Well, she'll need time to grieve." Helen tactfully disentangled herself from his embrace, careful not to knock either of them off balance. He was staggering from the booze, she from the unfamiliar shoes.

"Yes, she will." Ray knocked back the last of the drink in his glass, rattling the ice cubes for effect. "If you'll excuse me, I need to top this baby off. Can I get you one?"

Helen held up her full glass in reply. "I'm covered."

"Somehow I never figured you for a fruit-and-parasol kind of drinker." Ray grinned in passing. A couple of the group peeled off to go with him, leaving Helen alone with Beauchamp and Migos.

The temperature in the room seemed to drop a few degrees.

"What I don't get . . ." Migos began abruptly, speaking more to Beauchamp than Helen at first. He was a head taller than Helen, brown hair either greasy or styled, she couldn't tell which, eyes rimmed red either from crying or alcohol, and only slightly less wobbly than Ray had been. Helen recognized the belligerent tone, braced herself for the next words. Migos had been Ted's partner for two years before his tendency towards day drinking had forced Animus to swap in Helen as Ted's partner for the Ferguson's Asteroid mission. He'd never gotten over it. "What I don't get is how this could happen to a NAV. What I DON'T GET is how this could happen to a NAV like Ted."

Helen remained silent. She expected some resentment from Migos. She'd stolen his NAV. Ferguson's had made her and Ted a team, the kind of team that had brought in job offers from top-of-the-line operations. But the open hostility was new. As long as Far Reaches was investigating the circumstances around Ted's death, she couldn't say anything to defend him, or herself for that matter. All her conversations had been full of vague platitudes and personal stories, no one able to ask the questions or get the answers.

"The NAV is supposed to be the safe job." Migos was just getting started. "The NAV's supposed to be looking out for the OP. So exactly what the hell did you do out there to get Ted killed?"

Helen's politic silence became stunned silence. The seed of doubt in the back of her mind echoed Migos' statement. She hadn't been expecting outright blame.

Migos leaned closer, looking her in the eyes. He hadn't been drinking, not like Ray had. He was stone-cold sober, the wobble just an act to cover his words. Just over his shoulder, Beauchamp smirked.

So she put him up to this? Here? The idea of Beauchamp insti-
gating a fistfight at a memorial was crass and disgusting, but her
expression left Helen with little doubt. Yet while Beauchamp might
be the instigator, Migos was the more immediate problem.

"Theodore was the best goddamn NAV in the business. If you
think you're going to stay senior OP without him, you're sorely mistaken." The angry OP punctuated the announcement with a stubby
finger, stopping an inch from actually poking Helen in the sternum.

Helen let her gaze travel slowly from the accusatory finger up
until she returned Migos' watery stare. It took a moment for her
anger to catch up, to bolster her tone.

"What happened to Ted is not on me," she said firmly, enunciat-
ing each word carefully. Not that she believed it, but making sure
Migos believed it meant one less source of gossip she'd have to deal
with.

"An accident? What kind of accident kills a NAV? You ran into
a problem on your little special project, shunted the primary load
from the entanglement Feed, and cooked Ted's fucking brain." His
index finger completed its action, jabbed her squarely in the chest.
"You know it and I'm gonna make sure everyone else knows it too,"
he huffed, building up steam for the rant he'd been waiting to deliver.

"That's enough out of you, Migos." Beauchamp stepped in
smoothly, like she'd finally recognized where this was going. "Enough
conspiracies already." She directed her non-apology to Helen as she
steered him out of the conversation. "Forgive Migos; he's been driving moles for the past two shifts."

"Fine, but the truth will come out," Migos muttered. He allowed
himself to be led away.

Beauchamp cast an insincere smile over her shoulder. The damage had been done.

Is that really the rumor going around? Helen scanned the other
fifty or so faces in the room. Ted had been the social butterfly; the
size of the crowd at his memorial showed just how many people he'd
intersected with meaningfully. *That I threw Ted under the bus to save*

myself? She recognized about half of them, was on speaking terms with most of them. She collected herself, put Migos' words out of her head, took another sip of her drink, and moved towards another knot of Ted's friends.

The Wall of Shame expanded as the event moved on, now interspersing highlights and embarrassments from Ted's ten-year career among the eulogies and the photographs projected on the far wall. There were a few incidents on there that even Helen had been unaware of, a few pictures of girlfriends and boyfriends that Helen hadn't known. The goal was to give everyone a sense of the whole person, even the parts of their life you hadn't been there for.

It was humanizing in a way Ted would've appreciated.

Helen kept an eye on the wall as she met up with friends and coworkers. Some came just for a few minutes to pay their respects, some came to take full advantage of the bar and the company-sponsored ride home. Helen stayed until the very end. By the time Keller found her, she'd switched from club soda to something stronger.

"Hey, Helen. Time to wrap up."

Keller took the seat next to her, ice clattering in the bottom of his own glass. Helen startled out of her reverie. She'd been staring at the wall when the projector shut off and the images vanished.

"They didn't show it," she said quietly.

"Didn't show what?" The lights in the empty corners of the room switched off, darkness marching towards the seats she and Keller occupied. The dim threw his white, embroidered shirt into sharp relief against his skin.

"The eulogy. They asked me to record a few words about Ted, but they never put them up there." She waved her hand at the screen.

"Maybe you just missed it. There were a lot of distractions. Did you see they practically had to carry Ray out?"

"Nope. They just didn't use it. I even saw Beauchamp's pop up twice. And now I feel like I messed up the chance to say goodbye properly."

"I'm sure it was just an oversight. I'll look into it if it will make you feel any better," Keller said reassuringly. A member of the catering staff came over and collected Keller's glass, a not-so-subtle reminder that their event was over and they needed to leave. Keller gave him a thumbs-up.

Helen sighed, wrung out from all the talking and comforting. The alcohol was starting to make her head spin.

"No. The opportunity is gone," she said. "Did you hear Migos?"

"What, that lunatic theory about shifting the Feed resistances or whatever garbage that was? There's a reason he's always on mole duty, you know. Don't listen to him."

"Yeah." Helen resignedly got to her feet, wobbled a little as she rebalanced on the fancy, unfamiliar shoes with too high a lift. "Thing is, Keller, he's not wrong. This should never have happened to a NAV, and especially not Ted." She took a long look around the detritus of the wake. "I need to get back out there, I need an answer for this . . ." she grasped for words, ". . . complete and total fuckup."

"We're working on it," Keller said uncomfortably.

"Not fast enough, Keller. I'm going home. Any of the company cars still hanging around?"

"Should be. If not, I'll put you in a rideshare on the company card."

"Perfect."

They made their way up to the front of the restaurant where there were still a few mourners gathered. All less sad now, all well liquored up.

"I didn't see Ivester there," Helen said. "Did he stop by?"

Keller shook his head. "No, he didn't want to be a distraction. Ted's mother invited him to pay his respects at the funeral earlier, so I suspect he's recovering from that . . ."

"That was nice of her," Helen said, surprised.

"She read him the riot act, from what I hear. You know how Ted's family was," Keller said sourly. He showed his company ID to the first waiting car and Helen eased gratefully into the back seat.

"You coming too?" she asked Keller. He shook his head.

"I'm headed back home to Ethan and the kids. Everything is on hold on Line Drive so I'm taking a day. I'll see you day after."

"I will be there," Helen replied in a monotone.

"Only you could make that sound like a valid threat," Keller returned and shut the car door.

Helen leaned into the seat fabric as the car took off. She had to get back out to the Golfball to figure out what had killed Ted.

And if it kills you too?

Helen didn't bother with an answer to that.

CHAPTER SEVEN

THE ELEVATOR to the top floors of Far Reaches took longer than Helen was expecting. The walls of the elevator were blank except for a couple of tech-deco details and a single screen that displayed company announcements. The music piped in was almost loud enough to cover the whisper of the vacuum as the capsule slid upwards.

While Flight Ops sat in the windowless depths of the subbasements, Helen's new position was much closer to the clouds. The windows that lined the corridor to the Analysis lab provided a long view of the glittering, ever-changing mass of Launch City at first sunrise. In one of the observation alcoves, Helen pressed her cheek to the clear crystal panels. With a little effort, she could catch a glimpse of a strip of sidewalk twenty stories below. The rooftop patio at Wade's was just at the outer range of her view. Launch City was a perpetual work in progress. Built out in concentric rings from the ruins of the colony's original spaceport, the City had slowly consumed the suburbs where Helen had grown up. Tamer cousins of the eenies that built the Golfball could collapse a structure and replace it within days. The skyline, for Helen at least, was rarely the same twice. Most of her work life took place between Flight Ops, in the basements, and the ground floor. Getting a top-down view of the City, plus a moment to appreciate it, was a rare thing.

Hope the labs don't have windows or nobody's going to get anything done. With a touch of regret, she peeled herself away. Her shifts as an operator always seemed to fall right between the day/night cycle. Sunrises and sunsets weren't things she got to appreciate on a regular basis, but her new schedule almost seemed to be designed around them. Helen resolved to take advantage of it while she was waiting to be reinstated.

When she arrived, she discovered that the Analysis lab was, in essence, one very large virtual space. Helen paused a moment outside the door to don the thick-framed Insight glasses she'd been issued. She was aware that Far Reaches' teams were spread all over the globe, so projects could run around the clock as time zone dovetailed into time zone. That meant half the people in the lab could be there virtually, visible only through the goggles. *Glasses,* Helen corrected herself.

She walked through the door, the glasses shook hands with James the AI, and the room opened to her. The black-painted walls erupted into color and motion and the drab grey furnishings took on a sense of style and improbability. Helen stopped, absorbing the complex constellation of numbers and simulations that covered every available surface in a room that was designed to be all available surface.

"Helen, glad you could join us." The voice was the only actual sound in the room. The rest of the chimes and clicks and whistles, Helen realized, were being piped in through the frames of the glasses. It felt a bit like operating a waldo, since she was seeing through a different set of eyes, but here in a shared virtual space the visual noise was even more pervasive. It was more like being in a crowded cafeteria than a cockpit. *That's going to take some getting used to.*

The owner of the voice was a trim younger man, roughly the same height as Keller, dark skin pale from too many hours indoors. The tattoos on his face were highlighted in Far Reaches blue, the Insight inviting Helen to dig into their meaning. She declined.

"Thank you," Helen returned cautiously. "Is this all for Line Drive?" She gestured to encompass the room and its virtual content.

He grinned, teeth sharp and even between sienna-colored lips.

"Absolutely. I'm the only team member here on-site today, but we've also got Rachel on the other side of the planet in Emergent Seoul and Torbin's off-planet right now on Kilwa Station."

He indicated a half-dozen ghostly forms standing against the wall, skeletal steel frameworks covered in fabric to give the Insight something to paint a body onto. Each unit waited to be waldoed by an analyst from a distant office space when needed. "Time difference means it's just you and me right now, but we all have overlapping shifts, so you will meet them both between today and tomorrow."

"And who are you?"

"Dougal Monroe, sorry, usually the Insight takes care of introductions." The young man's handshake was cold, like he'd just been holding a glass of ice water. Helen disentangled her grip quickly. "You've got a desk over here, but we do ask that you limit personal items because when the team is in full swing, stuff gets knocked over. Go stow your stuff if you brought any and we'll get started."

Helen moved over to the "desk" indicated, an island of plain grey to the side of the room's chaotic center. It was more of a pedestal really, about chest height, stacked with drawers until it flared out into an Insight touchscreen surface at the top. The largest drawer at the bottom opened with push and she dropped the bag with her lunch and personal fobs into it. Everything work-related would respond to the NFC chip in her wrist.

Across the room was a coiling, surging waveform, positioned so you couldn't see it when you first entered. It roiled against the wall, twisting and unspooling, smooth and natural as water. It was compelling in the way that leaning over the edge of cliff was compelling. Fascinating and terrifying when the only thing holding you back was the abstract understanding of what would happen if you took just one more step.

"Is that it?" Helen asked, unconsciously moving closer. She felt the hairs on the back of her arms lift, as if a cool breeze had wafted through. "Is that the signal Ted and I picked up?"

"Here, come take a seat." Dougal avoided the question initially. "Until you get used to the room space, you're likely to walk into a table." Helen didn't really need his confirmation, the whispers in her head recognized it; muttered uncomfortably in the back of her mind.

"Or maybe not . . . your waldo experience might translate over just fine," Dougal continued, drawing Helen's attention back.

"Sitting is good." Staring at the twisting sine waves that had killed her NAV made Helen nauseous. She found the first available chair and dropped into it. It barely moved under her weight, like it was bolted down to keep the room consistent.

"Perfect." Dougal bustled over and pulled the waveform closer with a pinch of his fingers. "I'll give you the grand tour, starting with this guy."

"And this guy is?"

"This is a visualization of the corrupted entanglement Feed. We pulled it from your mission to launch the payload. Isn't it gorgeous? We just got the first alert ping letting us know the payload is still alive, by the way, so the mission is still on target."

It was hard to take pride in such an expensive success. Helen took some solace in the fact that the payload surviving meant the project was still alive. Helen still had the chance to get back into the rotation.

"Okay, so check this out." Dougal pulled up a second signal and showed it off next to the first. The difference was immediately clear: the new form crawled across the wall, jagged and polygonal. Every angle and twist screamed its artificiality.

"That's the way the Feed looks on a normal day. Now, when we pulled your NAV out, we got a huge influx of incomprehensible data. Everything that came back down the line on that link was garbage, so Ivester was kind of shouting into the void. Ten minutes after you dropped out, everything returned to normal. We've been working off the recordings. This here," he waved at the slick, oily waveform, "is our copy of that garbage. We've been trying different algorithms to see if we can get it to make sense, but so far we haven't cracked it."

"So why wasn't Ivester affected when he linked in?" Helen asked.

Dougal held up a finger. "That may have been blind luck. We used the emergency feed, which piggybacks onto the OP signal rather than the NAV signal. Ivester wasn't properly 'entangled' the way you OPs and NAVs are," he corrected. "But something happened to Ted, that much is clear. And we have a full copy of your biofeedback showing that something happened to you as well. As far as I'm concerned, the sneaky little fucker is in that recording somewhere. We're going to have some fun hunting it down." Dougal turned that finger on the stabby-looking waveform, poking at it in virtual space for emphasis.

Helen felt a little more queasy, and somewhere in the back of her head, a familiar chattering whispered.

Dougal picked up on Helen's discomfort. "Sorry, I'm not trying to be insensitive, but this is a once-in-a-lifetime problem. I know nothing we can do will fix what happened, but at least we can get you some answers, right?"

"It's all right." Helen forced a smile and turned her attention away from the corrupted Feed, away from the whispers that threatened to take up too much space in her head again. "So the primary NAV and OP Feeds are now clean?"

"That's what it looks like." Dougal cast the waveform back to its place against the wall. "Let's take a look at the rest of our space. I've got new data coming in from Rachel this afternoon. We can revisit that slippery little construct then."

"Can you give me the thousand-foot view of where the whole mission is right now? I'm only really familiar with my own little piece." Helen fibbed just a little. OPs had broad discretion when it came to information on any given mission they were assigned to. Most operators only paid attention to their own checklists, but Helen preferred a longer view. Knowing the endgame made it easier find the right solution in a pinch, so she had spent the extra time to read through Dougal's filed reports, the timelines and plan of attack. What she really wanted was to confirm that her impressions were correct.

Entanglement was blindingly simple, really. Two sets of quantum particles were entangled using the standard Kleinsberg-Yount method. One set of particles was kept in a magnetic chamber, and only accessed by the coffin computers. The matching set was packaged up with a thimbleful of eenies and sent through a teeny tiny wormhole to its final destination. Those particles could transmit data instantaneous-ish, across billions and billions of miles. Over time the eenies would collect the material they needed to build out a new waldo. You could have a freshly made remote-operated vehicle in the space of a few months.

Line Drive represented the farthest anyone had ever sent a waldo, bypassing every other human-inhabited station and planetoid by a billion miles or more.

Line Drive was the first attempt to make a change to this pattern. Instead of exploring by remote, the payload of Line Drive would lay the groundwork for a human-safe wormhole engine, more commonly called a jumpgate. The star's energy would be tapped to build a gate large enough to bring through something more human-scale, perhaps eventually transport ship-scale. It would allow them to establish the first live human foothold in that area of deep space.

If we can keep the project on track.

Part two of Line Drive was already being prepped. Dougal pulled up the simulation and walked Helen through the progress so far. With the payload's successful launch, it would be six months before the next phase of Line Drive. By then the payload should have achieved its final orbit and begun collecting material to build the jumpgate back home.

Helen was, or had been, on the short list of operators for Phase II. They had only six months to determine if Ted's death was a tragic accident or a case of industrial sabotage. Helen still could not shake the thought that, if she'd picked up on the problems a little more quickly, Ted could have been saved.

"What else did you get back from the mission? I heard the images, the micrograms that came back, were corrupted?" Helen turned her

attention back to the simulations, trying to focus on the problems ahead of her rather than the problems behind.

"It makes the best case for this being an accident of some kind, rather than industrial sabotage," Dougal said. "Quantum Feeds are un-hackable, so it's probably a hardware failure in the Golfball itself."

"The Golfball was messed up when I got there." Helen ignored the chattering that arose in her head, pushing it back out of the way.

"Eaten away, you said." Dougal called up Helen's post-mission report, tossed the image on the wall. "That's some pretty specific imagery. We haven't been able to find a failure state that leaves behind bite marks."

Helen ignored the implication. Hofstaeder had latched on to that and kept circling back around to the idea, like she thought it was a symptom. Helen had begun to carefully adjust her wording so she wouldn't get those concerned looks quite so often.

"Well, when the next round of data gets back, you'll get a better descriptor than my fifth-grade art skills." Helen guided the interaction back towards joking camaraderie.

"Yeah, I'm guessing you never took an art class."

"Never passed an art class, but I got an E for effort," Helen returned.

"Well, the shells you saw do raise a lot of questions. I should have you run through the images we have on file for our eenies and our competitors', see if anything pops."

"I was using a false-color microgram, if that helps. The colors ought to show where there were mistakes when the eenies were built."

Dougal gave her a surprised look. "I see you've been reading the material already. Yes, under false color we should be able to see wear patterns, color shifts to indicate a bad build or weakness. Our eenies are silver to the naked eye. Color, actual physical color, costs molecules we'd rather save for something else." Dougal reached up into the Inspace between them and tugged at one of Helen's sketches, turning it into a rough 3D model. "Let's have you run through the eenie designs first. James can knock out the ones that aren't even a close match. That should narrow the list to something manageable."

Helen pulled one of her sketches out of the Inspace, gave it a tug. Working in virtual was easier than working on the whiteboard, more like clay she could push around with her fingertips to match her memory.

"Okay, what happens if I find a match?"

"Just let me know and we can go from there." Dougal opened a connection to James and delivered the instructions. The Far Reaches AI came back with a list of a couple hundred designs for her to examine.

"This might take a little while." Helen eyeballed the list, watching the number tick upwards slowly as James added more obscure and harder-to-find designs to the list on the fly.

"Once we have the actual images, we can sic James on finalizing the matches. Once Rachel and Torbin get here, we can put together a better outline of what we need you to be working on."

"I think this is going to keep me busy for a week." Helen pulled the stack of images closer, peering at the differences in legs, in tails.

"Nah, James will keep updating his decision-making based on what you cast aside." Dougal pointed out the changing numbers. "See, there's another ten knocked off the 'possibles.' Take it back to your desk and we'll see where it goes from here."

Helen obediently headed to her pedestal, dragging the stack of eenies in her wake. She wasn't sure if she hoped to find a match or not. A match would mean that Ted's death was industrial sabotage without a doubt. No match meant they'd still have more questions than answers.

It's like eating an elephant. I just have to keep taking bites at the problem until it's all gone, she told herself. But saying it was one thing, believing it another.

CHAPTER EIGHT

"Congratulations!" Keller stuck his head into the Flight Ops cubicle where Helen had been hiding. His slicked-back black hair suggested he'd just arrived on-site, since the aircon hadn't had time to dry it to its usual raven finish, and the reddish flush in his brown cheeks said he'd been in a hurry. *The man spends way too much time on his hair*, Helen reflected.

She was busy sorting through the influx of documents that came along with her short-term reassignment. No one was using her old workspace. She'd snuck back down to the basement to go through the rest of the eenie designs on the large, flat Insight desktop. As cool as the multi-faceted Inspace of the analysis lab was, there was too much noise for her to focus.

"It's temporary, or at least it damn well better be," Helen groused. She had spent most of the previous night in the lab, digging through materials on eenie design. The dispensary in her apartment's kitchen had failed to produce any coffee and she had yet to make it to the commissary for breakfast. What should have been a perfectly shitty morning was only countered by the mood-balancers Hofstaeder had her taking.

"Please, please, tell me you've got good news for me." Helen kicked the office's only empty chair over to the head of operations and he dropped into it.

Like most of the closet-sized workspaces, it sported walls painted black from the top of the desks to the ceiling. A band of ferro-plastic ran around the bottom of the black, making it a place to stick bits of paper and personal memorabilia. Easy enough to see from chair height, but low enough so as to not interfere with serious work. Helen's cluster of printed-out theater tickets and still images huddled together in the corner, out of easy reach. Add to this an Insight touchscreen table and a reclining lounger and you had a space that was more than sufficient for an OP's paperwork.

Perhaps not the best space for an analyst. Helen was already on the edge of overwhelmed with the volume of information she was working through. Flight Ops school had been a hell of a lot of work, but she was beginning to think she'd taken the easy road. Shortly, a delivery of actual, physical documents would show up, each carefully printed onto non-biodegradable sheets and kept offline and out of Far Reaches' computers. The idea was to make espionage as big of a pain in the ass as possible. She wasn't entirely sure what genius thought that was a good idea or where she was going to put all the paperwork.

"Temporary or not, it will give you a sense of your next steps when you've finally aged out of Ops," Keller pointed out. Helen wasn't in the mood for the mentor act.

"I plan to retire and turn into one of those biddies with a dozen cats who pilots the slow cargo ships out past the asteroid belt," she said with a touch of acid.

"You hate cats," Keller said.

"I might meet the perfect cat."

"You might just take the promotion with good grace, too. There's no way I can let you back into a coffin without a new NAV."

Ouch. That was the one point Helen had been trying not to think about. She didn't feel right replacing Ted, but in order to get back out to the Golfball, she would have to. She silently gritted her teeth before asking the question.

"So who's available?"

Keller held up a hand. "Not a chance. You know and I know how this works. Doc's still got you juiced up, probably on a host of emo-blocking 'don't freak out in public' drugs, all of which have to be flushed out before you can be re-evaluated. Give everything a few more weeks to process before we even start to think about partnering you up with someone new."

He was right. Helen was in a much better mood than she should be, given the circumstances. Whatever chemical cocktail the doc had given her that morning was keeping reality, or maybe just the consequences of her actions, slightly out of reach. She was, admittedly, a little curious to see what would happen when the drugs wore off.

She was also a little terrified to feel what would happen when the drugs wore off.

There was a definitive hole in her soul that Ted had once occupied. She could feel it, like the strange concave divot left in your flesh after a hard object had pressed against it for a long time. Long enough for it to become a part of you in function, if not in actuality. It should still hurt. It should . . . something. Something should have come rushing in to try to fill that hole, but Hofstaeder's clever mix of chemicals kept it perfectly formed in the center of her being.

"Keller," Helen asked slowly, "why haven't I been benched?"

"You have, or didn't you notice your suspended OP access?" Keller replied dryly.

"No." Helen turned the idea around in her mind, examined it in the light of her mentor's influence. "No, but I'm not. Company policy says I'm supposed to be out, like off the Far Reaches campus, strictly enforced downtime. So why the exception?"

Keller tapped his fingertips together. Helen recognized the gesture. It meant he was about to tread lightly. He was "not-saying" something, something important, and she'd better listen.

"Line Drive is a significant project for us, you get that, right? The cone of secrecy right now is very small and losing people, losing OPs, is non-trivial. You are one of the most senior OPs we have; you've got experience we need out there, especially in light of what happened. I'm not sure another operator would have been able to get the payload launched," he said quietly.

"Don't get me wrong, I don't want to be on leave. Not even if Doc didn't have me on emo-blockers, but . . ." Helen paused. Normally Keller was her superior, normally he was cleared to hear every damn secret she might encounter . . . Except now he wasn't. The previous day's walk-through with Dougal had made that crystal clear. She'd been shifted to the analysis team, bumped up a grade. They were on the same level in the org chart now, but under different subheadings. She couldn't talk to her mentor about what bothered her the most.

That was disquieting, but the idea fell, ever so gently, alongside the loss of her NAV on the other side of the chemical barrier between her head and heart.

Don't forget, she reminded herself. *You might not care right now, but those things matter. REALLY matter.*

"I feel we're missing something. I need to figure out what it is," she finished lamely.

"It'll all come out in the wash," Keller replied, letting her off the hook. "While you're still drugged up, though, I thought I'd get your opinion on the operator line-up going forward. Since your temporary promotion has stuck me with your workload, I figure you could at least share some opinions."

Beauchamp's going to be pissed when she hears about this. Helen allowed herself the petty joy for just a moment.

"I thought Beauchamp was supposed to be filling my spot?"

"Like I said, we are utilizing every available resource. As a card-carrying member of flight-team analysis, you are now officially one of those resources."

"Fine. Hit me with it. But you keep my name on that rotation list. I'll be back as soon as I can get Doc to clear me." Helen cast her gaze upwards to the black-on-black office walls. Keller's file appeared, projected from Insight, bright against the dark painted background.

"You'll be back when you're ready to be back. Not the macho OP 'I got this' bullshit kind of ready, but really, actually ready." Keller frowned, irritated. "You know better than that, right?"

"I don't think I'm going to be 'really ready' until I can get back up there and get my head around what I missed on the mission." *Until I can figure out who or what caused Ted's death.* The last part she kept to herself.

"Have you had breakfast yet?" Keller asked abruptly. It took Helen a moment to switch gears to answer.

"Not yet."

"Okay, let's take a walk." Keller abruptly got to his feet and left the cubicle, heading to the office's outer door. Surprised, Helen followed, pausing only a moment to make sure anything personal had been swept into the drawers.

Keller led the way down the carpeted corridor, the soles of his dress shoes making no sound. They passed the big picture windows that looked out onto the city, but rather than heading for the elevator, Keller turned the corner towards the interior of the building. At his approach, a door appeared in the hallway wall, one of the service doors, designed to be invisible unless there was an emergency.

"The commissary's only a few floors down and I missed my workout this morning; mind taking the stairs?"

"Who the hell takes the stairs?" Helen started to ask, but Keller had already opened the door and stepped inside. Helen hesitated. The stairwells were dead-zones, cameras only, no access to James or the rest of the Far Reaches network. *The perfect place to say things you can't say.*

Helen followed Keller in, allowing the heavy door to close behind her with a click that echoed down the metal steps.

"Bright and Mira are prepping for a second attempt," Keller said without even looking back over his shoulder to see if she was there. Something in that idea made a shiver run through all the wires in Helen's body.

Keller started downward, not too fast and not too slow.

"Already? Isn't that pushing it?" She rattled down the stairs to catch up to him, trying to keep the disbelief out of her tone. "When are they going?"

"As soon as possible, maybe a week, maybe less. And no, it's not part of Line Drive proper, it's a side-jaunt. The engineers want to get a second look at the Golfball." Keller narrowed his eyes. He'd picked up on her concern; she could see it.

"After the feedback problem gets addressed, right?"

A long pause from Keller. An uncomfortably long pause.

"AFTER, right?" Helen pushed for a yes or no. A clear answer.

"Right now all Golfball- and Line Drive-related launches are officially on hold until they make a decision about the feedback you encountered, yes." He was giving her the official, public line, but as an OP she knew better. Officially was a keyword, almost like a shorthand, that meant "this is what we are telling people while we are doing other shit under the table."

Panic fluttered. Helen felt it even through Doc's magic no-care cocktail.

"But we are on the clock here," he continued urgently. "The payload launched, so in another month or so we are going to get the wake-up ping from the payload and we are going back out there again. We've got to use the Golfball to learn everything we can, even if we have to take a few risks."

"Officially?" Helen repeated sharply.

"The Feeds are clean, there's no reason not to try." Keller looked at her closely. "This is bugging you, isn't it."

"It wasn't a technological glitch of some kind, Keller, and I *know* this wasn't human error."

"I know, I know. Something 'ate' the Golfball. Your words. But if there was a sabotage attempt, we have to get ahold of those eenies and deconstruct who was behind it."

"I don't know what it was. I do know we need to figure it out before Bright and Mira get out there and put their foot into it the way Ted and I did." Helen didn't know why the panic was rising, why she was suddenly, absolutely convinced that a second attempt was a suicide mission.

Keller looked concerned. "Trust the team, Helen. We got this."

"I want to be there." Helen gripped the railing to stop her hands from shaking. "From what I saw on the analysis side yesterday, no one has a clue about what caused that feedback."

"It's just a quick jump back out to see if Mira and Bright can get some new data. Jump in, do a scan, empty the eenie traps, get out."

"And if that sound shows up again?" Helen dodged around Keller on the stairs, halting his downward progress.

"It won't. It was a one-time glitch."

Helen tried and failed to get Keller to look her in the eye. "And if it does?"

"We'll handle it. Trust your team. Which reminds me . . ." Keller stepped around her on the stair. "I cleared it with Hofstaeder to get you back into the training sims."

"You *what*?!" Helen's apprehension was completely derailed, vanished at the unexpected revelation.

"I've got you an hour in the training sim later this week, and if that goes well, I'll get you another one the day after that. You've got to work on trainee level stuff to start, but I managed to convince her that keeping you offline, cold turkey, was going to be a problem for Line Drive. We can't afford to retrain another OP right now, so she and I split the difference."

"Holy shit, Keller, thank you!" Even the no-care cocktail couldn't dampen the sense that abruptly, suddenly, things were pointed in the right direction again. An entire new set of actions was now open and Helen's mind tried, briefly, to explore each one. Her earlier focus on the new Golfball mission had been pushed to the bottom of the list.

"Don't thank me yet, you've still got to requalify. You've got to get clearance from Hofstaeder. Until you do *both* of those things, I expect you to bust your ass for the analysis team, figuring out how we keep from losing another NAV." Keller took a moment to burst her bubble before stopping on the landing and passing his hand across the key panel to unlock it. Helen could just hear the whisper as his NFC chip shook hands with James to let them back out into Far Reaches.

When they exited, Helen's Insight chimed with a series of message icons and informational signs. She grabbed the scheduling icon from Keller first and jammed it into her calendar, blocking out the hour in the training sim before anything else could pop up and claim the time.

"You know, you could just take the promotion with good grace," Keller reiterated.

"I could also find the perfect cat," Helen responded, calling back to their previous conversation. "Thank you, Keller. This means a lot."

"C'mon, I'll buy you a coffee while we're still peers."

"You know the coffee here is free, right?" Helen asked.

"I'll make it a double, then."

CHAPTER NINE

THE STACKS OF CONTROL PODS resembled nothing so much as the capsule-hotels that plagued downtown Launch City, offering single-user isolation on an hourly basis. Each rack in the brightly lit room held five "coffins" on vertical rails so OPs could work in shifts. The room was always too cold for Helen's liking, but today she felt the chill as anticipation, rather than server-dependent air conditioning.

What she hadn't counted on was the fear. Completely irrational, nipping at the back of her brain, fear. It told her if she got back into that coffin, she might not be coming back out again. Hofstaeder had taken her off the emo-blockers for the sake of her getting back into the coffins early. It meant she had to be on guard, examine each reaction a little more carefully.

Don't be stupid. OPs don't die in coffins. Helen lied to herself to put the hesitation out of her mind. She shoved the idea that if a NAV could die, an OP could go even faster, back into a corner behind the thrill of being back where she belonged. She was not about to step back now, not when Keller had handed her an opportunity.

After a week offline, her Far-Reaches-blue supersuit was a little stiff and took a bit of adjustment. Once the conductive gel was pumped in, it warmed to body temperature and fit on the inside like a second skin. It served as one of the hundred points of feedback allowing her to transfer her body awareness to a nanofiber and titanium remote-operated waldo across a million miles or more. Or in op-speak, it meant she'd be far less likely to bump into things on the other end.

"Welcome back, Vectorovich." The on-duty tech waved her over to the stack. A quick punch of a button and the coffins cycled until an empty one stood ready, lid open, interior lights aglow. "Ready to get back in the saddle?"

"You know it." Helen placed her hands on either side of the open coffin and quickly levered herself inside to conceal her shaking. She knew perfectly well she would be under scrutiny. Hofstaeder and Keller would be going over her performance, looking for signs that she wasn't ready to go back.

The connection points between her shoulder blades were a centimeter lower than Far Reaches standard. Helen had to adapt, piling the coffin's gel padding up behind her knees and scooching down until the magnetic connectors snapped together. The coffin screens lit up with the pre-mission display, time to entanglement counting down. She could see her outline reflected in the coffin above her, a humanoid shadow lit by the coffin's interior glow.

"Operator Vectorovich, are you ready to engage?" The tech read off the consent line and Helen stuck her arm up out of the coffin, thumb up in the universal symbol for HELL YES.

"Preparing for full entanglement," the tech replied.

Helen heard the rasp of protective gloves on the touchscreen controls as the tech ordered the coffin's computer to engage. She pulled her arm back as the coffin lid slid closed and the atmosphere started to pressurize. Helen could feel the change in her eardrums, in the back of her throat. The connectors along her spine opened up. She could feel the cold as nutrient fluid began to suffuse her veins, and the uncomfortable prickle as nerves fell asleep, then went numb. She closed her eyes and exhaled, a long deep breath, as the computer interface became the only thing she could see or feel or touch.

The waldo they'd assigned her for this retraining mission wasn't too much of a beater. The previous op had left it in good order. Slipping into a warmed up waldo was akin to finding the toilet seat already warm from someone else's ass. It didn't feel quite right. It took a few minutes until your brain caught up with what your body was feeling.

Welcome to the cryo-spa of Capricorn216. The words scrolled across the bottom of her vision, a joke left by the previous operator. Helen let the marquee text run and snapped a screenshot for her personal file.

"Mark local time 12:14:56. Station live, station live, station live." The NAV's clipped, abrupt tones were unfamiliar.

They've teamed me up with a rookie, Helen realized. On a mission like this it shouldn't matter much; she had to remember to be patient, to execute the requests exactly. Milk run, rookie NAV, should be simple enough. She didn't know what she'd been expecting, but a boring run collecting mineral samples might just be what she needed.

"Operator Helen Vectorovich, personal identifier T4T4-957. Waldo is live, beginning initialization protocols." Helen dropped back into old habits like she'd never missed a mission day. The waldo's responses were recorded, one by one, as she went through the checklist that had popped up in her line of sight.

The spherical waldo was a surface-only drone, sensors and cameras built into an outer shell made of reconfigurable panels. It was nearly indestructible as long as you kept it from getting submerged in whatever liquid hell they'd dropped you next to. She shivered in recognition.

Capricorn216 was a common training spot. The near-space rocky body contained enough frozen methane to power an off-world colony for decades or fuel the AI-driven drones that maintained the systems' solitary jumpgate. Far Reaches had been mining the frozen methane here for a couple of decades. The surface was beyond freezing. Lakes of methane being prepared for harvesting posed a challenge for OPs who'd trained on waldos with legs. The crystalline slush around the edges of the lake melted under her belly as Helen rolled herself into position. She hunted for a clean space where the previous operators had not yet ground the ice into the substrate.

The payload of eenies had been dropped onto the new mining site months ago. A couple of weeks of growth and they'd begun working to convert the methane ice to a stable liquid that could be shipped off site. The lakes and puddles were stunning on Helen's color camera, even more so through the eye of the spectrograph.

Helen continued her slow roll, enjoying the feeling of the ice crunching under her belly.

"Operator Vectorovitch, you may proceed with list item one," the NAV's voice in her ear continued with the crisp tones, precise pronunciations.

Oh great. One of those.

There were many different kinds of NAVs. Some were chitchatty; you could count on them to keep you focused through conversation, dumb jokes and the like. Helen knew of one who read poetry by long dead deep-space miners. On the other end of the spectrum, you got the clinicians, those who lived and died by the list and barely gave you five words in between. Low-level training missions like this one often matched NAVs and OPs at random. Partnerships didn't start to show up until year two or three, unless an OP and a NAV showed exceptional teamwork from the outset.

I didn't think they'd match me up with the "listy" type.

"Confirmed. I'm just moving so we can get the best possible samples," Helen replied.

"Negative, Operator Vectorovitch."

What? "Repeat, please."

"Negative. All activities are to be constrained to list-specific items only."

"Have you seen how torn up it is over there? Any samples will be compromised," Helen protested even as the list in the corner of her eye turned a dangerous shade of orange.

Deep breaths. Helen reminded herself. She was going to have to adjust her own attitude. OPs were supposed to have leeway, the ability to judge situations on the fly. That was half the point of having a live operator running the waldo instead of an AI. Conflict between NAVs and OPs never ended well, even on a mission-by-mission basis, but sometimes the lesson had to be learned the hard way. *I'm not supposed to be training NAVs out here,* Helen groused in her own head.

She had an opportunity to give a new NAV something to work with, to do some actual instruction. Under other circumstances that would be exactly what she would do. But the goal of these missions, for her, was re-credentialing. Her performance would be under review, which meant her goal had to be proving she could still do the job. Coloring outside the lines, even if it might help the NAV get some real-world experience, would likely be counted against her.

Suck it up and comply, then.

"Affirmative. Shall I return to the previous site, or shall I take the samples from here?"

"Do not continue your trajectory. Retrieve your samples from your current coordinates. Deviation from the checklist has been noted and logged."

Fuckity fuck fuck fuck. "Confirmed." Helen brought the waldo to a gentle stop and started the collection sequence. Its outside skin broke open and the panels folded back, revealing the robotic sample arm. The list returned to its original soft, glowing green. Helen snapped a set of images from the new sample site and attached them to the mission log. That, along with the sensor readings on the condition of the terrain, would serve to appeal the notation later.

Notations weren't the end of a career; any experienced operator collected a few dozen over the course of their lifetime. With Hofstaeder and Keller both keeping an eye on her performance, she'd wanted this run to be perfect.

Alongside that idea, the chattering in her head began again. Here in the waldo it was easier to put it out of her head, easier to ignore. It sounded much less like random noise and much more like communication. Helen found herself half listening, trying to pick out words she recognized as she went through the motions to follow the checklist.

By the time the methane was all gone, the space rock would be a little more than a collection of loosely related rubble. At that point it would be ready for consumption by an entirely different class of tiny machines. Instead of wasting the millions of eenies that had been built for collecting the methane, they'd be broken down and re-purposed.

Everything in space was disposable, recyclable, reusable if you had the right tools for it.

Helen found herself poring over the eenie operating data while waiting for confirmation between list items. She took the opportunity to examine the characteristics of different types and their tasks. Reading helped keep the chatter in her head at bay.

There was no waste. Every mite was set a task, and when it broke down or failed in its programming, it was consumed and recycled into another type of mite. There were no leftovers, no broken pieces.

No dust. The thought sent a shiver down her spine, but she didn't know why.

"Confirmed samples, Operator Vectorovitch. Please proceed to protocol step five."

Helen suppressed a sigh as she moved to the next item on the list. According to the readout, she'd been on shift for half an hour already. *Never been a clock watcher before.* But this mission and her temporary NAV sucked all the fun out of riding the waldo. Even an AI could do a better banter than this.

"Operator Vectorovitch, please begin item seven of your mission protocol."

Wait, what? Did I miss number six? The list turned orange again, again warning her about going off protocol. Item six showed the glowing green checkmark of completion. She didn't remember completing the item.

"Confirmed, NAV, sample taking has begun."

"Negative, Operator Vectrovitch. Please stop current activity and move to the new sample point."

Helen checked the list again. NAV was right, she was supposed to change locations before the next sample. But she could've sworn that step hadn't been there before. *Serves you right for getting distracted.*

"Of course, moving now." Helen brought the sampling arm back in and began her slow roll.

"Confirmed. Noted."

Helen held in her frustrated reply. She could go scream at her apartment walls after shift change if she needed to. One minor mistake after another was beginning to wear on her.

Maybe I wasn't ready to get back out into a waldo just yet.

That poisonous thought hung in the corner of her mind just above the imaginary list of very real errors.

Moving the waldo, when she got the chance to do so, was a joy.

For a spherical waldo in low-g, there was no "up," but there was a filter in place that kept the flow of information to Helen's mind properly oriented. The crunching of the ice and the hissing of the lake in near-vacuum were not "sounds," they were vibrations and structural data. Helen could turn them off, but the point of a human-operated waldo was the unconscious ability to process all that information as if one's own body were present.

So when the ice under the waldo cracked, Helen reacted without thinking, she just jumped. A million miles away, her body jerked in response, even through the restraint of the supersuit.

"NAV, problem." The two words were all she had time to get out. Helen's waldo popped into the air a few centimeters. It tried desperately to interpret the signals coming from Helen's brain and body, but it had not been designed to jump, only to roll. The new location she'd arrived at was a slab of ice that the eenies were *already* breaking down. It had been weakened, breaking it into independent chunks before turning it to a collectible gas. If she didn't get to solid ice, she'd be dropped into the depths of the methane lake, something the waldo certainly was not equipped to handle.

I wonder what that would feel like. Helen dropped the errant thought as the NAV's task list turned red, then got replaced with an emergency protocol list.

ENVIRONMENTAL INCIDENT

First mission out and I'm running emergency protocols again? The panic started to rise, but this time Helen was unconstrained. This time she was in her element, riding a waldo with an entire array of tools and actions at her disposal. Helen yanked open the interface and started digging for what she needed while the NAV chattered, unheeded, in the background.

A glance at the waldo designs told her it was way too slow to give her a proper shove off the failing ice. She had to find a way to use the mass of the waldo in her favor.

Helen pulled up the movement simulator and requested a speed and trajectory with all the waldo's sensor panels open. Combined with the rotational force, they should give her enough traction to get to solid ground. While Helen ran the numbers, the ball continued to roll like a tire stuck in the mud. The friction melted the ice even faster.

NAV kept talking and the list changed to green again, back to standard protocols. It almost gave Helen pause, but the readings from the waldo said she wasn't in the clear yet. *Why the hell is NAV re-tasking the list?* No matter, Helen was already into her sequence of actions, the waldo's computer giving her speed and rotation data she needed.

Riding a waldo meant an OP felt every surface, every joint. Helen opened all the panels and felt the edges bite in, launching her forward as the rest of the sheet passed through liquid to gas. The waldo touched back down on solid ice with a bump and a shimmy.

"Operator Vectorovich, please return to protocol or this mission will be terminated."

"Hold on, NAV, I need to verify the stability . . ."

"Beauchamp said you were a loose cannon, Vectorovich. Prepare for mission termination in five . . ."

What the hell? The NAV's words over the past minute suddenly came through Helen's action-oriented fog. The repeated demands to cease action made no sense, but the checklist flashed red in Helen's line of sight, indicating a mission failure. If Cat Beauchamp had been talking to the NAV before or even during the mission, looking to sabotage Helen's re-certification, then she had a whole different kind of problem on her hands.

"On what grounds?" Helen watched as the protocol shifted again. *You don't break mission. Ever.* Sure, if an OP cracks, or the waldo explodes, but otherwise you just don't do it. *So what the hell is up with this NAV and why the hell has he been talking to Beauchamp?*

"Mission is behind schedule due to OP's failure to stay on protocol."

"Stay on protocol? OP's discretion here, NAV, I can't take ice samples from the *underside* of the ice." Helen stayed calm and collected. Now that she knew, or at least suspected, that she was being sabotaged, she could move to counter. As long as she stayed professional, the NAV would be the one getting all the questions if the mission failed.

"Joyriding around the surface is simply not allowed."

"Of course not . . ." Helen took a deep breath and let it out to defuse the flash of indignation. The logs would bear witness that she was trying to keep the waldo from going into the drink. Because this was a training-level mission, everything would be recorded. If she could keep the NAV from pulling the plug, they'd both come out all right. If he declared a mission failure, they'd both be in the soup.

"The waldo's back on solid ground now. I can proceed with the protocol. There's only ten minutes left on mission, can we ride this out?"

There was a long pause.

C'mon, c'mon, c'mon . . . Off mission meant punitive response for both OP and NAV. An older, more experienced NAV would shrug off the black mark if things had truly gotten out of control.

Helen was willing to bet this NAV didn't know what Beauchamp was asking him to risk.

"I can get us back on schedule," Helen wheedled. The waldo had a backup set of instrumentation she could put into play. She'd have a hell of a headache later, it would burn her out faster than normal, but she was willing to risk it to see if calling the NAV's bluff worked out.

"Fine. But stick to the list."

"Of course. Next item coming up."

And then I'm going to have to go have a little talk with Catherine Beauchamp.

CHAPTER TEN

"They're going to make you fight the reprimand." Keller passed Helen a soda-bulb from the vending machine. "Sorry, HR changed vendors again."

The vending machine offering was his way of taking the edge off her attitude. Helen had stormed into his office to read him the riot act about saddling her with an incompatible NAV. Three weeks into the required retraining sessions and every NAV had been a mismatch since day one. She stuck her tongue out at the generic red label before popping the top.

"It's not that I care so much about the branding, it's that the knockoffs never actually taste like what they're pretending to copy." Helen took a sip, then made a face, showing the beverage's brown carbonated bubbles between her teeth.

"Ugh." Keller waved her off. "That's disgusting."

"I'm not worried about having to fight the reprimand." Helen took a moment to suck in the offending bubbles, then followed with another sip. "I'm worried about wasting time having to fight dirty." She paced the floor of the cubicle, trying to work off her agitation. "I'd rather just be better at being an OP, rather than being 80% OP, 20% politician. Beauchamp is trying to make sure I don't get back out there and I don't understand why."

"She wants your spot." Keller shook his head. "She's got the skills, you can't deny that. The only thing keeping her from being added to the Line Drive team now that you're down is the fact that Ivester's sequestered the group." He rocked back in his chair. "You're going to have to figure this out like a pair of grownups."

"So why am I dealing with the procedural bullshit? It will take a week to appeal the reprimand, if I get paired with another toxic NAV . . ."

"You *need* an advocate. You're not the easiest OP to work with."

"A crap NAV who goes to all the right parties." Helen ignored him and continued her pacing. The bad training mission had her on edge. Weeks out and she was still finding her way through the knots of checklists around getting her certification back.

"Ted wasn't a crap NAV," Keller pointed out quietly.

Helen felt a quick stab of guilt. She took a long, slow breath, waiting for the prickle of potential tears to subside before saying anything. Mentions of Ted did that, brought emotion to the fore, out of the space in her chest where she kept them locked away. They didn't wiggle their way out, it was more like they had a fast track to her brain. Feelings she'd thought she had a handle on waltzed past all her defenses like they weren't even there. One second she was fine, the next she could barely speak. *Get your shit together.*

"You're right," she said finally. "Ted was an excellent NAV. He was also the one who knew everyone, who to talk to, what to say. I handled the hardware, he handled the people. I can't even get my head around replacing him."

"I can set you up with a computer NAV for the next training session, it's allowed, but that won't solve the problem of finding you a NAV to get you back on rotation for the Golfball," Keller said gently.

Helen scrubbed her fingers through her hair in a gesture of frustration. "After today's mission, I'm open to more options."

"Oh?" Keller looked surprised. "It was *that* bad a match?"

"I'm up for review due to mission outcomes. *Five* separate incidents in one mission." Helen held up fingers to match. "FIVE.

When was the last time you had a senior operator get five write-ups? It was punitive at best, and the mission tapes will back me up."

"Five? What the hell did you do?" It was clear Keller had been imagining a single reprimand, typical NAV/OP conflict stuff. Now that Helen had dropped a number, he was suddenly much more interested. He pulled up the mission logs and threw them up on the wall so they could go over them together.

Helen grimaced. "I'm an asshole, I get that, but not a *five-incident* asshole. It was a routine sample collection. Some combination of bad circumstance and shifting conditions."

"So what, your NAV changed protocols too fast?"

"Do you think I'd have trouble keeping up with a rookie NAV? I'm in the middle of a course change because the ice was going right to gas under the waldo, and he's harping on me to get back to sample collection." Helen called up the last fifteen minutes of her shift and projected them onto the wall, highlighting the protocols as they popped up along the timeline.

"Could he have been getting bad feedback from the waldo, maybe?"

"Maybe, but we're supposed to have a certain amount of discretion up there. The NAV is supposed to trust the OP. Instead I'm getting dinged for trying to save the waldo rather than grabbing samples according to schedule." Helen blew out a long, exasperated breath. "Sorry. It's just, not enough time in a coffin, and I was expecting a nice, vacation-y stroll across an asteroid on a training-level mission. Now I'm just vexed."

"I'll run through the mission logs, put a different perspective in the report," Keller offered.

"Logs will bear me out, but it was weird." She waited a long moment before her next statement, aware of how it might sound. "Couple that with the fact that the Beauchamp's been talking behind my back."

"Hah. So you think she's gunning for you? She set the NAV up to wreck your mission?"

"Maybe, maybe not, but I just want it on record in case this kind of thing happens more than once. No point in leaving my backside unprotected."

"Beauchamp's going to be playing on the rumors." Keller closed the files, packaged them up again. "Since your line about the Golf-ball getting 'eaten' got leaked, some of the NAVs have added you to their 'incompatible' list."

"It doesn't help that I've been muzzled because of the investigation. I can't get out there and plead my case; everybody thinks I've been locked away in this weird 'not on the team' space because of the damn NDAs."

"So just step up, take the promotion. Let Beauchamp have the seat."

NAVs and OPs were allowed to blacklist personalities they didn't mesh with. It didn't always get you out of working with someone. Far Reaches didn't particularly care if you liked each other or not, but it went on record and was factored in if a mission went side-ways. Known bad matches were kept off high-value missions like Line Drive. Helen couldn't afford to wind up on too many blacklists, and she couldn't break the NDA to defend herself, otherwise she'd never get back out to the Golfball. She was losing the battle and she knew it.

"Dammit, Keller. I need to get back out there." Helen started to pace again, repeating the five steps from one side of Keller's office to the other.

"Look, Analysis wants you full time. You've picked up on the mission files faster than anyone expected of a waldo-jockey. Why don't you take the pay bump and run with it?"

"Oh hell, Keller, I don't know." Helen dropped into one of the room's empty chairs. "It just feels like I am being handled rather than having earned a new spot."

Keller chuckled. "Of course you didn't earn it, not if you think about it like your rotation seat. The earning comes after."

"Are you sure that's soda you're drinking?"

Keller eyeballed the label suspiciously. "Is anybody ever really sure what's in one of these things? I mean, it says 10% juice, but that could be eyeball juice or tuna juice for all I know, as long as it tastes good."

"I think you'd be able to tell if it was tuna juice."

Keller pulled the conversation back onto the rails. "There is no 'earning' once you get out of rank. It's more like a convergence, especially if you move up within the company. You have skills X and Y2, they have an opening that needs X2 and Y2, they respect your skills, don't think you're an HR hazard, and pop, you're in the new gig."

"I think that's a gross oversimplification."

"It absolutely is. But the point is, a certain percent of the 'earning' comes after. Rather than fight like the dickens to *get* the spot like you do as an OP, now you have to fight to *keep* the spot. If you're missing a skill, you have to learn it. If your team moves on to some aspect out of your wheelhouse, then you find a way to become enough of an expert to keep the rest of the team moving forward."

"That's . . . That's worth thinking about."

"Of course, that means you have to give up your seat to Beauchamp."

"See, you just shut down your whole argument with one, single sentence."

"You really hate Beauchamp that much?"

"Not at all. She's an exceptional OP."

"But?"

Helen paused, considering her next words. Ted would have known how to phrase it for best effect, how to get Keller to actually listen. "You already know this, Keller. She's cutthroat, she plays favorites. The senior operators set an example for the rest. I can only imagine what's going to happen to flight operations if she ends up being the benchmark."

"One woman is not going to turn a hundred OPs into cutthroat reprobates."

"I hope you're right about that one."

"Well, you're going to have to either fish or cut bait pretty damn quick. If you can't get re-certified, she's getting your spot." Keller polished off the soda bulb and chucked it, without looking, at the recycle bin. It rattled off the counter and wall before clattering in. There was a quick whiff of ozone as the eenies inside returned it to feedstock for recycling.

"We have an eight a.m. meeting on the final checklist for the return mission, and I could do with a couple hours shut-eye." Keller stretched his arms to towards the ceiling.

Helen checked her own schedule. "I've got it in for 8:30. Are you sure you're right?"

"Your friend Dougal booked it in."

Helen held up her tablet to show him. "See, 8:30."

"Well, one of us has the wrong invite." Keller scrubbed his calendar back and forth, looking for another.

"Ugh. I'm having a string of minor, stupid things going wrong, this is just another one on the list. This morning I had to wait an hour outside the lab for Dougal because my chip wasn't recognized. I better get there early, just in case." Helen closed up her files and jammed the tablet into her back pocket.

"It will give us some alone time with the breakfast selection." Keller tapped fingertips together in mock anticipation.

Helen laughed. Keller lived off-site, and his preference for the prefab, identical servings the commissary provided was nearly legendary. One of the other OPs had joked that anyone who hired Keller away would have to match dining contractors as part of the package.

Helen paused at the cubicle door. "I'll let you know what the committee comes back with."

"I'll get the review expedited. If you're staying on Line Drive, then we need you cleared as soon as possible."

"Thanks. See you at eight."

CHAPTER ELEVEN

"So is this going to be an ongoing problem with you?" Helen got right to the point. She didn't have the time, or the patience, for dancing around. She'd found Beauchamp, and her angry aqua pouf of hair, holding court in the commissary between shifts, seated at one of the tables in the back, telling stories to a handful of younger personnel. The other OP collected newly minted OPs and NAVs the way birds collected shiny objects. She was experienced enough in her own right, but she supplemented that skill by keeping a finger on any up-and-coming talent. If they got in her way, she encouraged them to make career-ending decisions under the guise of advancement.

"Is what going to be a problem? You getting your NAV killed, or is there something else I'm missing?" Beauchamp smiled. Helen resisted the urge to slap her. She hadn't expected confronting Beauchamp would expose that Ted-shaped hole again. The reminder that she was missing a piece, a complementary soul, burned in the back of her mind. *Do not lose your shit or she wins.*

"I don't know what you said to that rookie NAV to get him to throw the training mission, but he's going up for review." Helen cast a glance as the two or three rookies at the table. "If you're coming for me, then git gud, don't burn the newbies because you're afraid to lose."

Her words had some impact at least. Glances were exchanged

around the edges of the cluster of OPs and NAVs at the table. *Good.* If she could at least sow some doubt, then she might not have to put up with Beauchamp coming at her from the side. The OP rotation could be cutthroat, as missions were assigned based on skill, experience and seniority, in that order. Helen had two out of three over Beauchamp. In order for the younger OP to move up in the ranks, Helen had to come down. Ted had been the one to handle the Flight Ops politics. Helen had made sure every mission came out a success. It had been a perfect pairing, but now Helen was vulnerable and it looked like Beauchamp was using that to her advantage. *Beauchamp's not the only one who has to git gud.*

"I'm not responsible for Yoshi's actions," Beauchamp replied. "He's an inspired NAV, even if he is just starting out. I'm sure his review will sort out in the end."

"You really couldn't care less, could you." Helen eyed her would-be rival. "What's your goal here, Cat?" The two or three younger OPs and NAVs in attendance had begun to drift away as their Insights notified them of the shift change. Beauchamp got lazily to her feet and closed the distance between them. They were near enough in mass for it to be a fair fight, if it came to that. But Helen's goal wasn't a physical confrontation. She needed to call Beauchamp out, publicly. She needed to put the other OP on notice with witnesses so that any future issues between them would get a second or third look.

"Goal? Just watching you fail is goal enough. Why the hell are they even letting you re-qualify after Ted?"

"It was a glitch in the quantum Feed." The defense was out before Helen could stop it. *Shit.* Beauchamp blanched at the words. Helen pressed her momentary advantage. "Look, I'm not interested in a nasty competition. If you want me out, fine, we're both OPs, we can stay the hell out of each other's way and let our records do the talking. If this is more personal, then tell me what your problem is and we can have it out like adults."

Something wasn't right. Helen expected Beauchamp to rise to the challenge. She was expecting a fight, one way or the other. Instead the other OP looked vaguely ill.

"No problems. Excuse me." Beauchamp walked off without another word. She left Helen standing there.

"Excuse you? We're not done, Cat!" Helen called after the other OP, but she'd pulled out her Insight and was headed for the door with a singular focus.

What the actual hell was that?

Puzzled, Helen watched the other OP make her way across the commissary. She had come spoiling for a fight and instead Beauchamp just turned tail and ran.

Or something. Helen examined the faces she could recognize in the crowd. She hadn't heard Beauchamp's Insight ping, hadn't seen anyone signaling. Something had set her off.

CHAPTER TWELVE

HELEN CURLED UP in the comfortable chair in Hofstaeder's treatment office and stewed. The medical end of this latest "debrief" had taken an hour out of her day and she still hadn't been cleared to get back in a coffin. Worst of all, they'd left her in the pink room, the one that smelled like cleaning supplies. She hated the smell; it reminded her of childhood at the Crèche.

Beauchamp said you were a loose cannon, Vectorovich. The NAV's comment rattled around the inside of her head. Words that, according to Hofstaeder, didn't show up on the mission recordings. There was always the possibility that Doc was lying, but it didn't seem likely. She'd already bent the rules to allow Helen back into a waldo and made a deal with Keller to keep the operator in the queue for the Line Drive missions. There was no reason for her to be clever. Hofstaeder could simply sign an order keeping Helen out of the coffins and none could gainsay it.

There was always the possibility that Helen hadn't heard those words from the NAV at all. That some part of her subconscious might have filled in the gaps while she'd been struggling to get the waldo back to solid ground. That didn't feel right either, but she couldn't discount it entirely. Helen hadn't bothered to make a private record, since it had just been a training mission. It would be her word against the recording, and while she knew the mission data would bear her out, the fact that bits were missing had her rattled.

A mistake you won't be making again.

Presuming she wasn't in the early stages of some kind of mental break, that left deliberate sabotage. Helen turned that idea over in her head, tickled its underbelly to see how it moved. Direct sabotage by one operator against another wasn't unheard of. It was a much more common occurrence at smaller companies like Distant Sun or Animus. Helen had spent her first couple years as an OP for Animus fighting tooth and claw for her missions. While the Far Reaches ranking system wasn't perfect, it kept infighting to a minimum. What if Beauchamp had made a deal with the NAV to screw up the mission, to keep Helen out of the coffins? It would open up a seat on the Line Drive project. Helen was the only OP on the rails, the only vulnerable spot.

Yes, but why? This is a lot of work for what? Fame? Access? First in line for Chef's waffles? Competition was one thing; the slights and psychological tricks used to get a performance edge over another OP were common. Beauchamp had tried for placement on the Line Drive project a year before but hadn't made the cut. Waldos like the spider model were new units, custom-tailored to the needs of the Line Drive project. Beauchamp hadn't been able to get up to speed quickly enough. *That's cold. Do you really think she's capable of that kind of backstabbing?* Even for an operator as ambitious as Beauchamp, deliberately scuttling another OP to get access to their mission lineup was a brutal move.

I signed up to ride waldos, not play private detective. Ted had been much better at the internal politics, keeping track of who had an issue with whom. Helen keenly felt the empty space her NAV had left behind. She couldn't afford to trust someone else to solve this problem. She was going to have to dig into this herself, figure out if Beauchamp was truly gunning for her and what to do about it.

Helen had sunk so deep into her own thoughts the knock at the door surprised her. She swung her feet off the arm of the chair, straightened up into some semblance of professionalism despite the ache in her spine and bruises on her elbows and knees. She closed her eyes for a three-count to re-center herself before she responded.

"Come in."

"Ah, there you are. Is the queen of kill switches done with you yet?" Keller's voice bounced off the office walls. Helen popped her eyes open, startled to see he'd snuck in through Hofstaeder's office door.

"I'm waiting on something. Not sure what," Helen answered truthfully.

"Can't be too important then. Let's get a move on." Keller stepped in, and with exaggerated care, closed the door behind him.

"What? Where to?"

"I take it they didn't keep you in the loop?" Keller pushed the hall door open and glanced down the hall like he was checking for security.

"Nope. Still dealing with the fallout from my 'training mission.'" Helen bracketed the phrase with air-quotes.

"That's going to have to wait. They bumped up the reconnection mission to the Golfball, and the countdown's already started."

Keller shoved the door open wide and waved her over. She followed him out through Hofstaeder's office, only to find the Doc herself striding down the hall in their direction.

"What the hell, Keller? Already?" The idea filled her with dread; the feeling crept in and pooled like ice water in her chest.

"It's not a full-blown run, they're just going to reconnect to be sure you launched the payload. I'll cover with Hofstaeder. I promised you could be there, remember?"

"I did launch the damn payload. They shouldn't be doing this," Helen said sourly. The dread colored her mood, dampened her natural curiosity. Whatever had put Ted in the hospital was still an unknown. They wouldn't take another run at it unless they had figured out the cause of that feedback. She tried to convince herself that maybe something new had come down the line while she'd been on mission, but that thought rang false. Far Reaches was like any other company, perfectly capable of risky decisions when money was on the line. Perfectly capable of finding an operator or a NAV willing to take that risk.

"They're not getting any telemetry off it yet, and the PR fallout means they need to confirm it's out there. Just go, I'll meet you at the Fishbowl." Keller gave her a light shove in the right direction, then turned and trotted to intercept Hofstaeder. The physician didn't bother to raise her voice, just set her arms akimbo in a resigned gesture and waited for the department head to approach. Helen paused a long moment, the checklist in her head in conflict with Keller's instruction. She turned and jogged down the corridor towards the operations center. She hated working in the dark, and she couldn't shake the feeling that a big piece of something was missing.

It took her only a couple of minutes to get to the Fishbowl. The operations gallery served as the central command hub for remote operation missions. There were ten such "fishbowls" in the building, all identical. Each command space paired with a viewing gallery for trainees, press corps, investors, school fieldtrips, any group that might have a valid reason to observe an operations team in full flight. Line Drive had its own, dedicated gallery, identical to the others, but with more locks on the doors and more chairs in the gallery.

"Control, this is Operator Bright, personal identifier K45Y-T7M4, we are live, we are live, we are live." Nick's voice came over the speakers loud and clear as the door to the Fishbowl opened on Helen's approach. She threaded her way through the empty rows of seats to the glass wall at the front of the room. They'd all been full when Helen and Ted had made their run. Ivester wasn't risking an audience this time.

Beyond the windows lay the control gallery for Line Drive. Banks of screens covered every available flat surface. The space held half a dozen experts, including Dr. Ivester, all discussing the incoming data as it sheeted across the walls. At the center of it all sat the NAV in a reclining chair, surrounded in a half-dome of smaller screens and communications equipment. An OP's entire nervous system connected through the coffin directly to a waldo. In contrast, the

NAV was one step removed, hooked in with a brain-only connection handled by a delicate tracery of a helmet. Helen had never driven a NAV's chair, but she could imagine the frustration of only being able to give instruction, rather than take direct action.

Watching someone else finish the job she started was painful, but Keller was right. She needed to see it through.

"Confirmed, begin protocols." The NAV was fully helmeted, so Helen couldn't get a look at the face, but it sounded like Mira. No surprises there. The younger NAV was a risk-taker, prone to making big decisions quickly. Ted's death was an outlier, a one-in-a-million event. Barely a risk worth mentioning to someone like Mira.

Helen activated the touch panels on the gallery walls to get a direct look as the NAV computer reached out and shook hands with the Golfball. The mission details spooled out before her eyes. First order of business would be to see if the Golfball could still receive a signal. Next up was to see how much of the Golfball and the spider waldo remained intact. She got a good look at the current range of suspicions, ranging from "OP error" . . . *Thanks assholes . . . through* "asteroid strike" and "eenie programming malfunction." So they were shotgunning the information collection, trying out a few theories all at once from the get-go.

That's a relief.

Helen pinged Mira through the Insight to let her know she was watching, common courtesy, and got an upraised middle finger in reply. Ivester took note of the gesture and turned to glance at the mirrored surface of the glass. Helen held up a hand to acknowledge the look, though she was pretty sure he couldn't see her. The images started to come in every second or so as Bright, from his coffin two floors down in the Mortuary, began to test the remains of the waldo that Helen had abandoned.

"I'm getting red icons all over the board. Whatever went wrong with the waldo, it's not gonna make this trip an easy one," Bright said.

"Follow the protocols," Mira barked back.

It was weird being on the receiving end of things. Helen could watch, but she couldn't act. It was like wearing a pair of mittens while trying to play the piano. She began to pace along the glass wall that separated the gallery from the Fishbowl, eyes on the glittering data as it poured across the screens. The view from inside the waldo, the *memory* of her view, resolved itself in her mind's eye.

"Did you say gone?"

Helen pulled her attention back at the disbelief in Ivester's tone. She'd missed whatever had triggered it.

"Affirmative." Bright's response was confident enough.

"I can verify that. Two of the waldo's legs aren't registering with the system." Mira backed up her OP, throwing the feedback data onto the big screens for all to see.

Bright continued his report. "Looks like an active issue, guys. Whatever the primary team walked into, it's still going on."

"We didn't account for this being an ongoing problem," Mira said quietly.

"Yes, we did," Helen murmured to herself. She tapped the glass wall and singled out three dual-purpose tools, quietly reflecting them back to Mira. The NAV didn't acknowledge the help, not in front of Ivester, but quietly added them to her bag of tricks.

"Okay, Bright, let's start ticking off boxes," the NAV called out.

"Affirmative."

This was a smash-and-grab, so running all of the startup checks and corrections wasn't as important. The Golfball, like all remotely driven ships, carried traps designed to catch random eenies for quality control. The goal was to grab a few that had gone rogue so they could be deconstructed, their code examined.

"Control, the trap is dead on this end," Bright spoke up. "I'm showing a dead icon. No signal, not even a warning light."

"I'm seeing incoming code," Mira responded. "The trap is still alive, but it looks like the lines connecting it to the Golfball's main interface are offline. I can see it, but you can't."

"So much for doing this the easy way then," Bright quipped.

"There is no easy in space," Mira reminded him tartly.

Every pair had their ebb and flow, it was the kind of thing that developed quickly between a good NAV/OP team. The back-and-forth made communications easier and kept both parties focused and on task. Mira and Bright were no exception. It threw into sharp relief the absolute incompatibility Helen had just experienced on her training mission. It reminded Helen just how long it had taken to find a NAV that she could really work with.

"All remaining systems check out. Hey, Mira, you ever see what happens when a fish dies in one of those big saltwater tanks? All the other fish start nibbling off the extremities first, you know, the fins and the eyeballs. That's kind of what it feels like with the waldo here. The core architecture is all firm, but all the outlying stuff has gotten eaten away." Bright kept chattering as new and different information started coming down the Feed.

"Haven't we had this chat about your icky metaphors before? Stick to direct observation, Bright."

"Fine, but I'm just saying if any of the eenie behaviors were proto-typed off of a goldfish, you might want to look there first."

Mira's response could best be characterized as a full body eye-roll. Helen stopped the laugh before it reached her lips. *No distractions now.*

"Operator Bright, please move to protocol three of four and proceed."

"Affirmative. Hey, are you guys seeing all this dust?" Bright asked and redirected one of his cameras for a closer look. On the other side of the window, Ivester threw another sharp glance in Helen's direction.

Helen closed her eyes, took a deep breath. *Dust, dust, something about the dust.*

"Confirmed, but focus on that next. First we need to get to the traps."

"I'm going to recommend examining the dust more closely on the next go-round," Bright stated. "Primary team mentioned it in their report, but I think we underestimated the volume."

Helen flipped through the list of protocols she and Dougal had put together and with a silent motion of her fingertips popped a new one up on Mira's screen. Helen couldn't see Mira's face, but the shift in her shoulders said she'd got the instruction.

"Affirmative, Bright. Analysis suggests we take that one next." Mira's fingers played across her touchscreens as she rolled Helen's suggestion into her protocol list and passed it down the link to Bright. While a mission was active, at least, OPs backed OPs. Helen knew Mira would accept the suggestions with good grace as long as it didn't impede the mission.

"Great, moving to containment." New images began appearing, one after the other. Bright switched cameras for better magnification. There were places where the image was choppy, showing holes where the damaged sensors couldn't pull in enough data.

Having been there, plugged into that waldo, Helen could "see" the damage in her mind's eye, could tell exactly what sensors were offline. Her memory filled in the gaps, the location of this button or that. The images that were coming back painted a rosier picture. It was as if those cameras had been deliberately turned off to conceal some of the damage.

"Okay, I'm at trap 510-1311. It's empty, and you're going to love this."

"I don't love anything about this," Mira said distractedly as Ivester leaned close and asked a quiet question.

"It's busted open, nibbled away just like the extra legs on this waldo."

"Busted. Open?" Ivester asked, sharp divisions between the words. Mira repeated the question so that Bright could hear.

"Affirmative."

"Okay, record everything, then move to the next trap."

"Affirmative."

The queasy, crawling feeling was back. Helen typed in a question and sent it down to Mira's screen.

"Operator Bright, please make sure you get an electron micrograph shot at that trap. Molecular-scale, if you can crank down that far." Ivester made that request and Mira passed it along without question. Ivester asked Mira a second question, and she just jerked her thumb over her shoulder at where Helen was standing behind the glass. He turned and frowned.

"Ms. Vectorovich, I was told you were still in recovery." His message scrolled out across the touchwall. Inside the Fishbowl, his lips barely moved. *Neat trick, that.*

"Officially, yes, sir. Keller sent me down to observe." Helen spoke aloud to her empty room, relying on the microphones to carry her response through to the Fishbowl. His look turned pensive and he nodded.

"I'm sure you know not to distract the NAV on duty, Ms. Vectorovich. Carry on."

"Yes, sir."

Helen heard the door behind her open. She cast a glance over her shoulder as Keller entered. He gave her a thumbs-up and threaded his way through the disorganized seats, distracted by something on his own comm tablet.

"Got 'em." Bright responded to Mira's earlier instruction. Helen saw the micrograph shots appear in the manifest and checked the estimated download time. "Okay, moving to the next trap. This one's got a green light, must be full of something." The OP continued his roll.

"That one's dead to me. Bright, get everything you can," Mira responded.

"Want me to relink the trap to the Golfball's computer or give you direct access?"

"I'm showing backup arm two on the waldo still working. See if you can get me direct access."

There were always a handful of physical redundancies built into any waldo. As a rookie, Helen had been unimpressed by the extra cables and multi-purpose tools. After she'd saved a few missions with those "unnecessary" extras, she had changed her mind.

"Got it."

"Okay, connecting the controller to the trap. You should be getting access in three . . . two . . ."

"NAV, are you whistling?"

Helen had used those exact same words. Helen's heart felt like it had come to a stop and in her mind she was back in the waldo, listening to the noise building along the communication circuit. She backed slowly away from the glass window, stumbling into the free-standing seats as she unconsciously tried to put distance between herself and what was coming next. A last glance at Mira through the glass showed the NAV bolt upright, face nearly touching the half-dome of control screens. Long fingers curled into fists, arms pulled back against her body, Mira looked like she was struggling to escape something. Helen closed her eyes against the wave of unreasoning panic that followed.

"NAV, there seems to be some kind of interference." Bright's voice came down the line alarmed and confused.

Helen forced her eyes back open. Forced herself to move through the remembered interference in her head. She could see the inside of the waldo around her, a bizarre replaying of the last few moments of her own mission overlaid on the real world like a pale and sickly hologram. She forced herself to reach for the touchscreen on the wall before the screaming fear could catch up with her decision and stop her. Helen's fingertips skidded across the interface, seeking the abort button three menus deep as the NAV in the room beyond started to convulse.

"Helen, are you . . ." Keller grabbed her arm, but she had already keyed in the abort sequence.

On the other side of the glass, the room went nuts.

"WHAT. THE. HELL!" Ivester's voice exploded over the speakers.

Mira collapsed. Bright, fresh red trickled from under her helmet and down to the point of her jaw.

"Mira, what the hell happened? I've been kicked." Bright's anger and confusion rang out over the speakers as the EMTs rushed the room.

Keller pulled Helen back, half supporting, half insisting, and shoved her into the closest chair. Helen took one deep breath, then a second, afraid to look, afraid to see what had become of Mira. She had been aware, in the abstract sense, that Ted had been badly injured, but she hadn't been able to see what happened. She hadn't been able to connect with that idea until Bright had repeated those four words. *NAV, are you whistling?*

"Helen? Operator Vectorovitch." Keller caught her shoulders, turned her to face him. "I'm getting you back to Hofstaeder."

"No, wait." Ivester's voice came from the back of the room.

"Aren't you . . ." Keller started, shocked.

"What? Going to take command? Get in there and start second-guessing my people? My job is to stay the hell out of their way right now. I want to hear it from her first. Why the abort?"

Ivester's presence gave Helen something else to focus on, a new checklist to tick the boxes off. The CTO moved to the touch-wall and started pulling down data faster than Helen could read it. She could just imagine the whispers in the air as it exchanged information between his personal computer and the Far Reaches server.

"It was the sound," she began, then paused, mind racing to figure out what it was that Ivester wanted to hear.

Screw it, I'm fired anyway.

"Bright mentioned a sound," she continued, "but there's no interference on a quantum link, there's never anything other than what we put in there."

"How do you know?" Ivester pressed.

Helen was taken aback for a moment, forced to collect her thoughts, to look at the problem differently. "Bandwidth. Every bit has to be accounted for so we can push enough information as fast as we can. That's why we prioritize the audio Feed to the NAV over the images Feed to the Fishbowl. I picked up the same thing, just a few seconds before Ted . . ." She had to pause a moment, take a step back before emotion caught up with her. "Before my NAV started seizing."

"The analysis team determined that was an anomaly, probably due to the eenie overrun on the Golfball on the other end of the line," Ivester pressed on.

"There are no recorded instances of any kind of interference on the quantum link ever. Not even in the earliest research. It doesn't work that way." Helen held her ground.

"So it's not chance, you're suggesting."

"Once might be a chance." Helen waved her hand at the EMTs clustered around Mira. "Twice is a coincidence . . ."

"Science doesn't do coincidence, Ms. Vectorovich. If we cannot maintain a connection to the Golfball, we are going to have a problem."

Helen risked a glance through the glass at Mira. The NAV looked shaken and pissed, but was still upright and ready to argue, from the scowl on her face.

"So both times the NAV gets affected," Helen suggested, grasping at something to work on, something that would let her keep control of the chattering-whispering noise in her head. "What if we run an AI NAV? We use them for minor assignments now; more than a few of us know how to work with them."

"The AIs have to be tied in to James. We don't know what this interference is yet, but if it Feeds all the way back into Far Reaches' big computer, it could be catastrophic."

"So it's got to be live people."

"For now. Until we can find a solution." Ivester gestured at the window. "I think, however, that I owe you thanks. You might have made a mess of our mission, but you may also have kept Operator Mira from taking a trip to the morgue."

The morgue.

CHAPTER THIRTEEN

"WELL," HOFSTAEDER SAID CURTLY. "That was hardly the outcome I was expecting when Keller took you out of here this afternoon."

Hofstaeder's inner office was dimmer than the outside halls. Near-white paint coated the walls from floor to ceiling and lights stayed at half brightness. Here in the depths of the psychologist's inner office, the focus was on comfort. Thick rugs muffled the unfeeling concrete. The chairs were littered with mild-patterned cushions far better suited for a personal space. The entire office, in fact, was dead to the outside. No connection to Insight, no hum and buzz of day-to-day operations. The stillness should have been unsettling. After Helen's near-meltdown at the Fishbowl, the separation of mind and machine meant a place to hide while she collected herself.

"I needed to be there." The panic attack, if that's what it had been, had subsided, step by careful step as Keller walked her back to the office. Hofstaeder had been waiting, perched in the chair behind the desk like a vulture in a sharply pressed lab coat.

"That's for damn sure. What I want to know is why you pulled the plug. Ivester sent over the room footage. You picked up on something going wrong well before anyone else did."

"I don't know," Helen said.

"Yes. Yes, you do. What was it? What have you not been telling me?"

"I don't . . ."

"Don't. Bullshit. Me." Each word was neatly clipped short as it left Hofstaeder's lips. "If you ever want to see the inside of a coffin again, you will not bullshit me. This is now the *second* Line Drive mission with a body count—well, very nearly a body count. Mira Reseda's going to pull through, but this is a *very important* point. Waldo operations *don't kill people.* Psychosis, dissociative breaks, occasional blackouts, bedwetting, sleepwalking, none of these are ideal side effects, but they can be managed. Not one of these things gets you dead and none of these things *ever* happens to a Navigator." The psychiatrist fixed flat brown eyes on the Operator. "Once could be an operational glitch. Twice . . . there simply is no twice. So the question I put to you, Helena Vectorovich, is why did you abort the mission?"

Helen sat stunned. She'd been ready for professional platitudes, for encouragement and soft-shoeing around the edges. She had not been ready for shock and awe.

"No." It was the first answer that came to mind. Helen didn't know what else to say in the moment. She needed time to process, time to get her bearings. But she knew that she was already on thin ice. If she said something, if she presented her alien theory without proof or plan, she was done. Red-carded off the mission and off rotation permanently. *Done.* What she didn't get was why Hofstaeder didn't understand that as well.

"I don't know anything else." Helen softened the no, instinctively ceding authority to Hofstaeder without revealing anything new. "Look, you know Ted and I heard something out there. That's on the report. When Bright said he heard something, I paid attention." Helen shrugged by way of finishing the sentence.

Hofstaeder steepled her fingers and stared, unblinking, over the tips at her patient. Helen, having committed to her course of action, stared back. Despite herself, Hofstaeder blinked first.

"Bright's description of the sound, and its effects, matches up with your reports," the older woman conceded.

"I'm not sure that makes me feel any better."

"It should. It changes your diagnosis, or at least eliminates the idea that whatever you heard was all in your head."

"Ted heard it too."

"Ted can't provide corroboration," Hofstaeder murmured. She started to reach out a hand, then stopped and returned to her clinical demeanor. "Now that you're not the only one, how do you feel about that?"

"I think it's a little soon to know how I feel, but my hot take is that this was a very expensive way to figure that out," Helen responded bitterly. The chattering in the back of her head started up again; even in the stillness of Hofstaeder's office, she couldn't escape it, only allow it to slide by, ignored.

"That's why we need to know everything. Especially now."

"I don't know. . . . Wait. The pictures . . ."

Hofstaeder shook her head. "Nothing. All the data was corrupted."

"Not your pictures. Mine. The ones on my personal drive would have been downloaded over the uncorrupted OP's connection." Helen had put them out of her mind, waiting for James to finish crunching the data.

"Pictures?"

"I take screencaps on every mission." Helen gestured at her temple. They were more than screencaps; they recorded bio-response data. Ever since Ferguson's Asteroid, she'd taken memento shots on every mission. "Personal record, like a diary without the smelly-pens and cheap golden locks."

"You know we can't touch those. Personal drives are off limits. Union rules."

"Hands off for you, but you put me on the analyst team. I can put my personal experience to use."

"We put you on the analyst team because Dougal has a degree in psych and could keep an eye on you," Hofstaeder said and pursed her lips—not quite a sneer, not quite a scowl. "The Almighty Ivester insisted we allow you to remain active against my advice."

"Well, now that we have confirmed I'm not actually crazy, let's put it to use, since I'm already there."

"You're looking at a precedent the union might not be all that happy with. If you give us access to that personal drive, you're opening a can of worms bigger than one loose waldo mission.

"I didn't say I was going to give you access. I said I was going to see if I have anything I can make personal use of as a member of the analyst team. You're going to have to trust that I'm being accurate. I can tell you what I know, where to look, then you can go find your own proofs."

Hofstaeder frowned. "So there are things about the mission you haven't divulged?"

Helen caught herself. She'd gotten too close to the line, felt a little too safe.

"Doctor, I've divulged everything I know so far, but I don't know what those pictures will show."

"I'm still not convinced that's true, Operator Vectorovich."

Helen shrugged, back on her guard. "All I'm asking is for you guys to let me do my job. If you're not going to put me into a waldo, at least let me use what I have on the analysis team."

"You do realize I'm trying to help you, right?" Hofstaeder's frustration was becoming palpable.

Helen didn't care. She'd retreated again, choosing to protect her tenuous grip on the chance at getting back into a waldo.

"Fine, Helen. I can't help you if you won't trust me. You've been through a trauma. If today's incident doesn't put the punctuation on that for you, I don't know what will."

"Look, Doc," Helen replied. "I have one goal. Getting back out there. I'll do any therapy you like, but other than that, you, they . . ." Helen's expansive gesture included every part of Far Reaches' operations. "They all know everything I know, right here, right now. If I remember or discover anything new, I. Will. Tell. You."

The chatter, which had stayed in the back of her mind a low, staccato hum, suddenly faded out, leaving her alone in her own head.

"I want to solve this as much as anybody else. In fact, I want to solve it MORE than the rest of you assholes because Ted was MY NAV, he was MY friend and I had to sit out there, a billion miles away, and listen to him die while you decided launching the payload was the most important thing." Helen got to her feet and placed her balled fists on the desk. "So, no, I am not hiding anything, NO, I am not deliberately withholding information. The sound I heard in the Feed was not some kind of coping mechanism to deal with the fact that my partner, who was supposed to have the SAFEST part of this goddamn job, got killed on the highest profile mission that Far Reaches has ever run. I am trying to get back out there to FIX this SHIT."

The sound of water droplets hitting the desk clued Helen to the fact that tears were streaming down her face. She was shaking and, just for a moment, she felt like she might put those balled fists to work.

Across the desk, Hofstaeder was smiling.

"I think I believe you."

Helen sat back into her chair with a thump, all the angry, nervous energy draining away.

"I don't fucking care."

CHAPTER FOURTEEN

THE LAB WAS ABUZZ in the aftermath of Mira and Bright's Golf-ball run. Every screen was alight, every member present, time zones be damned. Helen walked into an empty room, but as soon as her glasses shook hands with James, the space erupted with the virtual avatars of people on a dozen different landmasses.

"HELEN! You made it! I wasn't sure Doc was going to let you out in time!" A real-life Dougal appeared out of the press of imaginary bodies.

"Where did all these people come from? I thought your team was just three?"

"That was before this latest entanglement." Dougal shook a finger at the puzzled operator. "That signal showed up twice now, two different times, which means what we are looking at is not an anomaly. This is something completely new."

"This is something completely lethal," Helen cautioned, wanting to take the edge off the analyst's dangerous delight.

"Yes, but not inescapably lethal. We've got a lead on that too. C'mere!"

Helen allowed herself to be dragged around the room. Normally everything in the imaginary room was flexible, but with so many people using it all at once, it had become as rigid as a real-world office space.

"I wanted to show you this bit first. Mira and Bright had the sense to send back snaps before the interference could get started."

Helen stared at the image that floated in front of her, trying to pick out the detail Dougal had his stubby finger on.

"Okay, so these guys look like our eenies right?" Dougal continued with barely a slowdown.

In the image, the microscopic clusters of silvery robots littered a pockmarked surface. The extreme magnification made them look as large as discarded sneakers on a badly mown lawn. There were thousands of them in-frame, many of them clumped together, whip-like flagella locked as if holding hands.

"Those are the Hoovers. Their job is to collect and package materials." Helen's knowledge of the eenies that went into the making of the Golfball had improved over the past few weeks.

"That's what it looks like." Dougal adjusted the magnification with a flick of his wrist. "We've been operating under the assumption that the software developed an error somewhere along the line." He swept a hand from right to left, bringing up the next image in the sequence. He repeated the gesture, jumping from page to page in the ever-growing report until he found what he was looking for. "And it had to be something higher up in the programming, because it affected more than one class of eenie."

Helen pulled up the relevant data and checked the comments.

"Right, but Far Reaches hasn't been able to replicate the error on our end," Helen responded carefully. "So far . . ."

"So far we've been working just off your report, which, to be honest, was a little bit out there. But this mission got us access to the code currently being run by those broken Hoovers."

"So the working theory is that the eenie instructions got a bit flipped when we passed them through the wormhole back at mission start a few years ago?" Helen frowned and tapped the image with a fingernail. "The same error across enough of them to cause this? Seems a bit of a stretch."

"Less of a stretch than your alien theory," Dougal chided.

Helen winced. She hadn't actually floated an alien theory, but Beauchamp had gotten a copy of the mission report. Give that asshole a one-liner she could get her teeth into and she'd flog it for effect for weeks. It was starting to grate on Helen.

"BUT," the analyst continued, "look at this!" Dougal isolated a few strings of the output code to make his point. "They ran into something. This piece here, this has re-tasked the eenies. They're not building the Golfball any longer, they're *rebuilding* it."

The eenies were supposed to construct the Golfball from available materials. Once done, they boxed themselves up to wait until Far Reaches told them what to do next. The code Dougal was showing her said that the Golfball had experienced massive levels of damage and had to be repaired. Constantly repaired. The eenies had never had the chance to shut down.

"Now this is pretty weird, because this is not the result of a bit error." Dougal continued enthusiastically. "This is a reaction to external stimuli of some kind, so we're not looking at all those eenies going rogue. And if they're not broken, that means we can get them back under control again. I saw the suggestions you sent Mira while the mission was live. We need more of those if we're going to get back out there," Dougal continued on. "The fact that the interference in the Feed is something we can actively track is a key element. We won't get caught by surprise again. There's a bucketload of unknowns in play already; we need more data so we can put those in the 'knowns' bucket instead."

"So how do we do all this?"

"We start by pulling apart the code Mira and Bright sent back, figure out what happened to our eenies. The eenie lab is in orbit and due to be decommissioned anyway, so if we do bring back an uncontrollable replication event with that code, it will be easier to contain. None of that stuff's getting down here."

Helen rocked back on her heels, considering. "So our own eenies are breaking the Golfball down and rebuilding it? That doesn't make sense. Why would they rebuild over and over again?"

"Well, we need to get back out there and get more data to know for sure."

The question of why the NAVs were the ones affected by the sound in the Feed remained unresolved. Helen would have preferred that this first mission back to the Golfball answer the question of why Ted had come away with his brains jellied while Helen had little more than panic attacks. Still, one step closer was one step closer.

"How familiar are you with Catherine Beauchamp?" Dougal asked offhandedly. Helen cast him a glance. The analyst had thrown the report up onto larger screens that covered the far wall, spreading out the pages so he could move between them faster. His stubby fingers moved quickly, flicking all the reports into order.

"Familiar?" The question seemed odd. Maybe Analysis didn't really have a handle on the underpinnings in Flight Ops.

"Mira and Bright have asked to be pulled off the project, so your Keller is working on lining up a replacement team. Beauchamp put a direct request to me to transfer over."

Helen spent a long moment in silence before speaking, then decided to choose the high road. As much as she and Beauchamp might be in conflict, the woman had skills. If it had just been Beauchamp, Helen probably wouldn't have batted an eye at letting her rival OP take on a risk like the Golfball. However, it wasn't just Cat. Her NAV would be taking the risk as well. Helen didn't have it in her to make Beauchamp's NAV pay the price. Making an end-run around Keller though, that was a bit weird . . . *Well, it fits Beauchamp's personality.*

"Beauchamp is a skilled operator, but she should have gone through Keller first," she said carefully, measuring her words.

"Keller thinks she's interested because she wants to show you up. She wanted the launch mission, and now she's got a chance to show everyone why it should have gone to her," Dougal replied.

Ah, so Dougal did *check with Keller.*

"Hell, now that I know what I know, I'm pissed she didn't get the launch mission," Helen said a little sourly.

"Think she could have done better?"

Helen paused again. *That's a loaded question now, isn't it?* Hofstaeder's words about why Helen had been put on Dougal's team still hung fresh in her memory.

"Does it matter? I can't fault her skills, but you'll need to be very clear with her protocols. She doesn't make good decisions working fast outside the box."

"We've got the opening, it's going to need to be filled."

"Yeah, and I can't get back out there if I don't have a NAV," Helen snorted. "But don't think for a second Beauchamp's going to be an easy one to manage."

"I'll keep it in mind." Dougal turned his attention back to the records hanging in the Insight space. Helen got the sense that a checkbox had been ticked off. It was almost like Dougal had promised to talk to Helen and now that the requirement had been met, the conversation could turn. She'd have to ask Keller about it later.

Helen eyeballed the eighty pages of mission data that she and Keller had been working on. The images were grainy. Nothing to be done there. The magnification had been cranked down so tight that the latticework of the carbon fiber control panel was clearly visible in minute lines and crosses.

"The camera sucks," Helen said.

"We're just working with what Ivester built into the waldo."

"So what exactly do we expect to see in these?" Helen reached up and zoomed the image out, a dizzying move that made her feel briefly ill. "Look, here's the dust from the mission reports." The surfaces on the console were smooth, but the crisp edges of the detail were all muddied, like the silted-over forms at the bottom of a river.

"Those are the eenie castings you talked about in your initial report." Dougal selected a second image and suspended it in the air. This one showed an even denser concentration of dust, puddled in the corners, the lines, in the control surfaces inside the Golfball.

"You know how engineering likes to bogart resources. All these castings should have been used up by the time the Golfball neared completion," Helen pointed out.

"If something interrupted the building process, the eenies would just shut themselves down," Dougal said, selecting a third image, this time examining a cutaway section where construction had just stopped. Helen had seen eenie building errors before—they were fuzzy, like tufted fleece, and sometimes poetic lattices were formed, delicate square tiles and gossamer fingers. What was on the screen now looked nothing like that. This was not an error in creation; this was a reduction. The edges were sharply cut, nibbled away as if by the teeth of minuscule rats.

First built up and then chewed back down again, Helen realized.

"Dougal, are you seeing this?" Helen shuffled through, eyeballing thousands of defunct shells that drifted and fetched up in the corners. They overlapped like fish scales, making little moiré patterns that danced in the camera image.

"Wait. Go back." Dougal took over the Insight. "See that there?" He slid the image back and hit the magnification to dial in on something Helen had missed.

There, among the loops and whorls of the discarded shells, was a tiny spot of color. Color was expensive; color would cost molecules that could be put to better use elsewhere. Everything developed, designed, and released into the wild by Far Reaches was a million different shades of grey.

Helen's heart skipped a beat. The color seemed to shimmer and shift as the computer zoomed in. She knew what it was. She'd forgotten, or maybe she had lost it in the rush and rumble of the mission drop-out. The chattering pressure in her head whispered, words that were just out of reach, but she ignored it, pushed it back, and focused on that tiny bright patch.

She saw it move. Between one frame and the next. Just a twitch, just a single motion like an asteroid skipping. Just enough to know it was there. Helen took a deep, ragged breath and for a moment she was back in the crippled waldo, feeling the nibbling at her fingertips and joints.

"Shit. Helen. We have to show these to Ivester," Dougal said breathlessly. "I think we've found our saboteur."

With an effort of will Helen pushed the memories back, reasserted her focus. It went a little easier each time, every time she had a bit more of herself back a little more quickly. Dougal opened another image in the series, giving James the parameters to look for. The computer identified even more tiny spots, more than a dozen. Nothing major until Helen opened the fifth and sixth images.

The screen erupted in thousands of points of color.

Around them the room fell silent as one by one the others caught note of what Dougal and Helen were examining and came over to look.

"Helen. This is important," Dougal breathed. "This is . . . this is unprecedented. If we can prove who designed these little scales . . . We have to get back out there."

"What do you think I've been saying all this time?"

CHAPTER FIFTEEN

HELEN'S ORIGINAL SKETCHES had been recalled and thrown back up on the whiteboard wall as a starting point, but they had already been forgotten. Dougal had placed the sequence of images Helen had found in Mira and Bright's data alongside and clicked through them, one at a time. The motion was clear to everyone. The room full of analysts and engineers was silent except for the hum of climate control.

"Play that again." Ivester's voice cut through the silence.

Click.

Click.

Click.

The images that Mira and Bright sent back somehow managed to convey a level of chaos that Helen's hand-drawn sketches had missed. The precise edges of the eenie shells showed up against the background in sharp relief. Greys and whites predominated until the third frame, when one of the supposedly dead eenies extended a brightly colored leg. Followed by another. The full set was only fifteen frames in total, but it had rendered the room completely silent.

At the back of the room, Ivester removed his glasses and tapped them thoughtfully on the palm of one hand.

"It would appear," he said carefully, "that we are not the only ones interested in our little orphan star."

The chatter began low as the engineers started talking in twos and threes. Helen stared at the now familiar intruder. Whatever they were, they had hollowed out the eenies, wearing their skins like hermit crabs. Mira and Bright had found exactly the right thing to turn the conversation from "OP gone crazy" to "industrial sabotage."

"So what we have here, ladies and gentlemen," Ivester said to the room, "is a nano-machine of unknown origin. These stills are from the images that NAV Mira had the presence of mind to take before the interference on the entanglement Feed began. It is still entirely possible that this is simply a variation our own designs." He got to his feet and gestured to the images projected on the wall. "It's still possible something went wrong during the eenie generation cascade. We need make sure we have exhausted that option first. But I don't think I'm going out on a limb to suggest there might be something more exotic than a simple case of cascade failure. Industrial sabotage is now the top item on our list. This microscopic Scale," Ivester placed quotes around the word with his fingertips, "has laid siege to our technology and we need to figure out exactly what is driving it." He pinched at the air and one of the images zoomed in, filling the wall with a single, brightly colored Scale. "Ladies and gentlemen, we are hearing hoofbeats. While we need to make absolutely sure it's not horses, unicorns are no longer off the table."

A hand shot up in the front of the room as the chatter began afresh.

"Are we trying to keep a lid on this? The press, and our various partners, have been keeping pretty close tabs on all the data since the mission went off book." It was Dr. Swati who spoke. Helen remembered her ice-cold acumen after the original debrief. She wasn't wrong. Much as Helen had been suffering the slings and arrows of gossip and rumor among the members of flight operations, Far Reaches had been suffering the same on the public front. Tabloids and competitors spun all manner of theories as to why the project had suddenly gone dark.

Ivester's look of resignation was legendary. It lasted only a moment before being smoothed back over into the million-dollar smile, but it was clear he intended for the room to see it.

"I will be sitting down with our liaisons after this meeting to go over our findings so far, but I'm not going to lie to you. Our relationship with pretty much everybody is going to need to evolve very aggressively in order to stay on top of the situation. As of right now, this still belongs to Far Reaches and damned if I'm going to let anybody take this project away from us." He paused for dramatic effect. "I hope you all feel the same."

There was a smattering of applause at that. The room was filled with realists who knew full well that some of Far Reaches' governmental strategic partners, notably absent, could steamroll them and take control. Their saving grace was that nobody knew the technology quite like Ivester's team did. The bodies in this small, dimly lit conference room represented the single best source of information about the Line Drive project.

Helen briefly felt a twinge of panic as she looked, really looked, at the people assembled in the room. Fewer than fifteen people. That wasn't a lot of institutional memory to work with.

Now you're just being paranoid. It was infectious, this need to keep looking over one's shoulder. *This shit is way above your pay-grade.* She cast a glance over at Ivester. He wouldn't go down without a fight. The man practically shone with purpose. The distracted look that had plagued his features since Line Drive went pear-shaped was gone. In fact, his entire focus was here in this room; she couldn't even spot the flicker of Insight in his heavy glasses.

"Our next trip back out will be in three days. Operator Helen Vectorovich is developing the protocols, so please be sure you copy her on all requests and questions."

A couple members of Flight Ops whooped at that; one held up a hand. Helen's Insight tablet chimed and ID'd him as one of the coffin-tech team.

"Do we have an answer about what happened to Vectorovich's NAV on the first run-through?"

His name was Ted. Helen's whisper failed to reach her lips. Reminders of the Ted-shaped hole in her life still stung. It had been over a month already, and the rawness of the loss was gone, but reminders still caught her off guard with disturbing regularity.

Ivester adjusted his glasses.

"At this moment, the consensus is that NAV Theodore Westlake encountered quantum feedback due to problems with the communications array. The medical technologies team will present their findings to any interested parties on Wednesday, but those of you who need the details now can find the raw data available on the secure server. Just message Kaitlin in infrastructure for access." Ivester shifted his gaze to encompass the entire room and continued, this time speaking to everyone.

Helen appreciated Ivester calling Ted by name, rather than using any of the more distant stand-ins she'd been hearing around the building to avoid admitting he was dead.

"The data we've collected suggests we have a five-minute window before the feedback kicks in. At four minutes and thirty seconds we will be triggering the exit protocols to give our flight team plenty of time to get out. Anything you want to do on this next mission out must be executable within that time window."

"Are we planning on tasking an AI to handle NAV for this mission? Would that allow for longer mission times?" Another question from Flight Ops.

Helen held her breath as the room felt silent. They knew already that the answer would be no, but hearing it out loud would make everyone feel a whole lot better. Funny how most OPs weighted the risk to the NAV versus working with an AI partner. The odds of death would have to be a whole lot higher to convince most of them to switch.

"I don't think anybody in this room would agree with the idea that this should be handled by a machine. Even a Turing-certified unit like James will lack the interpretive nuance we may need," Ivester responded. "However," he held up a hand, "we will be using all of our not inconsiderable resources to help interpret and analyze the data as it comes back. The AI team will be kept in the loop at all times. That is all."

And that's a hell of a lot, Helen reflected.

CHAPTER SIXTEEN

"WE ARE LIVE, we are live, we are live." Elliot's voice filtered in over the speakers from a billion miles away.

Helen forced herself to listen, to watch Elliot slowly pick his way through the protocols she'd put together with the Analysis team's input. Unlike the nearly disastrous "secret" run Mira and Bright had taken weeks ago, this time the gallery was packed. Even support personnel who only had a vague reason to be present crowded the back of the room.

Helen resisted the urge to move away from the Fishbowl window. This was on her now. She needed to set the example, to own her work. As much as she wanted to hide in the back of the room, it wasn't a place she could afford to be, not if they were going to push this project forward. Not if she was going to get out to the Golfball any time soon.

The soundproof windows between her and the Fishbowl lit up as the information from the waldo started to come down the line. The moment Elliot and Zai connected, the clock had started counting down. At the four-minute mark, the numbers would turn yellow, and with thirty seconds left, they'd go red. Easy enough to understand without thinking about it too hard. Nobody wanted to see it hit the five-minute mark.

Watching the mission from this perspective, a billion miles away, Helen felt very much like she'd been bound up in a strait-jacket. Unable to act, unable to affect anything in the room beyond. She clenched and unclenched her fists.

Two deep breaths to curb her frustration and Helen focused her attention on the data coursing across the big screens, the ones thrown up on the far wall for the spectators. Graphs and charts and images designed to convey the mission information to the layperson. She idly wondered if James ever got bored dumbing everything down for all the observers.

"So far, so good." The low voice off her shoulder came from one of the coffin techs. He wasn't assigned to this mission, but everyone wanted a look-see and people were sneaking their friends in.

"Elliot's got this," she murmured back. She'd managed to wrangle a spot near the front window.

"Is it really different?" he asked her quietly. "Running the spider waldo?"

Helen pulled her attention away from the data and back to the conversation.

"Not all that different. It's more complex. There are more working parts than on a mole or a jackrabbit. But the setup is the same," she replied.

"Did you hear the second mission's packet was finished? They're firing it through the wormhole towards Cygnus Three at the end of the week."

The coffin techs, Helen reflected, were terrible gossips. Being closeted away, monitoring coffin life-support and systems for days at a time tended to make them hungry for information, even bad information.

In the room beyond, Zai splayed his fingers out across his dome of touchscreens to issue instructions to the Golfball. In her mind's eye she could see the inside of the capsule, mission parameters sliding in and out of vision like ghosts of past mistakes. The checklist popped on Zai's screen. Helen could barely make it out from where she was standing. *Short list.*

"Hey, Helen, you forgot to put the parking brake on." Elliot's voice filtered out over the room speakers. "That's the last time I let you drive the new toys first."

The room chuckled, each OP adding their own particular note and cadence to the mix. Helen had no way to respond, even as Zai looked over his shoulder at her with a grin. Helen shook her head with a half-smile and flipped him the bird. Another chuckle from the room.

"I think you're going to have to pry the keys from her cold dead fingers, Elliot." Zai turned his attention back to the console.

"Oh man, too freaking soon." Helen heard the tech behind her mutter under his breath. He wasn't wrong, but it would never not be too soon and Elliot's mind was a billion miles away. Helen wasn't about to hold him accountable for the lapse in judgment.

"Okay, checklist complete." Elliot's voice rang down the line. "This waldo is significantly diminished. Please see the report and advise."

The observation room seemed to grow warmer as the mission clock cycled through the numbers on the far wall.

"Confirmed. Adjusting protocols." Zai consulted one of the other techs in the room and gestured at Keller, who joined him at the console. From her side of the glass pane, Helen couldn't hear what they were saying and she leaned closer, trying to catch a glimpse of their faces as they spoke. She couldn't shake the feeling that something was coming. Something had already begun to go wrong, they simply hadn't figured it out yet.

Don't be stupid. We're ready for this.

Helen resisted the urge to tap on the glass. The bodies in the gallery pressed just a little bit closer. Helen focused more closely to try and keep the slowly creeping feeling of panic at bay. She'd helped develop the protocols herself. She knew exactly what could be done with the tools they had. There was nothing out there that Elliot couldn't handle.

"Confirmed, new protocols have been set, begin at your discretion." Elliot's voice came over the intercom, and Keller and Ivester both moved away to focus on other tasks.

The chattering pressure in Helen's head lessened just a touch; the panic took a step back.

"This is kind of a lame list, Vectorovich. Don't you want me to do something cooler? Arm the cannons? Prepare to be boarded?" There was a touch of teasing in there. Helen ignored it, but she could feel the glances directed her way. Beauchamp had been running the rumor mill full-tilt in the off-hours. Helen's original "ate the Golfball" comment had been turned into an all-out alien invasion. Helen knew if she bothered to respond, she'd waste all her time spiraling down a tide of ignored denials. She assured her friends that Beauchamp was mistaken and ignored the jabs and insults at the commissary. As a result, though, she'd been spending less time with Flight Ops and more with Analysis. It weighed on her. The longer she was off-rotation, the harder it was going to be to get back out there.

Zai, to his credit, cast a wordless look over his shoulder to read the room behind him. Helen held her hands up to her face, framing her eyes with huge imaginary goggles like the eyes of a little grey alien. He gave her a thumbs-up to signal he'd keep the banter rolling. Anytime you had a mission with a casual audience, rather than just the higher-ups, it had the potential to become a show. Zai and Elliot were very good at putting on a show.

"Sorry, Elliot," Zai told his OP, "I can't send you the secret protocols until after you get properly probed."

"You can keep those protocols under lock and key then, thank you very much. Okay, NAV, beginning the secondary list." The room chuckled again. Beauchamp's campaign to keep Helen on the outs with flight operations was starting to backfire.

The displays on the far wall gave the layout of the Golfball as it was supposed to be with a glowing red dot showing the location of the spider near the middle. Helen was pretty sure Mira and Bright had ditched it out by the mite traps near the controls for the payload. Elliot's current position was a long way from where he should have started.

Helen had intended to stay offline. Her part was done, the protocols and checklists already in play. Flight control access codes, everybody's access codes, were locked out to avoid any accidental crossovers between communications. Ivester wanted a clean run, no interference from her or anyone else watching. But it was her mission; she'd been buried in the minutiae of it for weeks. Helen couldn't shake the feeling that this detail was important. There were no wind currents in space, no one else had driven the waldo since Mira and Bright had abandoned it. It should have remained pretty damn close to where they left it. The shift was unanticipated. Neither Helen nor Dougal had thought to add checking simple elements like the waldo's positioning to the checklists. It meant the shift might go unrecorded.

Helen might be locked out of the command communication, but that didn't mean she was locked out of everything. An Operator, any Operator, was far from useless as long as there was computer access handy. She composed a plain five-word sentence. Keller was offline, so any message would just sit in his accounts until end of mission. There had to be another way to get the idea in there other than just playing charades on this side of the window.

Zai and Elliot were entangled, so neither was a good option anyway. Talking directly to them would be regarded as interference, helpful or not.

A whisper in the ether caught her attention. She had been hearing them more clearly over the past few weeks, when she bothered to pay attention. Sensitivity to the building's pervasive wireless network went with the job. All operators could pick up on the ghost of communications. As the chattering of panic in her head grew less overwhelming, Helen had realized that her sensitivity to the wireless networks had been dialed up to eleven.

The whisper told her that Ivester had not closeted himself away from communications. The CTO had kept a line open, despite the protocols. That meant she could reach him through the communications system.

Helen sent the note before she even finished her train of thought. *Breaking protocol*, she reminded herself. *Interfering with the mission in progress*, the voice in her head pointed out. Well, Almighty Ivester left himself open for it so . . . She could not shake the feeling that this was important, maybe critically important.

Ivester approached Keller and the two exchanged words. Keller looked annoyed and the two disappeared back out of sight to one of the senior consoles. *That may not have worked as well as you hoped.* Helen stayed in her position close to the window, focused on the display data ahead.

Elliot was on the move, the bright red tracking marker sliding across the map.

"I wish they'd kept the spider," the tech said.

Helen glanced over. "The what?"

"When you were on the first mission, someone in the control room had mapped in a spider to represent the waldo. Keller was officially pissed about it."

"I wish I'd seen that."

Officially pissed was code for, "Very cute, now knock it off."

"OP, can you hold position for a moment?"

Helen refocused on the Fishbowl as Zai's fingers drummed frantically on the console's touchscreen.

"Affirmative."

The data sheeting across the glass stuttered. Keller reemerged, no sign of Ivester. He spoke to Zai, pointing at the table readouts, but Helen couldn't tell what they were discussing.

"Okay, let's return to protocol." Zai's tone was terse, clipped. Whatever Keller had said had taken the sparkle out of his attitude.

"Affirmative, moving to confirm."

"Roger that."

The countdown passed the two-minute mark.

The gallery began to clear out, people departing in ones and twos. The Entanglement, getting control of the waldo back again, that was the exciting part and now it was over. It was expected to be all data and long bouts of silence from here on in, nothing nearly as exciting as the potential for a spectacular failure.

Helen rubbed sweaty palms on her hips and stayed near the window, staring into the Fishbowl. She could see the cramped interior of the Golfball in her mind, illuminated not for the benefit of the waldo, but so the cameras could send back a good clear record.

"Looks like we still have a clean Feed. Moving to trigger Golfball reclamation and Phase II."

Elliot's voice over the speaker brought Helen out of her mental spiral. Data reclamation was the big archive. It would start the process of retrieving every moment, every second of information that had gone into building the Golfball. Following that, the Golfball would be reconfigured and sent to join the payload at Otlyan23. As long as the interference didn't kick in and corrupt the data, this mission was a success.

"Roger that. Linking up to the Golfball mainframe to verify." There was a long pause. "Hold please."

"Affirmative."

A smattering of applause had come from the remaining personnel in the observation room. A few high-fives and backslaps came her way and she gave as good as she got, putting up a grin for all to see. No matter what the follow-up, the core mission parameter had been achieved, which meant that phase three of Line Drive was one step closer to a go.

"Hold please."

Helen pulled herself back from the congratulatory swell. That wasn't Zai's voice, that was the automated system. The soundproofing in the control room had kept her from noticing the tumult beyond the glass.

"Hold, please."

Everyone was moving too quickly for Helen to get a look at Zai.

The countdown on the screen had gone to red, the numbers passing 5:05 . . . 5:06 . . .

"Hold, please."

Oh gods, not again. Helen held her breath.

No word from Elliot, nothing that Helen could hear over the speakers, just the flat, slightly scratchy sound of the recorded warning.

"Hold, please."

She stood, helpless outside the glass, debating whether she should signal the medical team. She couldn't see Zai's condition, couldn't tell what had happened, just a wall of rapidly working bodies around the console while Ivester stood in the middle trying to lock in the connection.

"Hold, please."

Helen refused to give in to the rising tide of panic. She turned and started shooing people from the room. If the team hadn't disconnected Zai in time, rumor would start to spread. There were no blinds to block the window between the observation room and the command center. Everyone piled out slowly, some still rubbernecking.

Helen waited until the room was clear, then shut and locked the door, preventing anyone else from entering. She took a seat in the back of the room, far enough back where she could no longer see Zai's console in the room beyond.

"Hold. Please."

It wasn't until the panic finally subsided that she noticed the stinging half circles in her palms from where she had driven in her fingernails.

"Control, this is Operator Elliot. Did Zai make it out in time?"

There was a very long pause.

"That's an affirmative, Elliot. Any sign of interference on your end?" Ivester's voice cut through on the line. Helen took a deep breath, pulled the sleeves of her shirt down to blot her eyes on the cuffs. It worked. *Holy shit, it worked.* The interference had failed to materialize in the Feed. The lag she was hearing meant they had commandeered the emergency channel to allow for continued communications between Control and the waldo. By removing the NAV from the equation before the five-minute mark, they had, very possibly, found their workaround.

"Not yet, Control, but rest assured, I'm dumping out of here the minute I hear something go boo!"

Another long pause. Helen counted off in her head. Almost three seconds of lag, which meant they were going to have to rely heavily on the OP to riff if anything went wrong.

"All right, Operator Elliot, let's move you to the next set of list items." Ivester waited as Zai finished disconnecting from the NAV chair and took over the voice-only emergency comm. "Take your time, this is all gravy. Since we seem to have some amount of communications lag, I'm going to have to ask you to be extra careful with my waldo. I want her back without a scratch."

"Sir, I'm missing three legs and I'm pretty sure half my face got eaten off. You're going to have to clarify what you mean by 'not a scratch,'" Elliot said. Beyond the glass, Helen could see Ivester grinning.

"Just carry on, Elliot. Save as much as you can. I'm sending the bonus protocols to you now."

Helen got to her feet and risked a look into the Fishbowl. Zai was on his feet, watching the readouts alongside Keller. The EMTs hadn't moved from their places along the wall. On the other side of the glass, Ivester gave her a long stare.

"Well, Operator Vectorovich, it seems we have our workaround," he said. "Be sure to congratulate your team for me."

CHAPTER SEVENTEEN

HELEN LOWERED HERSELF into the coffin and wiggled her butt into the gel lining out of habit. She'd talked Hofstaeder into clearing her for short salvage runs with an AI NAV. Nothing too stressful, nothing too fancy, less risk of Beauchamp mucking things up.

She'd been working short missions in around her regular schedule, squeezing them in where she could. She needed the time in the coffin if she was going to get re-certified and back onto rotation for Line Drive, but setting up Elliot and Zai's run had consumed all of her official work hours. Even the training runs Keller set up got rescheduled, leaving Helen to favor-trade and make deals wherever she could. Fortunately she had a few favors owed and there were still operators who hadn't bought in to Beauchamp's ever-present "loose cannon" innuendo.

"How's the coffin, Operator?" The tech on duty hovered near the control panel on the coffin's exterior.

"Perfect, as always." Helen keyed the switch on the armrest that slid the lid closed. She didn't bother to hide her excitement. This was her last run. Complete this mission and she'd be on track to get back out to the Golfball again.

"Ready to go?" The tech's voice sounded in her ear now. The coffin linked to the computer that would entangle her mind with the

Myrian23A5 particle. Insight came to life around her, icons and information popping up for her attention, then sliding out of the way. *One long breath in, one long breath out.*

"Abso-fucking-lutely," Helen replied. She wiggled her fingers and toes, feeling the slightly sharp tone as the waldo configuration was matched by the computer buffer first, giving her extra limbs and adjusting her senses. The transition was important. While it was possible to link a mind straight into or out of a waldo, it was always better to take the extra few seconds for a smooth transition. The buffer made sure you didn't end up with phantom limb syndrome for body parts you never had in the first place.

"Entangling now."

The lights spun, dropped to black and the waldo's senses became her own.

This was an older model "mole," one of the many assets acquired when Far Reaches had bought BrightWinds a few years back. *The same buy-up that had brought the pain-in-my-ass Beauchamp into the fold, in fact.* The other firm had poured far fewer resources into operations design; the Insight was all edgy greens and sharp right angles, not a curve to be seen. The mole had no eyes, worked almost solely by sense of touch, so everything came in as pure data. It was like surfing without a wetsuit.

"This is Operator Vectorovich, personal identifier T4T4-957. We are live, we are live, we are live." She turned her attention to waking up the sleeping waldo.

The Myrian23A5 mining project was on the outer edge of human expansion. The AI NAV that BrightWinds had been running had declared the mining site a total loss and ejected the operator. The entire operation had been abandoned.

Normally a waldo would be recycled, broken down into a new packet of eenies, quantum particle and all, and sent to the next closest target via a low-power micro-jumpgate. This one had been floating, unpowered and unused, in a zero-grav mining tunnel for a few years. Helen was mildly surprised when the mole booted up and began to report as if nothing had ever been wrong.

"Operator Vectorovich, confirmed you are live and are receiving signal. Your NAV is still coming online." Keller's voice sounded in the background, slightly tinny, she noted.

More glitches in the system. Helen signed internally. The NAV particles on the BrightWinds assets had gotten sold off to Beyond Blue along with their entangled AIs. Far Reaches had gotten the people and the OP entanglement particles. This ensured that neither company gained a significant advantage. That also meant that Helen had to run her mission with a NAV communicating through the emergency channel, the same back-channel that Ivester had used when Ted had been . . .

Helen avoided finishing that thought. *Doesn't matter.* She could handle a few bit-errors in the system if it got her the hours she needed to get back into a coffin.

"Confirmed, Keller. Aren't the AI NAVs supposed to be faster and better-looking than the rest of us? The waldo has woken up and is reporting all clear, which seems a little strange given the mission file."

"Well, let's dig in and see what we can find out. I'll get the AI NAV on here as soon as I can, but might as well warm everything up in the meantime." Keller let the "better-looking" quip slide on by.

Never a good sign.

Helen dug around in the mole's memory to see if she could make some space to store the mission data. *Goddamnit, this whole waldo's a piece of junk.*

"Confirmed. Remember, that NAV was built for AI/human team-ups using a standard NAV entanglement. Maybe there's something left in the cache. Check your settings," Helen reminded him.

"Hang on, let me double-check." There was a pause as Keller made some adjustments.

Helen found the log, a list of all the activities of this particular waldo since launch. In a moment, she'd copied the files over to her own system. She could trickle them back over her own Entanglement link to the coffin. It would be slower—tiny chunks of data squeezed into the gaps and pauses in her own communication, but it would get there.

"No luck OP, NAV's being touchy. Want to abort?"

"I can store the mission data files locally," Helen pointed out, "I'll trickle everything back over my Feed." *Anything as long as I don't have to abort. I need the hours in the coffin.* Next open mission wouldn't be up for a week and Helen only needed one more after this before Hofstaeder could re-certify her.

"Confirmed."

Flight Operations' shit show is my best day this week. She grinned.

"So far, the waldo is waking up just fine. What does that official report list its as condition as?"

"AI NAV registered catastrophic failures on multiple fronts, but the OP could not confirm. BrightWinds decided to go with the NAV's assessment and shut the whole thing down." Helen could hear the change in Keller's tone that meant he was reading the acquisitions report as they went. "That's . . . strange. Okay, stay on your toes, keep the cursing to a minimum, I'm recording everything."

"You got it, boss. This looks to be a third- or fourth-generation mole, so what do I need to do to trigger the eenie recycling sequence?"

BrightWinds specialized in asteroid mining operations, pushing farther and farther out to find more exotic materials. That made workhorses like this mole their bread and butter. Not a tool, joint, or jet more than needed for the job at hand. Helen relaxed and wiggled her fingers, feeling the side grips on the mole rotate in response. Helen's task here was to assess the mining site, confirm the available resources, and queue the waldo recycling process. Once she'd triggered the sequence, the waldo and the entire asteroid would be chewed up by eenies into feedstock. The resources would be marked as ready for reclamation and another OP flying a different class of waldo would be along to gather it up.

"Fourth generation," Keller confirmed. "So you're looking at a manual key code for recycling. You'll have to get to the main computer hub and plug the mole into it."

"That's a little old-school. Do we have the manual key code? Or do I have to go over to the NAV computer and dig it out of the memory? The mole's in great shape, though. I'm not seeing why BrightWinds abandoned everything." Helen flexed, feeling her external shell press up against the walls of the tunnel.

While "blind" and slow, moles were exceptionally flexible and tactile. She could feel the smoothness of the polished tunnel against her "skin," the warmth of the melted stone as it absorbed the waldo's waste heat.

"BrightWinds used AI NAVs pretty exclusively," Keller replied. "And you know how picky a poorly coded AI can be. Too picky, in my opinion."

"I'd expect to see at least a few warning lights. Maybe they just needed the insurance money."

"Let's finish running the diagnostics and see if anything pops," Keller advised.

"I'll add it to the protocol list." Part of this entire exercise, the main reason Helen had selected a lost cause for this run, was in order to practice building protocol lists on the fly. Working with the analysis team had given her a different perspective and she was itching to try it out in real time. But she'd expected to find a waldo that needed a software rebuild at best. Helen pulled back and fiddled with the controls, testing the motion on the stubby digging surfaces, feeling the hardscrabble of the tunnel floor under her fingertips. She unconsciously compared the action to the precision of the spider. The two waldos were so very different in feel, in responses.

Without warning, the chattering noise reappeared in the back of her mind, twisting her perception of the sensor data. Her heart rate spiked. She was alone, a billion miles out into the black, but she knew, as the audio tone shifted and her vision began to distort again, that whatever had killed Ted was coming for her now. There was no way back without encountering it. Her heart beat even faster, bleeding through the Entanglement link to shake the waldo where it clung to the wall of the Golfball.

It's not real. It's not then, she told herself. *Pull yourself together.*

"Well, shit." Keller's voice snapped her back to reality, the memory passing, everything reverting to her new normal. Her panic attacks were fewer and farther between. Helen had a handle on them now and, while she couldn't stop them, she could ride them out without anyone else being the wiser. *Except Hofstaeder, who seems to be psychic about these things.*

"What?"

"Are you okay? I'm seeing a heart rate spike, and my comms just lit up with Doc making angry eyebrows in my direction."

"I'm fine. Just off on a tangent for a sec," Helen lied. Her heartbeat worked its way back down. *Different place, different waldo*, she reminded herself and turned her focus back to the information scrolling across her view.

"Keller," Helen changed the subject, "this waldo is an absolute piece of junk, but everything is in working order. This salvage mission is getting weirder by the minute. I'm going to do some exploring, see what else we have out here."

"Ready for more weirdness? The gate's out of power."

"What?"

"There's a micro-wormhole gate already built and they sent something through it before they shut down operations."

"So?" Helen began her slow crawl forward, comparing what she saw through the mole's ground sensors to the maps made by the previous OP.

There was an established pattern to asteroid mining. First you opened a micro-wormhole to the asteroid and sent in your eenies to build a few moles and clear out the low-hanging fruit like solid ore deposits. Next, you chewed up most of the waldos to build a micro-jumpgate to ship the ore to a central location for processing. Lastly, you unleashed the eenies to turn the rest of the asteroid into useful feedstock. If everything had gone as planned, there would have been nothing left for Helen to entangle with. Nothing was wasted: even the quantum entanglement particles would have been sent along, leaving only a cloud of dust.

"I'm looking at the checklist from the previous OP. Nothing on here about the micro-gate being built. Nothing about shipping anything out to the next site. Helen, do you get the feeling we're missing some information here?"

"I always feel that way, Keller. Nobody tells us OPs anything. That's why I always read the mission briefs."

"I've got something else to tell you."

Helen came to the end of the tunnel and the floor abruptly dropped away. The mole went tumbling out into a large, open cavern.

"Ow." She felt it on her skin, the scrape of the mole's outer shell on the wall as it tumbled. "Tell me what?" She rolled, curling the waldo's flexible form around and bringing it back under her control as it reached the wall on the far side of the room. Helen fired off the engines, feeling the warmth under her belly as the hundred stubby legs scrabbled for purchase and brought her to stop.

"Guess who the operator was."

"No idea, never worked with BrightWinds."

"Catherine Beauchamp."

"You're fucking kidding me. I'm cleaning up Cat's mess here? That's choice."

There was no response of the end of the line.

"Keller?"

"Hey, Helen! This is Ravi from Operations."

A quick moment of panic, quickly squashed.

"What's up, Ravi?" And where the hell did Keller go in such a hurry?

"Keller asked me to take over the comms until your AI NAV gets booted up. Ivester grabbed him to review some data over at the primary console."

"How's that NAV looking?"

"We're rebooting. Looks like you were right about something being in the cache. He's approved you doing a full exploration run, so just let me know what you need on this end."

Helen wiggled, pulling her legs free from where they'd dug into the cavern wall. A fine powdering of dust rose into the vacuum. She could see the patterns as they messed with the sensor inputs. Whatever the dust was made of, it was starting to play havoc with her ability to "see." She'd have to move on, melting the dust ahead of her before she stirred it up. Without enough gravity to pull it down, it would hang, weightless, suspended in the empty space. Sure, the particles could be pulled together through their own minute gravity wells or static, but Helen didn't have that kind of time.

"There's a lot of dust, getting a little sensor trouble," Helen said out loud for the record.

"Makes sense. If the micro-gate is already built, they must have ordered the eenies to break down the rest of the asteroid."

Helen shifted her attention to the readout. "There's an awful a lot of organic material in there. It's not just silica and iron."

"Contamination, maybe? Pull a sample for review, maybe it's a starter-asteroid."

"Good idea." Unlike the spider waldo she could never quite put out of her mind, the mole kept all of his collection apparatus close to its chest. Helen kicked it into gear and moved forward through the particulate, opening the vents and sucking dust into the collection grid.

Dust again. Helen turned her attention back to the sensors as they compensated. Sand, regolith, gravel, ice, you name it, she had danced a waldo across it. This superfine dust could cause problems all across the board.

Except.

No. It was just dust from the mining process.

Just. Leftover. Dust.

She had to calm down and quit overreacting. Helen called up the electron micrograph.

"Helen, Doc says she's seeing an upset in your biochemistry. What's going on?"

"Tell you in a second. Just checking something out."

"It's only mining leftovers. Whatever process BrightWinds used must leave the dust as a side effect."

"I worked the moles for about two years, Ravi. I ran into a lot of different mining techniques." Helen elaborated on her thought process. "What the rock is made of makes a huge difference in the type of mining, whether you just dig through or heat it up or both."

"So?"

"Well, the tolerances of this mole are tight. If you get rock dust in between the joints, it's going to cause problems. There's no way you'd operate a waldo like this in a place like this if this kind of dust is your by-product."

"Maybe that's why they went bankrupt."

The data from the electron micrograph began to sheet across Helen's vision. She focused on the numbers, allowing the mole software to translate them into pictures for her. She held her breath, afraid that if she said anything out loud, the image dancing in the front of her mind would vanish.

The dust was the same, or at least remarkably similar, to the Scale left behind in the Golfball.

"Ravi, I'm going quiet for a sec so I can send you the scan I just got. Can you get these images to Keller, Dougal up in Analysis, and Ivester, and have them recheck what I'm seeing?"

"Roger that."

Communication cut out for a five count as the image was compressed and sent back down Helen's entanglement Feed to the Fishbowl. She was careful to use the opportunity to send a copy to her personal drives at the same time. It wouldn't stand up as evidence, but it would keep her sane if anyone tried to convince her she was seeing things further down the line. *Because we learned our lesson last time, right?*

"Helen, is this coming straight off the equipment? You're not running it through any interpolation software?" Ivester's voice came down the line.

"This is raw data." But Helen checked again to be sure.

Go very carefully. Helen held her breath and asked the mole to suck in a fresh sample. She carefully turned on every sensor, every analysis tool in sequence. She needed to find out everything before something happened to kick her out of entanglement.

You're not running away from this one. It's just you and the waldo, no one else out here to get hurt.

"Confirmed, Ivester, you have virgin data."

"Confirm it again," Ivester snapped.

Helen didn't mention that she'd checked twice already. She checked again.

"Confirmed."

There was a pause, then Ravi was back on the line. "Well, whatever you found, it sure lit a fire under him."

"How do you mean?" Helen asked.

"He dumped a copy of the file to the network and bolted out of here. Didn't say anything else."

If we're lucky. If we're very, very lucky, we might just have found a match for the eenies that sabotaged the Golfball. Helen felt . . . not giddy, but lighter. This was live data with a different set of entanglement particles. They might have a way to solve this without putting anyone else at risk.

"Okay, let's get back to exploring, shall we?" Ravi brought her back to task.

"Affirmative." Helen called up her protocol list and added a few new items. "This salvage run just got a whole lot more interesting."

The images in front of Helen started to stutter. The reactions of the mole grew more sluggish.

What the hell?

"NAV, I'm running into a feedback issue of some kind." Helen slowed the mole down, started engaging the parking sequence.

"Hold on, Keller's just back."

"NAV."

Helen's tongue felt thick and heavy, swollen. She tried to talk around it, tried to . . .

Oh god, bleedthrough. She was supposed to be fully entangled with the waldo, so what the mole felt, she felt. If she was feeling with her own body, while still under full control of the waldo, that meant something was going very wrong back in the coffin.

"NAV. Eject. NAV. Eject."

The techs on duty will catch it, will get you disentangled any second now. The thought was slow to come together. Helen could see the individual pieces that comprised it. Layered images in her mind's eye, but stringing them all together to form a whole was harder than it should have been.

Still no panic. That worried her. After the hundred little panic attacks her trip to the Golfball had cost her, there should've been a fight-or-flight response kicking in, pushing her to do something, anything. The bleedthrough must be going both ways. The waldo was fine, so she was fine.

Everything's fine here.

"Operator Vectorovich, can hear me?"

By the time Ravi finished speaking, she should have been yanked back to her own body.

"Keller wants you to stay entangled for ongoing feedback. You are being transferred to the buffer."

"Feedback, what the . . . ?"

"Helen, are you there?" Keller's voice came in abruptly. The readouts, the ones she could still read, showed Keller had taken over on the emergency channel. That got the panic going. If the strange eenies really were here, then there was a chance whatever had killed Ted was here too. That meant Keller was in danger.

"Keller, get the fuck off the line."

"Not a chance. Worst-case scenario, we have five minutes to get you sorted."

"Am I being handled?"

"Yep." Keller didn't screw around, she'd give him that.

"Okay, tell me what . . ." A sense of bliss flowed through her, the unassailable feeling that everything would be just fine if she stopped worrying quite so much.

"Helen, Doc just hit you with a big dose of ketamine, did you feel that?"

"Woo-hooo. I can ride this robot for days, man, dig every goddamn secret out of this space-rock." Helen started to bring the mole up out of parked mode, but the controls remained silent, unresponsive.

"Right. Now, something is going wrong in your coffin. Doc's working on getting you stabilized and out of there, but she needs you to keep talking to me while we do that."

"Goddammit, Keller, this was my last mission. I'm so fucking close to getting back out there and now THIS!" Helen kept poking at the waldo's controls, vexed at their lack of response. There was a feeling there, underlying the dreamy comfort. The need to get up, get out, and move was strong, but not as strong as whatever Doc had hit her with.

"Don't know, don't care, the techs will sort all that out later. Helen, I need you to do something for me—well, several somethings. All in order. Tell me each time you've completed one step."

A list popped up in front of her eyes. More tests, more shit to do in just the right order. Her entire life was governed by a long series of to-do lists. "I am the absolute QUEEN of protocol, Keller. I can check off your little boxes all goddamn day long." Helen giggled for no good reason. Then she giggled again because she really needed to be doing something to fix this and she just couldn't bring herself to care.

"Oh yeah?" Keller replied. "Prove it."

Helen tried to refocus, but it was getting harder and harder to think past the ever-present potential for giggles.

"Oh, and we shut off your control to the waldo, so don't worry about that. Thanks for parking, though."

"Noooooooo," Helen complained weakly. "Not my mooooole!

It's a nice mole. We should totally make more moles like this one."

"Wise words. Okay, give me number one on that list."

"Okay, fiiiiiiine." Helen stared for a long minute at the picture that had popped up.

"What do you see, Helen?"

She opened her mouth to speak, closed again. She recognized the image, knew what it was in form and shape and texture. She just couldn't find the word, any word.

This is a test, she reminded herself. *You have to get this right. Put a little work in.*

"Helen?"

Something changed. She didn't know what, maybe the doc had hit her with something else or whatever had crossed the wires in her head suddenly came uncrossed.

"Cat." She had the word now. "That's a cat. I fucking hate cats, Keller, you know this." With that, she found clarity; thoughts and concepts came back. *Not that they had gone anywhere.* It was more like someone had simply turned the lights back on. They were screwing with the wires in her head, and whatever they were doing with the coffin was affecting the connections that allowed her to entangle with a waldo. If those got messed up, she was done.

"Perfect. Next one?"

"It's a house. Hey, are you going to do the ink blot ones too? Those are lots more fun."

"Nobody does those anymore. Let's finish list item one, okay?"

Now that she had her right mind back, she had a better handle on the situation. *Oh, there it is. The creeping sense of panic.*

"Keller, why are they keeping me out here?"

"You're not out there any longer, Helen. You're back at Far Reaches. We've got you held in the buffer while we get the coffin sorted out. Doc wants us to move to list item two."

"So you're not NAV?"

"Glad to see you're feeling more like yourself. No, we shifted you into the buffer and James patched me into the simulation."

"I missed the transition. That can't be good. I should have been able to tell the difference."

"We can sort that out later. Doc didn't want you to panic."

"A little panic is good for the soul, Keller." Helen opened her Insight and dropped into the programming interface.

"So can we move on to number two?"

"Sure thing, bring it on." They had switched her Entanglement into one of James's simulations, disengaging her from the waldo. The space was normally used as a buffer for when an OP had to drop out of entanglement too quickly for the brain to compensate. It meant Keller was safe. The killer sound couldn't reach anyone in a simulation.

"Helen, get out of the programming interface and pay attention."

"Yep, hang on." There, she had it. Access to the security cameras in the Mortuary.

Oh fuck, that's me.

A coffin was being run out into the hallway by a pair of orderlies, Doc sitting astraddle. The lid had been popped and Doc was hooking an IV into the support system. Helen tried to get a closer look, but they'd moved out of camera range and she had to pull back to find another.

Her focus stuttered.

"Helen?"

Panic again: she could feel her heart pounding in her chest. It could be her own mind trying to give her feedback in the absence of any body, even a waldo's body. She felt, very acutely, that she been suspended somewhere in space. Someplace between the simulation and the waldo.

"Heeeeey, Keller." Words came together very slowly again . . . concepts out of reach.

"Hang on, Helen. Doc's moving you to the medbay."

"I can see that. I don't like the medbay. Can we go to the beach instead?"

"Nobody likes the medbay except Doc. And how are you seeing this? Stop hacking things."

"The doc . . ." Thought stuttered and matched the static that filled her vision.

"Helen?"

Helen was aware, she could hear Keller, but she couldn't respond. Her tongue was paralyzed. She couldn't see or move. Not even the Insight lines and windows survived the blanket of static that swept up to envelop her.

"Hey! Operator Vectorovich. Protocols. Get on them, now," Keller barked.

Helen tried to let the fear rise, to let the panic reach out to break her free, but it was like wrestling with a wet sleeping bag. She couldn't get a purchase on it, couldn't get a grip to tear or break through.

"Helen. Helen? You're online, I can see you in there. Knock off whatever the hell you're doing and get back on task."

Abruptly Helen had access to the security cameras again. Whatever had been in Doc's IV must have worked its magic. The coffin had been disassembled, sides pulled away, leaving her supersuit's umbilicals still connected to the main board. Pinned like a beetle.

Doc was moving quickly, single-mindedly. One of the techs was plugging wires directly in from the coffin's backboard to the bank of machines on the far wall, another rifling through the cabinets for something. Her vitals came up, displayed now on the far wall, but she didn't understand what any of it meant. Helen knew it was for the benefit of the cameras, just another blip in the never-ending layer of *cover your ass.*

A counter had been instantiated in her line-of-sight, seconds ticking past with regularity. One by one, the readouts were dropping into the red. The static in her mind chattered, shifting like densely packed like sand at the beach.

Ha ha, the beach again, wonder where that's coming from.

"Operator Vectorovich. Respond, please. Helen, respond." She could have sworn that was Ted's voice, but that was ridiculous, Ted was already dead. She missed his voice on the other end of the line, missed being able to trust her NAV.

Helen lost the camera, found the image in her mind's eye replaced by a series of still images. *Beach. Sand. Where are those coming from?* She hadn't been to the beach for nearly a decade.

Helen selected one of the images, one of the recent ones. Maybe her addled brain was pulling metaphors out of her personal log file. The stills she'd snapped on her Golfball run came spilling out, like grains of dust. *Oh, it's dust, not sand.* The pictures multiplied and filled the space in her head, her vision, her ears. Keller's voice, the Insight interface, everything vanished under an onslaught of static-colored dust that turned into billions of tiny waldos seeking something she did not have.

CHAPTER EIGHTEEN

THE INSIDE OF FAR REACHES medical floor was becoming far more familiar than Helen was comfortable with. After two days, she woke up in a brightly colored treatment room, still encased in her supersuit, strapped to the coffin's backboard. Doc had conscripted the coffin's drug delivery system rather than trying to hook her up to a more traditional medical apparatus.

Helen remembered at some point Hofstaeder storming on about heavy metal poisoning being obsolete and just who the hell would bring such a low-tech trick into her goddamn wheelhouse. The entire incident left Helen with an unshakeable feeling of exhaustion underpinned with an all-body ache that reached down to her bones. She was trapped in a ten-by-ten room painted dog-dick pink, tiredly regarding the lost pillow on the floor. She was trying to decide if it was worth alerting the nurse to get it back when Ivester came in the door.

Well, he looks about how I feel. He was pale on the best of days, but now dark circles and red rims around the eyes suggested a chemical-driven lack of sleep. He stepped in, not quite furtively, but with the air of someone out of place. His usual entourage was notably absent. Even in her diminished state, Helen caught the glimmer in his glasses as his Insight spoke to the cameras in the room and they powered off.

"What's up with the cameras?" Helen chuckled around the tightness in her lungs. It was funny to think about a project lead being constrained, just like everybody else. Whatever he had come here to say, he didn't want it on the record.

"You caught that?"

"Of course I did. Your gear," Helen tapped at a set of imaginary glasses, "isn't really subtle."

"I haven't heard that one before." He dropped into the chair closest to the door.

Helen stared him quizzically. She expected something from management, an apology, a statement of some sort. Not a personal visit, and certainly not a secret personal visit from Ivester at any rate.

"Why, exactly, are you here, Dr. Ivester?" Doc had been keeping her pumped with enough chemicals to keep her in the bed, and presumably, out of trouble. It was making Helen a little less careful of her tongue than she would otherwise be. *Clearly trouble has other things in mind.*

Ivester adjusted his glasses self-consciously. The movement pushed the nose piece a little higher, a little closer to his tired grey eyes. "Well, for one, I wanted to see for myself how you were doing. My team was getting reports, of course, but it's not quite the same thing."

"And for two?"

"Line Drive operations have been completely suspended."

Helen just stared at him. Suspended? That was . . . She searched for a word in between stunning and depressing, coming up empty. She felt momentarily sick, almost like she'd been punched in the gut.

"The eenies are on autopilot," she managed to say. Then her brain started working again, latching on to the train of thought as if it led to a way out. "If everything's on schedule, our payload just made it into orbit and the jumpgate is getting built whether or not we shut down Line Drive on this end."

"Well, yes." Ivester leaned back, a frown sketched across his features. Helen waited for some elaboration from him, but it became clear that this was going to be one of those conversations where she had to ask the questions. Keller did the same damn thing.

"Until the communications array comes back online with Phase II, we can't even talk to the payload to stop the jumpgate being built," she continued, stubbornly forging ahead.

"Also, yes."

"That's a big project. We need those resources. Why are we stopping?"

"That's not the right question."

Helen stared him down. Ivester opened his mouth as if to speak, closed it again, brow furrowed.

"Why do I get the feeling you're going to say something I'd better consider when thoroughly sober?" Helen groused.

Ivester's snort turned into a laugh—not his "on camera" laugh, something far less well-trained and nervous. "That's exactly what I'd advise you to do, if you get time."

"Time?"

He sighed, took his glasses off and fiddled with them nervously. "They're shutting down the first stage of the Line Drive program completely. The Golfball's become a liability the board doesn't want to deal with."

Helen's sick feeling coalesced into anger. Scrapping the program meant Ted's death, the pain and suffering of the other NAVs, that was all just going to get swept under the rug. All those months of work rendered null and void. *They've closed the goddamn door. There's no way to get back out there*, she thought bitterly.

Ivester seemed to sense the shift in her mood, held up a hand to forestall her next words. "I'm serious when I say scrubbing. They're going to terminate as many people involved with the Golfball portion of Line Drive as possible. The board wants to sell the whole thing off, but I think I can keep them off that idea for the moment."

"Sell everything off? Ivester, we might have discovered an entirely new life form and they want to chicken out?" Helen clipped her words to keep the anger under wraps.

"They can't terminate your contract, legally, as long as Doc has you under her care. It's policy." Ivester got to his feet and started pacing. It was clear his mind wasn't on the loss of the Golfball, not the way hers was. *He's saying something else.*

Helen shifted gears. "Wait. What?"

"The Golfball is officially being scrubbed, but arranging a sale will take time. The Board knows full well that if our partners at XERMo learn that we are looking at a new, possibly grumpy, life form, the government will simply seize everything and they will have to eat the loss as well as the responsibility. They don't want to take that risk. I'm personally taking project lead on all the assets until a sale is arranged. IF a sale gets arranged. I need you here, at Far Reaches, for the next steps we take." His eyebrows were down into a thin line. "I'm asking you to make sure Doc doesn't discharge you just yet."

In the unforgiving light of the LEDs, Ivester looked like a man who'd had his worst week ever. Not defeated, just wrung out, like he'd lost track of one too many moving parts and had suffered a complete train wreck.

Which is probably a fair assessment.

"You're taking the Golfball underground?" Helen caught up.

"Let's just say, I need you, and you specifically, on a special project."

Helen eyeballed him critically. "I don't even know if that's possible."

"It can be handled as long as you're still working here. Look, we put our foot in something out there. You know it, I know it. You've encountered these things twice now, twice. They didn't come from here. They cost you your NAV and now very nearly your life. Don't you want to find out just what the hell is going on out there?"

Helen recognized that look, that evangelist's stare. Ivester thought he had put two and two together and discovered a secret everyone else had missed. It was the kind of mindset that would push limits, break rules . . . end lives.

"Ivester," Helen said slowly, "someone just tried to kill me over this. As much as I need to get back out there, I'm not sure I want to risk my life on it." It was a sobering thought—another one best considered well after she was off whatever Hofstaeder was pumping her full of.

"I know, I know. Just think about it. I promise I will do everything I can to keep you safe."

Helen sighed. "Is Keller in?"

"Is that a yes?"

Helen held up an arm, the tips of her fingers still a bluish tint as the machines continued to scrub the selenium out of her system. "I reserve the right to come to my senses after Doc is done with me."

"Fair enough." He got to his feet. "Now if you'll excuse me, I think security is going to come chase me out of here."

"Good luck."

"I make my own luck, Ms. Vectorovich." Ivester left as quietly as he'd come in.

"Make enough for the whole team this time!" Helen called after him.

Helen tried for another deep breath and came up short. She didn't know what happened if you actually died while operating a waldo. Some operators said it was possible for your mind to get stuck in a waldo's computer permanently. Judging by the experience she'd just had, that was a fairy tale, something to deflect from the creepy horror of knowing your body could die and you would be helpless to take any action.

Like dying in your sleep. You'd never know what happened.

The room felt a lot colder and she dragged the hospital blankets closer. Doc had taken away her Insight tablet, so she was left with nothing but the insistent humming of the monitoring devices and Ivester's visit to chew on. *And a near-death experience*, but now, right now, was too soon to dig into that.

She steered her thoughts back to Ivester's half-formed proposal. She'd been a part of scrubbed projects before, seen the soul go out of the company, even if it saved the bottom line. Far Reaches was about to change. Ivester had said that the Golfball was about to get canned, which meant that any of the other exploration firms that caught wind were going to start "expert shopping" in very short order, if they hadn't begun already. If she wanted to jump ship, go someplace safer, now was the time.

"Hey, how's Doc treating you?" The door popped open again, this time admitting Keller and an insulated bag that smelled like heaven.

"I am not dead. That's all I got for you today."

The door swung shut behind Keller, and she caught a glimpse of the uniform.

"Why is that guard outside my door? It's not like I can go anywhere hooked up to this damn thing." Helen gestured at the mostly disassembled coffin parts stacked up between beeping medical machinery.

"Since Doc came back with the toxicology results, there's been a warm body outside your door. Ivester read security the riot act. No one allowed in here except medical."

"And you." *And Ivester, apparently.*

"Well, I have a relationship with Lutipo out there. That's why I recommended him."

"So are you going to explain Lutipo?"

"First, lunch. Had to promise Ethan I'd bring you this."

"Ethan? He's sending you with home-cooked lunches now?"

"Exactly. Remember that pho I brought in last month? That was Ethan's. Anyway he sent this over, so I'm bringing it in to share."

"Um . . . Thanks." Keller dragged the room's tiny table over and unpacked the bag. Helen's stomach reminded her, none too graciously, that she'd been eating through an IV for the past few days. Keller grinned and handed her a black neoprene-wrapped container.

"Here, that one's yours. Just broth, no noodles."

"Awww."

"Eat that and I'm going to walk you through what happened when you were busy dying in your coffin."

"Malfunction," Helen corrected. She didn't want to think too deeply about the alternative, even though between half-heard Hofstaeder rants and Ivester's admission, she was well aware of reality.

"You were totally dying. Doc's a fucking miracle worker." Keller peeled both containers open and handed Helen a fat black straw. His own soup was far more interesting, with brightly colored protein cubes and long thick noodles.

"Fine," Helen said firmly, using the force of her tone to push that feeling of panic back down so she didn't have to think about it too closely.

"Someone tampered with your coffin right after the start of the mission. Introduced selenium into the coffin water. Over time it kept building up until, whammo."

"Someone?"

"Someone. We don't know who yet: the cameras in the Mortuary were compromised, no one was recorded coming in or out, but James clearly shows your coffin being tampered with, we just don't have a record of who it was."

Helen tried to get her head around that idea while Keller unlimbered a set of wooden chopsticks and fished a nest of noodles out of his own bowl. Helen popped the lid off hers and took a long sniff at the contents.

"Oh, you're a lucky man, Keller." She took a careful sip without the straw. "Pho's a clear liquid, right?"

"Absolutely. So here's the thing, and you did not get this from me, but Beauchamp's gone. Vanished. Poof, gone."

Helen threw him a skeptical glance. "What?"

"Gone. Her letter of resignation's in the system. She just walked out." His eyebrows put the lie to that sentence, and he stuffed his mouth with noodles before it could betray him too.

"That . . . That makes no sense. Beauchamp's been trying to get onto the Line Drive team for weeks now. She went over your head, right to Dougal."

"And failed, I might add."

"Oh bullshit, you know she was going to be slotted in as soon as they took off the hold."

"She was one of the top picks to bring on board, I'll admit, but her ability to work with others had been on a downhill slide, complaints were starting to stack up. She got an offer from one of our competitors, Beyond Blue. Ironic that she took off the same day you got taken back out of action. If she'd held on two more days, we'd have been forced to put her in rotation."

"That's . . . that's a little creepy, Keller. You don't think she did this?" Helen tried to put two and two together. Beauchamp's slip-ups in performance had raised a few eyebrows among Flight Ops, especially with her publicly stated goal of knocking Helen off the top spot. Still, the fact that Beauchamp had walked away from a fight when Helen had confronted her had been out of character as well. Maybe she had already received the offer. Maybe Ted's death had affected the other OP more than Helen thought.

Maybe she jumped ship because she knew she was losing her edge. A stray, petty thought to be sure, but it didn't ring true.

"I don't, but Metro will make the call. Beauchamp was an excellent pilot, but I don't know if she could have convinced the security system she wasn't there. And like you said, she was an in for Line Drive, so there was no reason for her to take a stab at you literally. Unless there's something more serious going on?" He raised an eyebrow. Helen shook her head. Whatever disagreements she might have with Beauchamp, she didn't think they had reached the "murder you in your sleep" level of hostility. Helen took another big sip of soup, trying to stave off the chill that accompanied the idea. It helped.

"Also, if you get a call from Harcourt Tamlin, take it. He's your union-appointed lawyer."

"My what?"

"Lawyer. This whole thing . . ." he gestured with his chopsticks expressively, ". . . was not an accident. You didn't get a bad chemical mix, there was no negligence, the coffin is in perfect condition. Even if you don't decide to sue, Far Reaches is going to have to assume you're going to. You can't negotiate for shit. I've seen your employment contract."

"Fuck. We don't know who did this, right? How can that put Far Reaches at fault?"

"That's not what it's about. Metro's handling the investigation for that. This is about Far Reaches covering their asses, so talk to the lawyer and do whatever he says. Okay?"

Helen took another careful sip of the soup, mind reeling.

"Aren't they going to be pissed about you giving me the heads-up like this?"

"Heads-up? I'm just here on a mission of mercy." He jabbed a chopstick at her. "You know how Doc's idea of food involves protein slurry and ice water. Besides, she doesn't permit any recordings from here. That particular camera . . ." another flip and expressive stab with the chopsticks, ". . . has a long-running history of catastrophic failures when it comes to recording just about anything. Doc uses this room for her particularly sensitive cases, when she doesn't want things going on permanent record."

Helen wondered if Ivester had known. "What about the Golf-ball?"

"The Golfball is still on the rails. We've got a meeting in half an hour. Since you're off rotation again, I've got to scramble."

"Ivester was just in here. He said it was being scrubbed."

Keller slurped the last of the noodles and chased them down his throat with the remaining broth. "Dammit, that guy never tells me anything. Okay, that's going to cause some problems. I gotta run."

"Hey, keep me posted."

"You bet."

As soon as Keller packed up and left, the tightness in her chest increased. It felt a little like panic, but it was much more physical. The feeling had been building and she'd been able to ignore it because of the string of revelations she'd just been hit with, but now it had the upper hand. *Dammit, not now.* Helen took a big gulp of the soup to try and clear her throat, hoping the warmth would relax the tightness away. The resulting paroxysm sprayed pho all over the coverlet. She had to focus to breathe. Her lungs felt full and inhaling too deep just made it worse. The machines hooked into her suit started to react with lights and atonal sounds. Helen leaned forward, knees drawn up to her chest. She could breathe in short gasps, but it felt like she was operating on half a lung.

The door slammed open, framing Doc for a second before she strode into the space. "Looks like pulmonary edema," Hofstaeder called over her shoulder before the doors swung shut. "And who the hell brought food in here?" Doc keyed in a code on the keypad beside the bed and immediately Helen felt herself relax, her lungs opening up.

"You. Lie back down."

Doc pressed her palms to Helen's shoulders, pushing her back. Helen resisted. "It's a side effect of the selenium, you've still got fluid in your lungs and it's going to take a time to clear that out."

Helen felt like she was operating on half oxygen, her vision flickering around the edges. She laid flat for a second, then struggled back to a sitting position as it got harder to breathe.

"You weren't supposed to have any visitors in here until we made the decision whether or not to transfer you to Metro General. The more you talk, the faster you overtax those lungs." Doc punched the button to bring the bed into a more upright position.

"Didn't."

"Of course you did, there's soup all over the place. I presume it was Keller. He's the one who recommended Lutipo to guard the door. Did he at least have the sense to keep the noodles out of it?"

Wordlessly, Helen nodded.

"Well, at least he paid attention to the medical briefing." More typing on the keypad. "I need you to stay here in this bed and be quiet until we finish. You're lucky the coffin computer picked up on the problem at all. It started scrubbing your bloodstream almost as fast as the toxins could get into it, but since you've already got selenium supplements as part of your allowed chemical mix, it wasn't as aggressive as it should have been. Someone just introduced a highly concentrated version of something you were already microdosing. We'll get you clear soon enough—even the heavy metals you might have picked up as a kid will be gone."

Helen nodded again. She still couldn't breathe well enough to talk, and she had so many questions.

"What?" Helen managed to work the word into the exhale.

"What? You mean whom." Hofstaeder's lips compressed into a thin line that was about as angry as Helen had ever seen. "We don't have an answer for that, but until we do, there's a guard on the door. All these damn cameras," she waved a hand at the same ones Ivester had hacked and Keller had dismissed, "have been hardened against interference, and I will be handling your recovery personally. I will not lose another member of Flight Ops to this cursed project."

"How long?" Helen asked, Ivester's request still weighing on her mind.

"Until you can go? Let's see how long it takes to get your lungs clear. Lucky for you, bodies are much easier to fix than minds."

CHAPTER NINETEEN

THE LOWEST POSSIBLE LEVEL of Far Reaches smelled of uncured concrete and hot machine oil. The sub-sub-basements had a checkered history, most likely invented by bored support staff. The flaking paint on the walls had a shimmer that meant the maintenance eenies were already working on the resurfacing. Given a week, the concrete walls would look and feel as professional as any other space in Far Reaches' multi-story campus.

Ivester convinced the board to let him take the Golfball as a spin-off. The ultimate goal, on paper, was to develop it into something that could be sold off to recoup the costs. It also meant that "out of sight, out of mind" was the expression of the day. The Golfball project split off from Line Drive and hid underground, literally and figuratively.

Helen's recovery time had taken longer than expected. Heavy metals from the selenium poisoning had bound to the connections that let her link to a waldo. As a result, some of those needed to be removed and redrawn. She'd been able to make a few upgrades, spread out the processing load, refine the level of control she'd have when piloting a waldo. It also meant her hands had developed a tremble that came and went. Hofstaeder had assured her it would go away in time, but Helen felt compelled to hide it.

She shifted the bag on her shoulder with shaking fingers and reached for the door handle. Helen had gone back and forth in her head about whether or not to accept Ivester's offer. The only way to nail down what happened to Ted was to get back out to the half-eaten Golfball on its final approach to Otlyan23. So the decision was simple in the end.

The NFC chip in her wrist shook hands with the lock and allowed her in. The new lab space was still a work in progress, furnishings still wrapped in shrinkwrap, light fixtures still being extruded. The center of the space had already collected stacks of servers and touchscreens.

"Hey! You made it!" Dougal emerged from one of the office cubicles along the far wall. "Welcome to Recovr." The analyst had narrowly dodged being let go along with the rest of the Golfball support team by approaching Ivester about joining Recovr as soon as the proverbial ink was dry. Helen was delighted that the team would be made up of familiar faces; it meant she could focus on the waldo.

"I see we have some recovery of our own to finish up first." Helen picked her way through the room-in-progress.

Dougal laughed. "Oh, this is just the cosmetics. Ivester made sure they got your coffin hooked up before we did anything else." He spread his arms wide to encompass the rest of the space, the smattering of overhead lights making pale patterns on pale skin. "This room will be dedicated to support and development, when they get all the walls in anyway. Over there are the offices." Another wave of the hand. "Ivester's already using one. We're going to trick one out as your ready room." He deftly avoided tripping over one of the conduits that crisscrossed the floor like a snake in the sunlight.

"Okay. What else you got?" Helen took a few steps over to the "ready room" and dropped her bag by the door.

Dougal rubbed his hands together. "Oh, wait 'til you see where we got the coffin set up."

Helen wasn't entirely sure what she expected, given the half-finished state of the rest of the space. The next set of doors opened up onto a room that might have started as a fair copy of the Far Reaches Fishbowl upstairs. A single, solitary coffin was bolted into a wall rack meant to hold at least half a dozen operators. The touch-screen wall was covered in images and frames filled with numbers. It looked like Ivester was working on several bits of the coffin software almost simultaneously, jumping from screen to screen as he went.

"You've been busy," Helen commented.

Ivester turned away from the control panels, a broad grin working against the tired lines behind his glasses.

He looks like he needs another week off.

"Like it? We've got a limited window to take advantage of, so we needed to get the entanglement gear up and running first." Ivester closed up whatever he was working on and came to join Helen by the coffin.

Helen took her time, checking over the equipment. Not brand new, but certainly on par with the rest of Far Reaches' gear. The conduits in this room all descended along the walls from the floor above, leaving the rubberized mats clear under their feet. There was no real separation between the coffin racks and the controls, no observation theater. One team, one room. *Cozy.*

"Are these the CAT23 pods we replaced two years ago?" she asked as she cycled the coffin open and stuck her head inside. The interior had been re-kitted, new gel pads, new touch panels. It even had that new pod smell. Helen was impressed. Ivester wasn't fooling around. "Looks pretty. Has anyone taken it for a test drive yet?"

"Not yet. We needed our damn operator to show up for that." Another familiar voice rang out.

Helen turned, delighted to find Keller approaching from the far end of the space.

"Well, since I was only poisoned this time, Doc cleared me pretty damn quick," Helen said, and gave him a hug in greeting. Keller had been spared the axe, since he oversaw Flight Operations. Recovr was officially tucked into his queue just like any other mission set. As an R&D project, they'd have less oversight than income-generating missions or even exploratory projects like Line Drive. Helen felt a bit less uneasy. Having Keller on the team gave it a feeling of legitimacy, like they had a shot at succeeding.

"Now that you're here, we need to get the gear calibrated. I presume you heard about Beauchamp and Beyond Blue?" Keller shooed Ivester aside and began flipping switches and poking screens.

Helen grimaced. "Yeah, here's hoping she's a better team leader than she was a follower."

"She'll do fine. Did Dougal show you the ready room?"

"You mean the closet with aspirations?" Helen cast a glance over her shoulder at the half-repurposed office. "At least it's got a door."

"And it's all yours. Go get your supersuit on and we can get started with calibrating the coffin to your Insight. I've got the list of upgrades—I forgot you never rolled back to the GEN2 interface like most of the OPs so I had to make some changes."

"GEN3's faster, cleaner." Helen headed for the ready room. "I don't suppose you managed to get a shower installed in here?"

"It's on the list."

"Ugh, that means we're using the evaporative gel?" The layer of conductive gel excreted by the supersuits had to go somewhere when you changed back into your clothes. A hot shower usually did the trick, since the stuff broke up easily in water. The in-orbit labs, where showers were a luxury, had come up with a gel you squeegeed off like an all-over body sanitizer.

"Yep, we got lavender or shower-fresh scented. Operator's choice." Under Keller's experienced touch, the coffin powered up with a comforting hum.

"You know neither of those actually smells like the name, right?" Helen grabbed her bag and closed the door behind her without waiting for an answer.

It was over an hour before Helen came up for air. Whatever half-finished state the rest of the lab might have been in, the Insight interface with the coffin was downright stunning. Clean lines, responsive, attentive. Ivester had put the time in on the software, even if the room didn't have enough chairs for the whole team to sit down.

It wasn't until they broke for lunch that Ivester outlined the entirety of the plan.

"I'm sure you're all wondering why I called you here this afternoon . . ." he began in a sonorous tone that belied his wiry frame. It elicited a chuckle from the team.

"Well, I'm not, but we probably should get the new kids up to speed now that they're on the payroll." Keller threw in his two cents.

"And under NDA," Ivester returned.

"Up to speed on what?" Dougal spoke first. The news Feeds had been buzzing with speculation about the recent announcement from Beyond Blue. Helen held her tongue, let Dougal do the digging.

"The Recovr team," Ivester made a gesture that encompassed all four people present, "has taken over Golfball operations. The Board wants us to do a little R&D, figure out how to make this thing safe, and then they want to sell it off to the competition."

"So we're *not* building a salvage operation?" Dougal seemed confused, still eager, but not quite on the same track. Helen wondered just what had prompted him to sign on. An analyst like Dougal should have had no issue finding a new spot at a rival firm. Whatever he thought Recovr was going to be going after, it had to be big. Ivester folded his fingers together.

"Let me explain. The official goal of Recovr is to prep the Golfball assets for sale. You're all still Far Reaches employees, we still have access to those resources, but we are no longer a key asset. However, while we are crossing all the Is and dotting all the Ts, we have an opportunity." Ivester paced back and forth in front of the group, trying to assemble his phrasing.

Here we go.

"You've all been privy to the . . . unusual circumstances surrounding the Golfball, the first phase of our Line Drive project. More to the point, you've all been exposed to some of the . . . broader implications of those circumstances."

"Oh my god, you really do think those are aliens." Dougal said it first.

Ivester paused for a few moments, staring at the analyst in bemused silence. Then he cracked a grin. "Well, let's cut to the chase then. Yes. We've run out of horses to examine, which means there are only unicorns left in the stable. I don't know what kind of life form these . . . Scales are, but I would very much like to find out."

That cleared up any confusion. Dougal turned to Helen, an incredulous look on his face. "So after all that crap you caught for saying it was aliens, it turns out it's aliens?"

Helen opened her mouth to answer, closed it. She hadn't realized they'd brought the analyst in without full disclosure, so she chose her words carefully. "It didn't really work out that way. What I saw on the first mission certainly wasn't anything I'd seen before, but the first theories about sabotage were a hell of a lot more likely."

Ivester raised an eyebrow at Helen. "Right," he said, "we explored those options, and came up empty." He tapped his fingertips together. "Now, engineering is pursuing the idea that those strange eenies we found are likely a mutant generation. It's still more likely than aliens, true, but it's the kind of thing that will require a ground-up redesign to root out. It will take months of time and the payload is already in orbit around our little orphan star, collecting material for assembly of the jumpgate."

"According to Far Reaches' annual filings, they've declared the Golfball portion of Line Drive a total loss and are turning all resources to support the jumpgate that will connect Otlyan23 with our solar system," Helen added.

"Nobody reads the filings," Ivester interjected.

"I was in the hospital for days; I read the filings. Do you want me keep speculating or not?" Helen asked.

Ivester nodded, taken aback.

"Here's the thing: the Line Drive mission is a success. As long as the eenies do their jobs, the jumpgate is going to be open in two months. When the gate to Otlyan23 opens, there might be a whole new nano-scale lifeform waiting for us on the other side." Helen took a deep breath and reminded herself not to flinch at how crazy the next part sounded.

"We think we encountered something alive," Helen carried on, "something that got to the Golfball and killed my NAV. So, the plan is to confirm and evaluate what we're dealing with before that gate gets opened up."

Dougal's eyes lit up. "You're talking about a first contact scenario?" he said somewhat breathlessly, then pulled himself back to reality. "We've never encountered anything more alive than amino acid sets with an attitude problem. Why the hell isn't anyone all over this? This is *huge*."

"Also, not technically first contact. Helen already came *into* contact, she just didn't know it at the time," Keller cautioned.

"And Theodore paid the price for it," Ivester added sourly. "Far Reaches is in the business of salvage and exploration. If we start blowing the 'first contact' horn without being careful, some of our government-level partners are going to walk in and take everything off our hands without so much as a penny to pay us back. The board's logic is that someone else can take the financial hit if this does turn out to be a living organism. They want to dump the project and let someone else take the risk."

Ivester and Keller exchanged looks before the CTO continued. "I can tell you that every mention of your recent findings at Myrian23A5 was diverted, buried, or simply deleted. The only reason I put two and two together is because Keller came and filled me in during the salvage mission. Close on the heels of that, someone tried to murder Helen in her coffin and I was handed a leave of absence from the board."

"So someone else within Far Reaches wants to keep it a secret?" Helen asked. The idea that someone had been actively working against her, that Beauchamp was part of a larger effort, gave her a chill. Operators and management had issues all the time, but Beauchamp had been a devil she knew. She was even more worried about the devil she didn't.

"Maybe, but I don't yet know who or why," Ivester said. "With most of us being on the outs, we are unlikely to get a satisfactory result on that front. So we need to turn our attention to the things we can do from our well-appointed little basement here. Which, right now, is getting back out there to Otlyan23. Since our unknown adversary did such a splendid job of keeping the board in the dark, they, in turn, were willing to let me keep the keys to the Golfball."

This elicited a couple of grins. Getting away with the entanglement key was a pretty big deal. Helen wondered what else he'd had to give up in return.

"There is something else to note," Ivester said, more quietly this time. The shift in tone gave them all pause. "Far Reaches is about to open a full-sized jumpgate into deep space. That's a permanent, two-way, star-powered wormhole, which means that we can visit Otlyan23 anytime we want. That also means that anything near Otlyan23 can come and visit us if it has a mind to. Once we link that gate to its power source, it doesn't turn off until somebody blows it up."

He paced the end of the table, hands clasped behind his back.

"Even if we're not talking about an intelligence, we're talking about something that can interrupt our entanglement communications on a quantum level. Even if it's just some flavor of galactic space bacteria, incapable of getting through the gate unassisted, it's only a matter of time before it comes through stuck to the bottom of a cargo container because someone got sloppy.

"We have to get back out there and prove whether or not there is SOMETHING there and what it's capable of. We may need a valid and compelling reason to delay bringing that jumpgate online."

"Can we even do that?" Dougal asked, incredulously.

Helen sympathized. They were talking about bringing a multi-year project with a price tag in the trillibits to a screeching halt. The inertia alone might flatten them all in the process.

"Let's get our proof first. Then we can better evaluate what we're up against."

Dougal sat back and drummed his fingertips on the tabletop. The vibrations made the paper wrappers left from lunch shift and crinkle.

Helen studied the analyst. He was giving the plan his consideration, but there was a hesitancy. Things weren't quite clicking. Helen had come to her own decision well before she'd accepted Ivester's offer, but she'd had a view from the inside. Add to that the need to resolve, and maybe now avenge, Ted's death was still rattling around in the back of her head. Dougal's motivations weren't so clear, and Helen wasn't sure if she should appeal to his vanity or his skillset.

Keller picked up on Dougal's hesitance too. He passed a glance to Ivester, then back to Helen.

"I'm on clean-up, since Recovr paid for lunch," Keller announced, gathering together empty containers and motioning for Helen to do the same. She gratefully took the hint and helped collect the wrappers.

"Let Ivester talk to him. He doesn't need three people at once pressuring him into this," Keller said once they were out of earshot.

"I don't get it. Didn't you guys give him the heads-up? Why bring him in cold?" Helen kept her voice low, risked a glance over her shoulder to where the engineer and the analyst were talking at the table.

"Dougal came to us. Once rumor got out that you'd joined the Recovr team, he wanted in." Keller chucked the trash in the recycle bin. The flash as the wrappers and other leftovers came in contact with the eenies inside made his pupils contract to pinpoints. Helen was silent for a moment, digesting that information.

"I'm . . . I'm not entirely sure what to do with that."

"Do good things. We need an analyst on the team if we don't want to screw all this up. Dougal's a rock star. Having his name on the documentation and analysis means it's going to get taken way more seriously. If you're right, and if Ivester's right, then we need every advantage we can get."

"So if Dougal bows out, do we have a second option?"

"If you added your two cents, asked him to stay . . ." Keller countered.

"Asked? You mean help Ivester put the screws to him? Didn't you just tell me to do 'good things'? If we're wrong, he's going to take a career hit. It's one thing helping to package up a trillibit asset sale, quite another to be on the 'ooOOoooo it's aliens' side of the table. I've been there for months. It sucks."

"We don't have a lot of options."

Helen ran arguments through her head, looking for something that might be interesting enough, amazing enough to make it worth the professional risk to Dougal.

"We don't need a lot. We just need one. Remember Myrian23A5?" she asked.

"The one that almost killed you?"

"Look, the whole super-secret point of Recovr is to figure out if those little Scales are actually alien. Let's use Myrian23A5 to get the system properly calibrated. We can test the limits of the new setup and maybe get the whole team in sync. We know the Scale were there. The mission's been mothballed—I know, I checked."

Keller hesitated, but not for as long as Helen thought he would.

"All right, let's try it."

"I got this." Helen headed back over and stepped into the pause in conversation. Dougal looked distressed. Ivester was putting some kind of full-court press on him for sure.

"Gentlemen," Helen said, "lunch break is over and we have things to do if we're going to pull this off."

Ivester was annoyed at the interruption. Helen saw him cast a glance at Keller, but whatever signal Keller gave him, it was enough for the engineer to put a lid on it.

"But we haven't . . ." Dougal protested.

"Save it. Keller and I need to get the gear calibrated anyway, so stick around and see what comes back down the pipe. If you change your mind later, we'll chalk it up to a short-term contracting gig." Helen cocked an eyebrow at Ivester. "We're going back out to Myrian23A5."

"I . . ."

"Great, let's go." Helen pointed in Keller's direction, the Flight Ops lead already calling up the information on the wall of touch-screens. Dougal gave in and went to join him with a shake of his head.

"Ms. Vectorovich, I don't appreciate . . ." Ivester began.

Helen held up a finger, waited a beat until Dougal and Keller were in conversation before beginning.

"Look, we need him, right? Let me show him why he should stay. You said Myrian23A5 was the tipping point for you, so let's show Dougal what we found out there and see if it convinces him too."

Ivester considered a moment. "Okay. See what you can do."

CHAPTER TWENTY

IF THE MOLE HAD MOVED, run out of power, maybe turned into a giant space worm while she'd been away, Helen would not have batted an eye. Finding it right where she'd parked it was a bit anti-climactic.

"Operator Helen Vectorovich, personal identifier T4T4-957. We are live, we are live, we are live." She repeated the official communications identifier. Going back out to Myrian meant Helen was flying without a NAV. The AI NAV had failed to connect on her previous mission, the computer simply never answering. Keller was playing a lite version of the role through the emergency channel, just in case. It meant they wouldn't have access to anything that was normally under the NAV's control. The micro-jumpgate and any remaining eenies would be useless unless she could access the NAV computer array using the mole.

Ivester's voice came down the line. "Okay, Operator Vectorov-ich, let's see what else we can find on this rock."

"Get off the party line, boss, NAVs and OPs only," Helen re-turned.

"I can see we're going to have to revisit the team structure before the next run." Keller's voice now.

The emergency line could be accessed by anyone at the console for communications. Ivester had used it to take over for Ted. Keller and Ravi had used it on her last trip to Myrian. There was potential for distraction if Helen didn't establish the boundaries up front. She made a mental note to talk to Ivester about it later.

"Okay, Keller. What should we go check out first?" Helen settled back into the sightless body of the mole, flexing the outer carapace and trying out each of the paddle-like feet in turn. A quick ping with the sensors showed her the network of tunnels closest to her, unchanged.

"Let's pull the local activity logs. We've got a jumpgate built, and the NAV particles not responding, and a bunch of bogus data in the reports. Hopefully we can get more accurate information from the NAV computer on-site," Keller said.

"Okay, open up . . ." Helen caught herself. "Sorry, forgot you're not entangled like a NAV. I'm going to head over to see if I can plug this waldo into the computers." Manually interfacing a waldo with a NAV's computer array was an emergency measure, a backup of a backup.

"According to the schematics James has on file, everything's in a central location, but we haven't been able to access it from here. It ought to be easy enough to find in there," Keller said.

"That's efficient." Helen tickled the mole's computer and called up a map of the tunnel system that BrightWinds had bored under the asteroid's skin.

"Well, BrightWinds was trying to develop a completely AI-run system. Automation all the way down."

"I take it that didn't work out well." It was bad enough that most exploration got done by remote first; removing humans entirely from the equation left Helen cold.

"They explored farther out than the rest of us—took bigger risks. The AIs started to run into stuff they couldn't handle and they had to bring in live NAVs. That's about the point the cost-benefit ratio went sideways," Keller elaborated.

"Hey, Keller." Now that Helen was back in the mole with all its information and sensor logs laid out before her, things had stopped adding up. Whoever had decided that Far Reaches should buy up BrightWinds' mining assets clearly hadn't looked too deeply into this one. The maps and tunnels didn't match up. Like the moles had started to dig and then lost their sense of direction. The tunnels crisscrossed and went every which way, erupting to the surface, diving to the center of the asteroid, more like tunnels dug by real-live moles rather than waldos. "It was the AI NAV that declared this a total loss, right? Not the human OP?"

"Not just Myrian23A5, but about a half dozen of BrightWind's operations out on the fringe," Keller confirmed.

"What are the odds that BrightWind's AI NAV ran into that same signal that killed Ted?" Helen directed the mole to return to the micro-gate, allowing it to set its own route. An idea had started to emerge and she was in a mood to air it out.

"That's . . . Well, that's not the worst idea I've heard. You're thinking that BrightWinds kept it under wraps?"

"Maybe. The tunnels here don't match the maps at all, it's like all the protocols went haywire. If that signal got to the AI NAV, it might have caused this kind of breakdown. Tell Ivester. See if he has any insight."

"I can hear you just fine, Ms. Vectorovich," Ivester cut in. "There was no mention of any kind of disruption in the files, but we clearly don't have all the information at hand. Maybe the local mission logs will tell us more."

"I'm on it." Helen called up her list of protocol items, shifting things around as the mole trundled its way forward. The ground-penetrating sensors had been mapped to Helen's visual input. Whenever she sent out a pulse, she got a 360-degree image of the surrounding wall densities. The effect was akin to the way a dolphin could "see" underwater, just much more robust. When the waldo exited the tunnel into the cavern carved to house the jump-gate, Helen was immediately, intimately, aware of the sheer size of it. Way too big.

"Hunh," was all the comment she made aloud. Within the mole's computer system, she brought up the original plans, checking the differences against the final result. Helen let out a long, low whistle.

"Got something?" Keller's voice again. He would be tracking her presumed location on Recovr's shiny new mission console, relying on James to predict her location based on the limited data coming back.

"I just hit the staging cavern about a hundred feet too early. According to the plans, it's supposed to be a heck of a lot smaller. Hold on a second and I'll send the information back." She interrupted the emergency line to transmit the updated maps.

Here in the airless void of the cavern, Helen adapted: flipper-like legs moving in sequence, using their own kinetic energy to help her steer. The asteroid was too small to have its own gravity. Instead, the air jets along her sides, normally used to clear mining debris, propelled her forward.

"Okay, Helen, we're back. That cavern is a whopper."

"According to the mole, the instructions were changed sometime after the original cavern was created."

"Do you have a record of who issued the change?"

"Not in the mole's database, but that should all be available once I hook us up." Helen put out a series of sensor pings in order to pinpoint the NAV computers. She found them huddled in a cluster against the far wall. Just a stone's throw away, the micro-jumpgate had been constructed and now stood dormant. Through the basketball-sized maw of the gate, the glitter of stars in empty space lay in wait.

"Helen, I've got something interesting for you." Ivester's voice now. Helen would have rolled her eyes if the waldo had any. The engineer's repeated interruptions were bad for the mission flow. *Really going to have to lay down some ground rules.*

"Can it wait? If I miss and hit the gate, I'm going right out into the black." Helen kept her focus on the box that housed the operations hub. If the cube-shaped structure had been any more plain, it would have been invisible and Helen had to hit it head-on. The mole didn't have any "hands" to grab on with, so if she missed, it meant she could go bouncing right out through the gate and into space. She lined up her nose with the cube and fired her air jets in sequence, splaying out the mole's paddle-like legs. The mole shot gracelessly across the cavern, the slow axial spin making absolutely no difference to its trajectory, but it made Helen feel like she had a little more control.

"Consider this your incentive," Ivester said. "The last Operator to ride that waldo was Catherine Beauchamp, back when she was working for BrightWinds."

Helen hit the smooth metal cube face-first and collapsed the mole's body in around it, scrabbling with all her legs until enough of them had locked on to bring her to a stop.

"We are way ahead of you on that one. Didn't Keller loop you in? I think this has gone way beyond coincidence." Cat's direct attack on Helen had come while she'd been out at the asteroid the first time. Finding out that there was a lot more to the operation than the reports had logged was barely a surprise.

Helen snuffled along the outer skin of the cube, looking for the access panel. The sensitive wires along the mole's snout found a hard edge, followed it along until it turned a corner, then worked their way across until they found a series of holes just big enough around for the feelers to fit into. A quick thrust and a turn of her head and Helen had access to the computers inside the cube. She felt the shudder as the access door came loose and banged along her side before spinning off into the void. *Hope I don't need to go get that back.*

"Helen." Dougal's voice now. *What, are they just passing the receiver back and forth between them?* "Remember, we are completely blind on this end. If you're not saying anything, we have no idea what's going on."

Having all the voices right in her ear made it easy to forget that she was all alone. On a proper trip with a fully functioning NAV, there was more than enough information to go around. The NAV controlled everything: Insight, the computers, and the passive data collection apparatus that could program the eenies to do just about anything needed. The only data going back and forth now was the quantum Feed that allowed Helen's body to run the mole.

"Roger that." She pushed herself back into the familiar patterns, into the routine of working with a NAV and a full control team, even though she had no such thing. "I've landed on the local y-positive axis of the hub and removed the cover to the access hatch."

The technical jargon was harder to reel off, but meant there'd be fewer "your right or my right" questions down the line. With cardinal directions being relative, any given object had to have each facing clearly labeled and named. If you didn't have that, then you used your local *xyz* axes to indicate where you were in relation to that specific object, rather than the space around you. She hoped Keller hadn't been out of the coffins too long to remember the rules.

"I'm attempting to link the waldo computer directly to the NAV computer. Give me a moment, it's like trying to push spaghetti through a keyhole . . ." Helen focused her attention on one of the mole's prehensile whiskers, worming it into the computer, searching for an access point by touch. She found the edge of the access slot, worked her way to the middle, and finally made the connection.

"Here we go." The computers came online instantly, recognizing the mole and accepting the salvage protocol. *Again, not a damn thing wrong with them. Something really weird is going on here.*

"Dougal, there's a lot of information here. I'm going to cut comms and send it all straight to you. We can leave the mole connected without me."

"Before you sign off, can you double-check the NAV computer? If it's still working, I'd be a hell of a lot more comfortable if we could get a second person out there with you." It was Ivester who answered; they'd passed the mic again. "Keller's got a friend over at Beyond Blue who might be able to get us access to their half of the set."

"One sec." Helen dug through the files, looking for the NAV communications logs. They were corrupted, un-openable on her end, but she packaged them up to send back down the line anyway. James could try to make heads or tails of them. From there it became a scavenger hunt, trying to find pieces of software that directly communicated with the NAV particles. Helen came up empty every time. She was working blind, on the outside of a box with only a single connection inside. Out of frustration, she "hit" it with her sensors, a wordless, angry pulse meant to release a little tension.

The image that came back stopped her cold. The entire inside of the cube was riddled with holes. Perfectly excised sections of the computer had been taken out while still leaving much of the function intact.

In case anyone came back to salvage the operation? The thought came unbidden, accompanied by a familiar chill. Helen snapped images and sent them down the line without hesitation, interrupting communications as she did so. *NAV particles are gone, a couple of the memory units are gone—some of the internal housing?* Everything was eenie-built, so everything could be broken up and repurposed.

So why just the NAV particles? Where the hell did they go?

A little more digging into NAV computer's memory gave her insight. *The gate. THIS is what had been sent out through the gate.* Not mined materials or the resources the moles were supposed to be harvesting from the asteroid. Whoever, or whatever, had sabotaged this BrightWinds mission had sent the NAV entanglement particles through the gate to a new destination.

"HELEN, WHAT THE HELL?" Keller's voice again. "Do not just cut out like that, warn us next time."

"Did you see those pics?" Helen spoke in a rush. She needed to explain, somehow impart everything she'd just realized to Keller as quickly as possible.

Deep breaths. How would Ted . . . Screw that. How do I handle this . . .

"Not yet, Ivester's getting them. . . ." There was a long pause. "Holy shit."

"Yeah. The NAV particles are gone." Helen interjected into the surprised silence, "They must have been sent out through the gate, that's why I can't get a connection through to them." Helen continued digging, sorting files and information into packets for transfer back. "I can't tell where. A bunch of these files are corrupted, probably starting when their connection to the NAV got cut off."

"So someone stole the NAV particles?" She couldn't tell if that tone in Keller's voice was shock or disbelief.

"Well, they're gone, or at least the portion of the NAV computer that dealt with those particles is gone. Which means that whoever has your end of those entangled particles might know something we don't."

Another long pause. Helen hated those long pauses. Each one meant conversations she wasn't a part of, decisions made without her input.

"Okay, we need to you to transfer everything, and I mean everything, back to us. Don't trigger the recycling sequence, just in case we need to get back out there again, and I want full mapping of every single inch of that NAV computer." Ivester's voice came down the line now.

Helen had to stay entangled as long as the data transfer was piggybacking on the emergency communications channel. Mapping the cube would give her something to focus on in the meantime so she wasn't just spinning her wheels.

"I'm going to do some digging into what Beauchamp was up to last time she was out here," she said. "The waldo's got have its own version of events and I want to understand just what that was."

"All right. Don't hesitate to break into the download if anything we need to know pops." Keller again, sounding worried.

"I'll disentangle as soon as we can close the connection. Operator out." Helen cut the connection before Keller's worry could infect her too. She started the download, making sure the NAV logs went first. It was eerily, blissfully silent, the only sounds the clicks and pings of her own Insight and the faintly singsong responses from the mole.

Okay, Cat. Let's see exactly what happened to you out here. Helen instructed the mole to start its mapping of the computer cube and turned her attention to the waldo's memory.

CHAPTER TWENTY-ONE

"You might be on to something here." Dougal was hanging out on the couch in the back of the Recovr space. The eenies had finished painting the walls and had seethed up into the naked framework of the ceiling. Helen could see them from the right angle, as if the beams and cross braces were dusted with silver glitter. Despite the new information they'd found, he was still doggedly pursuing the idea that the Scale were a form of industrial sabotage, rather than a new form of life. Dougal had filled the Insight space with panels upon panels of information detailing out just how the "corrupted eenies" had made the jump. What he couldn't come up with was: *Why?*

"These are two entirely different kinds of data. We can't be one hundred percent sure based on this. The mole out on Myrian23A5 is using a whole different set of sensors than the spider out on the Golfball," Dougal patiently explained. *Again.*

Helen let out her breath in an aggravated huff. "So the problem is we're comparing apples to oranges?"

She'd just closed out an hour in the coffin, holding open the connection to Myrian23A5. The logs from the mole and the remnants of the NAV computer gave them a clearer picture to work with, but nothing definitive. After BrightWinds abandoned the site, it was clear the jumpgate had been used to send the Scale to meet up with the Golfball. So the invasion or sabotage or whatever you wanted to call it had a helping hand. So the second question on the table was: *Whose?*

Keller had left to meet up with his contact over at Beyond Blue. Now that they knew for certain that the NAV particles had been stripped and sent through the jumpgate to the Golfball, Keller thought he could get them access to the matched pair here in Launch City. With that kind of access, they might be able to get a handle on how the Scale were operating and who was directing them.

"It's more like comparing one apple by touch to a second apple by sight. Both sets of data support each other, but without collecting the same kind of data in both locations, the results are always going to have room for questions," Dougal said, reasonably enough.

Helen held her tongue. They were in Dougal's wheelhouse now; this was the whole reason they'd brought him onto Recovr in the first place. Proving that the Scale were more than just badly programmed eenies was key. That meant collecting data, getting evidence, and doing all this the right way. Dougal's way. *No matter how frustrating it might be at times.*

"So we've got to get back out to the Golfball proper." Ivester joined them, taking up position at the other end of the couch.

"Only if you want your arguments to be bulletproof," Dougal pointed out. "I can make a sketchy case based on this, but I could make an unimpeachable case if we could compare like to like."

"Then like to like it has to be. If we're looking at a new life form, then we've got to make it as clean and clear as possible." Ivester fell into line.

Helen rolled a shoulder. The feedback sensors on the refurbished coffin were out of alignment. She'd returned to a case of minor muscle strain, like what you'd get from sleeping in an armchair. Time in the coffin was still shorter than she'd like—they needed Doc to finish approving the drug delivery system. Helen would be limited to runs of an hour or two, so a quick run to make sure the entanglement with the Golfball still worked should be simple enough.

"Can we get what we need within a five-minute timeframe?" Dougal asked the next reasonable question.

"That timeframe only matters if we try to work with an entangled NAV. An entangled NAV only matters if we need to interact with the eenies that are repairing the Golfball." Ivester ticked the logic off on his fingertips. "The waldo by itself is still completely safe. Helen can run the waldo, and Keller can talk her through anything that needs outside support through the emergency comm link."

"Hold that thought." Helen's personal tablet pinged for attention.

The message was a video Feed from Keller, his face oddly lit by streetlights and colored LED strings.

"Hey, Keller, downtown tonight?" Helen opened with the observation, spoken out loud for Dougal and Ivester's benefit. "I thought date night was on Tuesdays."

"Not quite." Keller's tone was uncharacteristically clipped, tight. Something had him really pissed off. It took a lot to piss Keller off.

"What kind of problem?" Helen switched to her inside voice, ignoring Ivester's curious stare.

"Beyond Blue is about to announce they're sending a salvage team out after the Golfball."

"Bullshit."

"Oh, it gets better."

"You mean the bad kind of better, don't you?" Helen opened up the conversation, holding the tablet so everyone could listen in.

"Beauchamp is leading that mission."

"So?" Helen wasn't following. Beauchamp jumping ship was annoying, but not out of line. As far as Helen was concerned, having Ted's angry ex out of the mix was the best thing to happen for weeks. Undoubtedly Beyond Blue had offered her a better position—lead on something like a salvage run to steal the Golfball certainly qualified.

"There's a good chance she took a bunch of the Line Drive data with her when she left."

Helen shot a look at Ivester, who nodded and replied quietly, "There's a bit more to her departure than we looped you in on."

"How the hell did she manage that?" Helen demanded of Ivester, but Keller interjected.

"You have a hell of a lot more privacy when you live off the Far Reaches campus." Keller shrugged, the gesture making the handheld camera jiggle. "She must have been working on this in her off-hours, bringing them up to speed before she left us."

"So you think she was actively working against us?"

"We have to treat it as such. I'm headed back in, already called for damage control. We're going to have to speed up our timetable."

"Need anything from us?" Ivester asked.

"We have to presume she's giving them whatever she knows, both about Line Drive itself and our whole Recovr side-project."

"Beyond Blue can't get there for at least a year, even if they dump all their resources into a new wormhole," Dougal chimed in.

Keller scowled and whipped his head around as if listening for something, the lights throwing multicolored streaks in his hair. All Helen could pick up were the hums of electric cars and ambient chatter. He turned his attention back to them. "I've checked the records. Beyond Blue launched several deep space missions around the same time as the Line Drive went off. Most of those have already been resolved, but there's a few that look suspicious." The handheld camera joggled, showing bits of the background as he increased his pace. Helen got the impression he was troubled, keeping an eye out for something.

"A few?"

"One of those projects was launched from Myrian23A5, and it looks an awful lot like it was aimed to intercept our Golfball. I have to cross-check the numbers before I'm sure, but I think that's our little mystery launch with the NAV particles. I'll bring you up to speed once I get back to the building."

Helen caught a glimpse of cloudy sky and brightly lit signage before the connection closed. *Downtown indeed.* The light pollution restrictions meant he was on one of maybe a half-dozen streets in the City between the Far Reaches campus and Wade's, each with varying degrees of safety, none of which Helen was comfortable being on after dark. *No wonder he's jumpy.*

Helen dropped into one of the plastic office chairs and set the tablet on the closest flat surface. "Ivester, Beauchamp is an excellent OP. I might even buy her being a saboteur because she had it in for Ted. But this is way too big and way too hands-on for her. She's not an actor, she's an instigator. She never takes direct action."

"You only know the half of it," Ivester returned. He scrubbed his fingers through hair that had gotten longer and wilder while they brought Recovr up to speed. Helen caught the whispers in the air as he shut down all the cameras in the room and asked James to engage the privacy settings. "I went back and reviewed my notes. We had a bidder working against us when we were trying to acquire the BrightWinds assets. I mean, there's always people looking to pick up discount salvage rights, but this time we had an actual fight on our hands."

"Let me guess," Dougal interjected. "Beyond Blue wasn't *just* after the computer assets?"

"Exactly, but the lawyers had packaged everything up separately to get the most cash possible. So the timeline, as I see it right now, is as follows." His glasses flickered as Ivester began to sketch out the order of events with his hands. Helen quickly slipped on her own lenses so she could follow along. A white starting point appeared in the air. "BrightWinds' mining operations were supposed to be entirely AI-driven, with as few humans as could possibly be involved. They anticipated it could cut costs by billions and allow them to operate literally around the clock. No breaks, no downtime, no medical issues. Their pitch was that an AI-driven system would slash operating costs, allow for greater risk-taking, and, of course, bigger profits."

"Which didn't work out as planned," Helen responded.

Ivester began to pace, drawing lines in the air with broad, sweeping gestures. "The idea wasn't a new one, but the problem with true human-form AIs is that they don't like getting hurt any more than humans do. We don't bother to fix them, we just junk them and compile a replacement." He wagged his fingers in frustration. "At the end of the day it got too expensive, so they started bringing in human OPs again on the sly while they tried to get their computers back on track."

"Enter Catherine Beauchamp." Helen regarded the engineer from her chair.

"Exactly. There were four human OPs that BrightWinds brought in quietly. When we acquired their assets, all four of them came to us, including Beauchamp. Beyond Blue got some of BrightWinds' smaller operations, took over all the AI assets and computers, but Far Reaches wanted the people as much as the salvage." He eyeballed Helen. "I'm sure I don't have to tell you how hard it is to hire experienced OPs." A gesture of his fingertips and a node labeled Beyond Blue appeared along one of the two lines he'd drawn, Beauchamp along the other.

"So you're thinking that Beyond Blue used their NAV particle to sneak in to Myrian23A5 and encountered these . . . Scale there before we did?" Dougal interjected.

"But Cat was out at Myrian while she was working for Bright-Winds, and the logs don't show anyone else accessing the mole after shutdown," Helen put in.

"That line's a little less certain. We opened the micro-wormhole to send the Golfball to Otlyan23 right about the same time Beauchamp came on board." Ivester gestured at his timeline and another node appeared on the line. "It's possible, just barely, that Beauchamp could have introduced some of these Scale into the delivery."

"That's . . . that's really tight. Onboarding a new OP takes weeks, so she'd have to have foreknowledge of all our procedures, get access to the R&D floors. She'd have to be some kind of super-spy to pull all that off." Helen found herself defending her fellow OP without really intending to.

"Or someone else planned this out and Beauchamp was just the hands. But espionage is still more likely than our alien theory,"

Dougal hastened to add. "If we're going to posit any of this seriously, we can't handwave those details. It's possible Beauchamp had help, that there are other people at Far Reaches involved. We can't afford to ignore that."

Ivester nodded. "True enough, there's always a small percentage that could be compromised, or who hate their jobs or teammates, or who are in some kind of financial straits that makes a little industrial espionage seem harmless. We try to keep a lid on it as much as possible, but no system is perfectly airtight." Beauchamp's node turned into a little cloud of yellow speckles. "So the information here is a little fuzzy."

The next node to pop up was an angry red. Helen appreciated the sentiment.

"When we connected to the Golfball we discovered a fatal interference in the NAV Feed. We also discovered the presence of Scale, active Scale, unlike the dust you found out at Myrian23A5."

Helen stared at the pulsing red node that represented Ted's death. The Ted-shaped hole in her life was still there. She figured it would always be there, but for every piece of the puzzle she slotted into place, the edges grew a little less raw, a little less angry.

"There's too much coincidence here." Dougal broke in to Helen's introspective moment. "Every time the Scale pops up, Beauchamp is involved."

"Yeah, but Beauchamp isn't an engineer, she's not building these things. She's not a hands-on person. I mean, even when she's being bitchy in the commissary, she's got other people doing the real work, she's just winding them up and pointing them at a target." Helen got to her feet and stepped closer to the timeline. "Maybe she's a middleman of some kind."

"Then we come to our own discovery of the Scale at Myrian23A5." Ivester pulled the conversation back on track and drew a new node on the timeline. "Helen, as soon as you passed this information through to our system, everything started to escalate."

"How so?"

"Well, for starters, someone tried to kill you."

"Which makes no sense either. I drive a waldo. I'm not an engineer, I'm not one of the brains driving this boat."

"You're the one insisting we take a closer look. You were the one who brought the Scale to our attention. Not just in the case of the Golfball, but also Myrian23A5. As an operator, you're the only one out there who can take action. We can talk, theorize, and compare the data, but you're the person on the ground, therefore you're the biggest threat."

"A threat to what? It's not like a waldo has rocket launchers and ray guns strapped to it."

"After we moved you to Analysis, the work you and Dougal did was a key step towards preserving the entire Line Drive project. Your insistence that there was some kind of interference in the Feed, the initial observations on the Scale, your constant pushing to go to get another look when it would have been simpler to transfer out, all of those elements have been a driving force behind keeping this project moving forward."

A series of windows opened in the air as Ivester paced back and forth, comparing lists of information, deleted files showing in alarming red. "In the chaos that followed, all the Myrian23A5 information got scrubbed from our computers. Lucky for us, James is obsessive about redundant backups. In that case, we know Beauchamp handled the deletions. It's very possible, in fact, that she's the one who poisoned the nutrient mix in your coffin, but we don't have proof of that yet."

"She . . . what?" That idea rocked Helen back a little. Rivalry was one thing. Constant sniping and undercutting were par for the course, especially given Cat's status as the angry ex, but out-and-out murder was a step too far. Helen wasn't sure she could get her head around Beauchamp as a killer.

"The log records don't show her in the Mortuary while you were out at Myrian23A5, but one of the coffin techs made a note in his daily report that someone was there—they heard them but didn't see who it was. James notes the changes to the mix were entered manually, but the cameras can't see anything other than a couple hardware racks out of place."

"What about Ravi, the NAV on the first Myrian mission? Is he okay?" Helen realized that, one by one, almost everyone who had been involved with the Golfball was now gone from Far Reaches. Mira and Bright had transferred to the Helsinki operation; Elliot and Zai had been let go, snapped up by Lightflyer. Analysts and support staff had been let go or transferred off-site. If someone made a move on her because of what she'd discovered about the Scale and BrightWinds so far, did that mean everyone else was a target too?

"He moved to Animus when we started shutting down the Golfball portion of Line Drive."

"You don't think he's at risk?"

"Maybe, but he's out of our circle of influence for now. I've given Animus the heads up. They think I'm trying to poach him back."

"And you guys? And Keller?"

Ivester and Dougal exchanged a glance. Helen got the sense this had already been discussed behind her back.

"Now that Beauchamp is gone, any real risk is likely gone with her. They've done a fair job making us all look a little dirty on the outside."

"Likely gone?"

"When Metro completes their investigation, Beauchamp's going to be arrested and charged. In fact, the PR hit to Beyond Blue might be enough to put us back ahead of the game."

Ivester's constellation of events coalesced at the last mention of Beauchamp and moved from a solid beam of light to a series of dots.

The future, the image said clearly, was not yet certain. Helen stared at the lights, following the train of logic in her own mind.

"So what's our next step?" she asked.

"Simple. We take another run at the Golfball," Ivester replied.

CHAPTER TWENTY-TWO

HELEN DIDN'T REALIZE she had been holding her breath until she exhaled with a long, low, "Whoa . . ."

She'd known the spider waldo was slowly being consumed by the Scale. What she hadn't expected was how far along the process had gotten.

"Operator Vectorovich, please confirm you're connected." Ivester's voice was the only one on the line. He was sticking to the stricter protocols that Helen had laid down for NAV conduct. She didn't expect him to stick to them for long, but with Keller running late, Ivester would have to fill in.

"You're not going to be-fucking-lieve this." Helen reached and stretched, settling into not the spider waldo's body, but a new configuration. Something not in the design specs. *Too many legs, not enough eyeballs.* Much like driving the mole, she couldn't "see" things quite the same way. It was like keeping your eyes closed and having everyone in the room whisper the details to you. Whatever she had entangled with, it wasn't the waldo, it didn't feel like anything Far Reaches-related at all.

This is going to take a little getting used to.

"Operator Vectorovich, are we live?" Ivester asked over the emergency link, clear as a bell, even with the rest of the "noise" that had begun to creep in. It was the sound in the NAV Feed, the sound that had she'd been trying to avoid. Here, in this body, it was different, soothing. It fell across her senses like a veil. Even Ivester's voice was different, as if it registered on a different level somehow, more feel and color than sound.

Helen didn't respond immediately. There was a lot to take in: the change in perceptions, the absolute delicacy of the waldo's motion, and . . . that noise. She wasn't getting it directly. The signal was being transmitted through her sibs. This waldo, whatever it was, was only one part of a larger network. Millions of Scale were connected and communicating. Somewhere, out of the edges of that vast impression, something was going wrong. Horribly, horribly wrong.

Holy shit. This isn't the spider. It's a Scale. . . .

"Operator Vectorovich, are we live?" Ivester's voice, more urgently this time, impinged on her wandering attention. She had to pull herself back and re-center, keep her attention on this one problem. Something must have consumed the entanglement particle from the spider waldo and recycled it to build a Scale. Helen had to work to maintain focus, but the noise of a million voices was alluring, distracting. Helen wanted to stop and listen, really listen, but she kept herself on task.

"Control, this is Operator Vectorovich. We are live, we are live, we are live."

With that utterance, Helen found it easier to settle back into old patterns. The screens in her line of sight came to life, interposing like a barrier against the whispering minds of the Scale. The lists and protocols she and Dougal and Keller had been agonizing over started to emerge.

"Helen, just what the hell happened to my waldo? The coffin is showing anomalous readings all across the board."

"I think it's fair to say that this is not your waldo I'm riding," Helen responded. *Let's see what we have to work with here.* The feeling was invigorating. She'd stepped into a wholly new, wholly different kind of waldo configuration.

It made some kind of sense that a Scale, if they truly were tiny robots like the Far Reaches' eenies, could be ridden like any other waldo. Waldos in general were empty husks, waiting for an OP to act as their mind and will. This Scale was different. This Scale knew what it needed to do with absolute certainty. It acted according to instructions passed to it from its sibs. At the moment, Helen was just along for the ride.

Helen leaned back, trying to assume control. She had to fight it, to keep pulling as it attempted to return to its programmed series of actions. It wasn't so much that it could think, or want, but it had a very, very specific set of calls and responses. Getting it to do anything outside of those for more than an instant required Helen's total focus, like trying to keep a dog from chasing a car.

She could feel the shift in attention as the Scale's sibs around her imposed their will. They chattered at her, delivering new instructions, telling her to get her back in line. It was a powerful pressure, like the disapproval of a parent or a lover. She had to fight her Scale to keep it from relenting and she was losing.

"Wait, you need to stop that. Right now." Ivester's voice broke in sharply.

"Hang on, I've almost got it."

"No. NOW." Sharper tone this time, maybe a touch of panic?

Helen relented, relaxing and allowing the Scale to return to its position, to fit back in where it belonged.

It was too late.

An instruction came down the line, echoed through the thousands of sibs close by. It was paralyzing. Her Scale's limbs locked up and Helen found herself unable to control anything at all.

"We have a problem." Helen tried again, but the microscopic robot was unresponsive. She could feel herself coming undone as her sibs approached and started nibbling, picking apart her body for re-use. The panic started to rise . . .

"Pulling you out now."

"Wait, don't." Helen's protest was cut short as she was unceremoniously dumped back into her own body. She opened her eyes to the soft blue interior of the coffin, felt the backlash of too quick a transfer burn on the inside of her skull, behind her eyes.

"WHAT THE HELL, GUYS!" she roared at the screens on the inside lid of the coffin. They couldn't hear her through the soundproofing, so Helen burned her frustration off before she popped the latches and said something she'd regret. She thrashed a bit for good measure, throwing elbows and knees at the padded walls to no real effect.

In Ivester's inexperience, he'd dumped her straight back to her own body without any of the precautions dialed up. Once the initial adrenaline rush wore off, Helen still had shooting pains running down her spine, through her arms to her fingertips. Her mind tried to adjust but the supersuit kept firing random signals, making her fingers slip as she fumbled to pop the emergency catches. Helen retreated into the black inside her own head, trying to separate herself from her own body long enough to get a handle on the disjointed sensory input and confusion.

This fucking ROOKIE team, she thought unkindly.

Deep breaths made the pain worse. She tried not breathing at all. Even the soft lights inside the coffin were too much, and once the lid slid open, the lights from the lab were even worse.

"Here, I've got it." Hofstaeder's voice was way too loud, and the injection that followed burned like a brand on contact, then cooled down and moved through Helen's skull like a wave. The pain and disorientation weren't washed away entirely, just dimmed enough to allow Helen to open her eyes, catch a glimpse of silver hair.

"Thanks, Doc." The light and noise were tolerable now. Her head was still filled with the chatter from the Scale, making it even harder for her to sort out her own limbs.

"Good thing I was here this time," Hofstaeder admonished. "You do not have the full nutrient setup in this 'pod yet, which also means no drugs on demand."

"This is what I get for leaving Keller behind," Helen groused. The last of the umbilicals wormed its way out of her supersuit, freeing her to climb out. She managed to get a hand on of one of the brackets to pull herself up, then a second.

"Sorry about that, but we were getting shutdown readings across the board. Whatever it was you entangled with was going to be dead and gone in less than a second." Ivester and Dougal clustered at the control panels, comparing data points and information. Helen sat up in the coffin, elbows hanging over the edges.

"Ivester." Helen tried to get the engineer's attention. He and Dougal were still discussing the information sheeting across the touchscreens. "IVESTER!" Helen raised her voice, ignoring the stab of pain in her head. He whipped around, surprise evident on his face. Dougal looked alarmed, darting looks from the furious Helen, to Ivester, then back again.

"You. Do. Not. EVER. Dump an OP without a BUFFER." She ground out each word against the pain in her head. It was just bad backlash, she could work through it, but the need to emphasize following the proper steps was paramount. If she couldn't trust Ivester and Dougal to follow the rules, she was going to be running a risk whenever they swapped in for Keller.

Hofstaeder stayed back a step, keeping clear of the reprimand being delivered.

"You designed this fucking system, Ivester. Why the hell is it so hard for you to stick to your own goddamn rules?"

"I'm sorry. . . . I was just trying to get you out before whatever that was shut down." Ivester's stunned expression shifted to contrite. Helen's anger abruptly found itself without purchase and started to evaporate, leaving her feeling wrung-out and foolish. It would have been easier if he'd been an asshole about it.

"Right impulse. Wrong action. Next time we do this with Keller at the helm. You two . . ." Helen stabbed her finger first at Ivester, next at Dougal, "need a crash course in flight ops. Set it up before we go back out there."

"I just told you, whatever you were riding has shut down. There's nowhere to go back to," Ivester responded.

"There will be. The Scale have incorporated the spider waldo's entanglement particles. Whatever I was riding was one of a billion just like it. I think we've got some very interesting work ahead of us." Helen managed to get both arms together over one side of the coffin and rested her forehead on them where they met. "Doc, can you please give me a hand out. I've got half as many legs as I think I do."

"Of course."

"What do you mean, incorporated the particles?" As contrite as he might have been about screwing up Helen's return to the coffin, Ivester's natural impulsiveness got the better of him again. "Are you telling me you linked up to a Scale? You waldoed a SCALE?"

Helen winced as his excitement drove his voice louder, and swung her legs out, reaching for the floor with all five sets of feet. *Wait. Ten toes, two feet.* Getting up and walking around was the quickest way to get settled back into her own body, but every motion resulted in tingling pain.

"That is what I'm telling you right now. I may change my mind after I've recovered a bit. Call it first impressions."

"Dougal, we need . . ." Ivester turned, paused. Helen caught the whisper in the air as Far Reaches communications tried to get his attention. He held up a finger. "Hold that thought."

Helen managed to keep her feet under her long enough to get to the couch at the back of the room. *It will have to do.*

Ivester's expression grew grim at whatever he was hearing. "When did this happen?" He headed briskly to his office, one of the small cubicles along the far wall of Recovr's space. It was an angry motion, the door closing behind him with a sharp snap.

"What's that about?" Dougal came over to join Helen on the couch. "He sounds pissed."

"It's bad news, whatever it is," Doc said sourly. "Almighty Ivester doesn't handle bad news well."

They could see Ivester's outline where he paced back and forth behind the frosted panels that separated the office from the rest of the lab. They could hear his agitation, muffled beats of sound without enough definition to become words.

"He'll tell us when he's done. Or he won't." Hofstaeder fished a hand-scanner out of her pocket. "Now, since we don't have access to a full medical unit down here in this dungeon, I'm going to have to ask you to sit still for a minute."

"Yes, please." Helen leaned back on the couch while Doc held the scanner up against the side of her head.

"So explain to me what happened out there." Dougal reached out and pulled the constellation of screens floating in the air a little closer. Helen couldn't see them without her glasses, but she recognized the gesture. "I thought we were just reconnecting to see if we could still get to the Golfball."

"We were. That's why we didn't wait on Keller, right? This was supposed to be a quick drop in and drop out. A connection check. But whatever is going on out there is escalating. The whole waldo seems to be gone, maybe the whole Golfball too. It was hard to tell."

"If there's no waldo, what did you entangle with?" Dougal asked the most reasonable question.

"My best guess right now is one of the Scale. I couldn't tell for sure but it didn't feel like something programmed by Far Reaches. I was not prepared for this."

"This entire project gets weirder all the time," Dougal remarked.

"Can we even identify a Scale from the inside?" Helen responded.

"It looks like we will need to find out. But if you were, in fact, riding an eenie of some kind, my bet is that it's one of our Far Reaches models. My gut reaction is that your coffin tech would have an easier time talking to a Far Reaches eenie then it would talking to someone else's."

The quiet conversation was interrupted by the vibration of something hitting the wall of Ivester's office. Helen and Hofstaeder exchanged an alarmed glance.

"What the hell?" Helen headed for the door, Hofstaeder right behind. Ivester's outline had disappeared.

"Nate? Are you all right in there?" Hofstaeder raised her voice, reached for the door handle. Just inside the empty cubicle, Ivester was seated akimbo on the floor, staring through his personal Insight in front of him. The light in his glasses was guttering, like it was passing commands faster than he could think.

"Ivester?" Helen asked. "What was that?"

"Fine." He answered a question Helen hadn't asked. His tone was flat, uncharacteristically so. The expression in the cold grey eyes was utterly devastated. In the sudden quiet Helen could hear the whispers in the ether as he communicated, until suddenly the lights in his glasses winked out, like he'd thrown a switch, cut himself off abruptly. He refocused on the three Recovr team members standing in the doorway, settling on making eye contact with Helen. He took a deep breath, let it out.

"Keller is dead."

Dougal made a high-pitched sound. When Helen turned to look, he had covered his mouth with his hands in shock. His skin had paled, throwing the linework of his tattoos into sharp relief. Helen hadn't arrived at shock just yet, all of the plans in her head, every thought she'd been forming about next steps to get back out to the Golfball simply imploding, leaving a Keller-sized hole right about where the Ted-sized hole had been healing over. She leaned heavily on the doorframe, waiting for the now-familiar moment to pass.

She exchanged a glance with Hofstaeder, who looked as stunned as she felt. Ivester got to his feet and shook his head.

"Keller never made it back from his meeting. They found him in the lake about two hours ago."

Helen hunted for a question to ask, already doing damage control inside her own head, trying to stay in denial long enough to act. "Has anyone told Ethan?"

"Next of kin gets notified first. Ethan's already talking to Metro." Ivester straightened up, reassembled his composure. "Doc, Keller's family is going to need some support. It's probably a little outside Far Reaches' purview, but we should do as much as we can."

"Of course, I'll take care of it."

"What happened?" Helen asked the next question that came to mind. The timing was too convenient to be coincidence. *First someone made an attempt while I was helpless in the coffin, then the news about Beyond Blue making a run on Line Drive broke, now Keller winds up . . .*

She couldn't bring herself to finish that sentence.

"We don't know anything yet. Just that they found him when someone's dog got loose by the lake and went in after a body. They should know more in a few hours."

"You know this is whoever Beauchamp's working with." Helen said the words quietly, soft enough to keep them from Dougal.

Hofsteader heard, pressed her lips into a thin russet line at the idea.

"There's no proof of that yet, but I don't think we can ignore the possibility," Ivester responded.

"Nate, this is going to need both of us," Hofstaeder interjected. "Are you okay for the moment?"

Ivester nodded. "Helen, I need you and Dougal to figure out what the next steps are going to be for Recovr. This is going to take all my attention for a while."

Hofstaeder held up a hand to stop him. "Nate, this project needs to be canceled. Now. You've already lost two people to it. Whoever is trying to take it from you has crossed a line. Let them have the whole damn thing before anyone else gets hurt."

"I'll take it under advisement." Ivester pushed past them and headed for the lab exit.

Helen watched him go, a concerned Hofstaeder trailing in his wake.

"So what now?" Dougal had recovered from the shock.

Helen cast about for something to hold on to. Something that meant she wouldn't have to think about Keller and yet another gaping hole in her soul.

"You heard the man." She turned back to her work for a place to hide, as she always did. "Let's figure out how to tell these eenies apart from the inside."

CHAPTER TWENTY-THREE

WHEN HELEN HAD FIRST MOVED IN from the commuter-burbs of Launch City to the Far Reaches campus, she'd found that if she entered a room quick enough, she could catch everything still in low-power mode. It was like poking a friend who had fallen asleep during a movie. The lights came up, but it still took a second to restore consciousness. Tonight she waited after turning the door handle so it would feel less like she was walking into a tragically empty space.

Helen let gravity carry her aching frame across the room onto the lab's only couch, burying her face in the throw pillows. She had spent the past few hours in the commissary with the rest of Flight Ops, watching the shock of Keller's death move from OP to OP and NAV to NAV. The room full of pathos was too much to bear and she'd finally retreated to the lab to escape.

The couch smelled vaguely of plastic and dust.

Dust, dust, something about the dust. The thought came unbidden. *That part of the mystery's over,* she reminded herself. *You solved that bit.*

WE solved that bit. She rolled over and stuck her feet in the air, staring pensively at the gaping black void of the ceiling above. *But there's something still not quite right about it.* It was exactly the line of questioning she needed, something she could dig in to. The lights in the room shifted from their warm, welcoming glow to a cooler, more businesslike tone as Helen fished her tablet out of her pocket and started to call up the mission files.

Something about the dust.

The dust was comprised of the shells of dead Far Reaches eenies, that much had been clear. But eenies were rapacious; each generation was supposed to consume the one before, making use of every scrap of material they could get a hold of, from silicon to stardust. Inert material like the dust should have all been consumed long before moving on to something active like the waldo.

So what if the Scale were programmed differently? If they were supposed to attack the active elements, it might explain why the Far Reaches eenies had been stuck in rebuilding mode. *They were trying to undo the damage.* This wasn't a glitch or an eenie overrun, it was a fight on the smallest possible level.

She rubbed her face with her hands and retrieved her Insight glasses from her pocket. The room lit up with the windows and strings of code that Dougal and Ivester had abandoned earlier in the day. Following her line of thought, James began opening up all her Golfball mission files, from that first catastrophic contact on forward to Myrian. She thumbed through them, separating out the observations from the team in the Fishbowl from notes made by Keller on the fly.

Oh, Keller.

There had been no new information. Ivester had broken the news of Keller's death company-wide, stopping just short of calling it murder. Hofstaeder had made sure psych services were available to anyone who needed them, but especially Flight Ops. Helen sat quietly for a moment and reflected on the empty space in her soul that had been filled by her mentor. Losing Ted had been a huge blow. Losing Keller was going to be even worse, but for now, while she remained suspended in denial, she could act. Helen could bury herself in the problem and figure out just what the hell her friends had died for and who was going to pay for that.

Beauchamp might just be the hands, but in Helen's mind she co-alesced into the stand-in for whatever person, corporation, or alien was behind the Scale.

High-resolution images played out across the ceiling above her, the mix of hard and soft edges of the eenie shells painting an uncanny landscape in monochrome.

The pounding on the door interrupted her thought process and kicked her heart rate up a few notches. She disengaged the privacy locks before rolling off the couch. There were no weapons in the lab. There shouldn't *need* to be any weapons in the lab. She cast about for something to throw and asked James to be on alert, just in case.

The pounding came again, which was puzzling. Anyone who belonged in the lab should have access through the locks. She checked with James, but it returned no data.

What the hell?

The door bounced inward, narrowly missing Helen and depositing a tangle of limbs and suit into the foyer. The door bounced closed equally quickly and Helen found herself standing over a very under-the-influence Ivester.

"What the hell?" She said the words out loud this time.

The engineer accepted her help to get to his feet, and straightened his jacket. "I have a question."

"That's nice. Are you even sober enough for answers right now?" A quick glance told her no, but whatever dragon he was chasing, it was occupying his full attention.

"No. Not one bit. It has been . . . a very poor evening and I am looking for someplace to hide until I sober up. Do you mind?"

"Don't you have an apartment?"

"I started by meeting with Keller's family. Then I went to the apartment, now I am here." He held his hands out in front of him and stared at them bemusedly, like they belonged to someone else. "It wasn't helping. I have questions, and this is where I should be to get answers."

Helen stepped aside. Ivester headed for his office and left the door hanging open behind him. There was a clattering that sounded like he'd swept everything off his desk and onto the floor. Helen stared after him for a few moments before reapplying herself to the couch. She couldn't blame him. She was here in the lab looking for the same thing. She perched her Insight glasses back on the bridge of her nose and pushed more photos from her tablet out into the room, working her way back into the eenie problem.

"Why are you here?" Ivester asked, like the thought she might have somewhere else to hang out had only just occurred to him.

"Same reasons, fewer drugs," Helen responded.

"In my defense, Doctor Hofstaeder failed to warn me of the side effects."

"Yeah, that's not fooling anybody." Helen stretched out to occupy the full length of the couch and started calling up information on Far Reaches eenie designs. *The answer to identifying an eenie from the inside*, she reflected, *might be as simple as counting legs.* She closed her eyes and tried to recall the sensations of her most recent entanglement with no real luck. She tried, as a test, to count her own limbs with just her mind, no motions, no actions. It was harder than it seemed.

"Fair enough," Ivester said.

Helen sighed, train of thought broken again. "If you're going to be chatty, why don't you come out here and help me brainstorm on this."

"On what?"

"How to identify an eenie from the inside. Dougal and I think we need to start by figuring out if I'm Entangling with a Far Reaches model, or one of the Scale."

"Wait, you couldn't tell?" There was a thump from inside the office that sounded like feet hitting the ground. *Was he lying on the desk?*

"You try counting how many legs you have with your eyes closed and let me know how that goes," Helen groused.

Ivester got hung up on the office doorway, trying to look down at his own legs. He corrected his path, wandered a few extra steps into the room and came to a halt, distracted by the images Helen had been hanging up in the virtual space.

"It never occurred to me to pull that kind of information from a waldo. We always know what the waldo looks like from our end and we apply the feedback to our local simulation."

"Really?" *Makes sense, otherwise entanglement keys wouldn't be so hard to lay hands on.* "That's one checkmark in the 'Scale' column, I think."

Ivester pursed his lips and waved his arms like he was conducting an aria. A tidy set of columns appeared in the Insight space, one labeled "Scale," the other labeled "Fucking Boring."

"I see we're not screwing around," Helen quipped and added "entanglement particles" under the arguments for the Scale column. "As far as I know, nobody has ever operated an eenie like a waldo before. I feel like a total badass. That's boring to you?"

"It's marginally less exciting than a first contact scenario, but it is pretty cool." Ivester gave up standing and dropped into a seated, cross-legged position. He managed to maintain it for about six seconds before giving up and stretching out full length on the rubberized floor mats. Helen threw a couch pillow at him.

"Thanks." He stuffed the pillow behind his head. "I mean, can you imagine it? We might have just run into the explorers of an entirely new life form."

"They could just be the new life form. Some kind of space ant or space termite," Helen theorized.

"I will be sorely disappointed if they are space termites." Ivester held up an admonishing finger. "And since I am under the influence, I reserve the right to dream big. At least until the next in-house investors meeting. Then it's back to profit margins and five-year plans."

"Can we get that kind of feedback? I mean, something is coming back to the coffin software, otherwise I wouldn't be able to operate anything. Is there a way to read it to tell us the layout of whatever we connected with?"

"Yes, I think I can adapt the coffin software. So what else do we have to work with? What do you remember about the entanglement experience?"

"Well, the eenie or Scale was still running under its own software, so it was hard to get it to respond at all. It wasn't like running a waldo, which just waits for my input."

"Internal software? Did you get the sense it was intelligent, like an AI?" Ivester sat bolt upright.

"It had a purpose, and it had instructions. I don't know if you could call it intelligent."

"Was it receiving instructions from outside? The eenies we build hold everything in a cache until it gets cleared, then a new protocol gets loaded from the outside by a NAV. So if whatever you waldoed was more like part of a hive mind, that's going to suggest it was a Scale." The idea had lit a fire under the engineer. "But if you're getting external commands, we should be able to listen in, capture those, and cross-check it against our own programming." He got to his feet and pulled open a larger window in the Insight, opening up the coffin's programming.

"Can you please wait until you're sober before you start reprogramming my life-support?" Helen griped.

"I'll comment all the changes, don't worry about it."

"Ivester, I am worried about it." Helen sat up and leaned forward on the couch, elbows on knees. "OPs and NAVs aren't machines. We're already dealing with entanglement problems that are beyond the pale. Let's not get clever with the software at the last minute."

She'd touched a nerve she hadn't known was there. Ivester looked pained. "It's not the first time I've been lectured on that." He was quiet for a few moments. "I'm trying to find the perfect ideal, a way to entangle with the remote systems with zero risk at all. Far Reaches' entire entanglement system was designed to minimize the risk. And then . . ." He sighed and scrubbed his hands through his hair. "Today I was reminded that no matter how careful my engineering is, there is still no way to keep everybody safe."

"Safe is relative." Helen got off the couch and approached the engineer where he sat on the floor. "Safe is not what I need out there. Stable is what I need. Consistent is what I need. I have to be able to rely on what this coffin and software is going to do. I can work around limitations. I can get clever. I can push the boundaries. But if I can't rely on where those boundaries lie . . ." Helen reached up and closed the programming window. "Then the ground's going to collapse under my feet."

Ivester was silent, considering what she'd said.

He failed to meet her eyes when he asked his next question.

"So you think we should keep going?"

"Aren't you the one who showed up in my hospital room arguing that all this would be worth it?" Helen headed back to the couch, angrily scattering windows and numbers about the Insight as she went.

"People keep dying."

Helen recognized the tone in his voice, the darker notes of depression creeping in. *Shit, how do I fix this?* Whatever Ivester had been on must be wearing off and taking his emotional state down with it. *Get him thinking about something actionable.*

"Well, look, if someone murders you, I promise we'll stop. Until that point . . ." Helen turned and frowned at the engineer. "Until that point, I am getting my ass back in that coffin and figuring out just what we ran into out there. They took Ted, they took Keller, and they very nearly took me. As far as I'm concerned, I'm already all-in on this one."

"There are only three of us," Ivester mused.

"Four if you count Doc, but she's bitey. I don't think anyone will bother her." Helen kept a careful eye on her temporary companion. Glib dismissals weren't going to keep him from heading into a funk; probably only some actual sleep could help there. She changed gears, trying to draw him back into the discussion.

"While I was looking through the files we have from Elliot and Zai's Golfball mission, I had an unpleasant thought." Helen opened up a window on her tablet with the Golfball specifications and tossed it out into the space between them. "The Far Reaches eenies are designed to break down the inactive elements of the Golfball first."

Ivester stared muzzily at the information she'd floated. "Correct. We leave the active components alone until the last possible second. Once those get broken down, we're in the dark until the eenies finish building the new hardware."

"If that's the case," Helen said, "then we have another item on the 'Scale' side of your list. Whatever is out there began attacking the waldo way back during my first mission, while it was an active component. Our eenies shouldn't have touched it. Mira and Bright, then Elliot and Zai, both confirmed that was an ongoing problem. So whatever that is, I think it's safe to say it's hostile. Maybe not 'take me to your leader' hostile, but it's actively moving against our tech. Why else go after the only piece of hardware that can act?"

"That's why we're evaluating, to see if the Scale is hostile. If we can allow that gate back home to be opened at all."

"It may be worse than that." Helen wasn't finished with the bad ideas. "We control the opening and closing of the gate from this side through a redundant set of entangled particles. We own the only key on this side, and we own the only key on that side. But if these Scale have the key . . ."

Ivester's already pale face went ashen. "Then we may not only have built a door back home, we may have left the key under the mat." He stared at the mission specs for a long moment.

"We need to get back out there to see what information we can get from the Scale," Helen said.

CHAPTER TWENTY-FOUR

"Holy shit, it worked!"

Despite herself, Helen grinned at the surprise in Dougal's voice. Ivester's *sober* adjustments to the software meant the information coming back from the Golfball made more sense this time.

She rolled her shoulders and wiggled her fingers and toes, trying to get a sense of what she was driving this time. That was the tricky part. With a little help from James, she needed to figure out what she'd connected to and how to control it. Her clumsy attempts last time had resulted in the Scale getting torn apart and recycled.

One more checkmark in the "Fucking Boring" column, I suppose, she reasoned. The Far Reaches eenies were programmed in swaths, all keeping an eye on one another. If one tiny robot started to get out of line, the rest of the tiny robots in its swath would tear it down to its component particles and recycle it. It was the key reason the engineers shot down the "rogue eenie" theory that had been floated early on. It was simply hard for them to go rogue.

But, insofar as telling a Scale from an eenie, it might not be much of a help. Just because Far Reaches had programmed in a behavior didn't mean the Scale couldn't or wouldn't have a similar behavior of their own.

"We are live, we are live, we are live," Helen responded, the call sequence putting her into the proper frame of mind. "How's it looking on your end?"

Helen's screens lit up, giving her a look at the information going back to Recovr's computers. Ivester's software was busily crunching numbers, sorting out what all the data meant before she tried to control anything at all. This time the eenie/Scale she was waldoing was different. There were fewer legs, a greater variety of sensors, but the chattering, the sense of information passing from sib to sib to sib, was still there.

"We've got something to work with. Wait until we give the word before you start making things move. By the numbers, if you please," Ivester responded. Helen called up the protocol she and Dougal had put together, a long list of signals to map out. She could feel the eenie/Scale resisting in new places, adapting to her presence.

In the space around her the Golfball started to resolve, the vault of the inner wall rising overhead like a starfield, sputtering idiot lights standing in for celestial bodies. Helen was struck by just how small this borrowed body was in real terms.

The spider waldo had been completely consumed, the remnants only visible as a massive collection of carbon black boulders floating in the midspace. The Scale—she presumed they were the Scale—swarmed over the remains en masse. From Helen's new point of view, they resembled an army of sea urchins, shells wild with color, almost identical copies of one another. As Helen's gaze passed across the scene, each type triggered a different response in the eenie/Scale she was riding. New datasets came in: health, rate of consumption, and a host of other things Helen's Insight couldn't decipher just yet. They methodically chewed their way across the surfaces of the waldo's remains, gouging tiny trails in the surface. They added the consumed material to their shells, the spines growing longer and branching like a forest on a turtle's back. As Helen watched, they rose in waves off the surface to be collected by a completely different class of Scale, this one with fins and jets, to be carried away.

"Ooooooh, Ivester. Those do not belong to us." Helen exhaled the words, afraid that if she spoke too loud they'd startle and all fly away like a flock of sparrows. Through the Scale she was riding, she got a sense of the ebb and flow, the way that systems upon systems braided together towards a larger purpose. Every system had a way to get at that information flow, whether it be a log file or a debugger of some kind. If she could get access to it, or rather, if Ivester could get access to it, they'd have an eye into the Scale's greater goals.

So just what are you up to? Helen whispered, half to herself. She asked the Insight to record and pass pictures of the fields of Scale back down the line to Ivester and Dougal.

"Make sure you guys are saving everything," Helen said. "I don't know how long this will last."

"Don't worry, we are double-redundant on this end." Ivester's voice this time. After much back and forth, Dougal had convinced them that having as many eyeballs on the entanglement as possible could only make their case stronger.

"Holy shit, Helen. Is this what you're seeing?" Dougal's voice now. "I mean . . . are those that colored dust we were seeing in the images from the first couple of missions?"

"I think so. We're just looking through this little guy's eyes this time. The waldo . . . Well, as you can see, there's not a lot left of it, so I think our theory that the entangled particles got re-purposed may be right on the nose," Helen responded.

"See if you can give us a mosaic of your field of view. Start with as far left and up as you can see and then take snaps from left to right and so on." Dougal again. "We're looking to document as much as possible as quickly as possible in case something happens to the line."

Helen obliged, giving the images priority transmission back down the entanglement Feed. Less because they had to go first than because they were breathtaking. She took another moment, just for herself, then turned her attention back to the Scale she was riding.

"Okay, let's take this little guy for a ride."

"If you push too hard, it's going to get shut down again," Ivester warned.

"Not again. This is a different Scale than last time. Between our last trip and now, the entanglement particles changed hands, got re-incorporated."

"Are you sure it's a Scale?"

"It recognizes all its little friends over there, so I think it's safe to say. I'll try to be careful about what I ask it to do."

"We need to be operating under the assumption that any Scale that starts to act up gets attacked and turned back into feedstock, just like we do for our eenies. There's no guarantee the particles will keep getting re-used every time in a fashion that we can use to connect, so be very careful with this guy."

Helen relaxed into the "waldo," trying each connection in turn. The images in her Insight shifted constantly as it dialed in on the specifics. She didn't try to force it to do anything. Instead she just went along for the ride, feeling each motion, listening for snippets of conversation and instruction while James chewed through the signals coming in. This was an information-gathering mission, and as long as information was flowing to her, she didn't need to push too hard.

The first time, Helen had had a sense of lateral information flow. The instructions were accepted and repeated across millions of tiny selves. This time, it was much more vertical, and she was higher in the hierarchy. The Scale she was riding was the one receiving and disseminating instructions to a class of subordinates more often than sibs. She could almost visualize the layout, an inverted tree of command units and subordinate units. It was logic she could get her head around. The farther up the tree you went, the more sophisticated the unit. It was an eerie reflection of the fractal command trees the Far Reaches eenies used. She idly wondered if James used a similar system in dealing with the hosts of tiny robots that maintained the building.

"Ivester, I'm sending you what looks to be the command framework."

No response from either Ivester or Dougal, but Helen barely noticed. Entranced by the ebb and flow as the Scale chewed up and harvested the remains of the spider waldo, she was listening, listening, listening to the much more conversational chatter between them. She still couldn't understand what was being exchanged, but she could sense the stops and starts, the long pauses and abrupt endings. It was hypnotic, a perfect system of actions, reactions, and expectations. Every Scale had a task, every rank had a purpose.

So just what the hell are we going to call you? Helen idly formed the question in her mind.

To her surprise, the Scale answered in words she could understand.

Then it turned on her.

Holy shit.

Helen found herself pinned, unable to act as the Scale she was riding asserted full control. She thrashed about in her mind, willing fingers, elbows, knees to move in an attempt to find one joint, one muscle that could still cause a response. *Nothing.* All physical control had been cut off, restricting her to input only. She could still see and hear and feel, but the active physical connection to her body had been severed.

She still had control of her Insight and it was still pulling input information from the Scale. Out of desperation, she canceled the remaining images to be transferred and simply streamed the raw data back as quickly as she could, grabbing as much as possible before everything went ass over teakettle.

"Helen, what's going on in there?" Ivester's voice again. "We're getting a massive influx of information, but no feedback, can you move at all?"

"Something's pissed it off, I'm under some kind of attack, can you see it?"

"I can see something, but it's all gibberish. Hang on."

Helen cast about for an action, something to do. *If all you have is a hammer . . .* She started digging around in her Insight for a software option. If the Scale was a machine, then she might be able to mess up its programming, force a hard reset. *Let's see what running our own debugger does.* She engaged the program, following the checklist that presented itself. She might not be able to move her body, but any operator, once linked into their coffin, was far from defenseless. This Scale was, as far as Helen was concerned, just another recalcitrant waldo.

The Scale reacted violently. Helen felt it jerk and twist as her Insight software started aggressively passing commands back and forth.

"I'm going to have to abort." Helen ground out the words, trying to keep her focus.

"Hold on for just a few more seconds," Ivester replied. "I've almost got a handle on it."

"That's not what I meant."

The fields of spiny colored Scale had erupted into the air like an explosion of dandelion fluff, frantically fleeing something Helen couldn't yet see. The Scale she rode, however, knew full well what was coming their way. The only word Helen could find for it was "terrified." It began to issue orders, canned sets of instructions streaming out over the thousands of connections that Helen could see but not directly affect. As Dougal and Ivester worked behind the scenes, Helen's Insight mapped all those connections to get a sense of the battle plan.

That's when she saw them, droplets of translucent glittering grey streaming towards the Scale from every nearby surface like rainwater shaken from a tree. The Far Reaches eenies were faster, better controlled and clearly on a mission. As each droplet approached, it broke up into a host of much smaller units, coating the surface of each Scale they encountered, consuming then moving on to the next closest Scale. They didn't leave anything behind: the consumption was total, and the mass grew larger as it consumed more.

Well, that's *terrifying.*

The surge didn't last for long. As Helen watched, the wave of silver-grey eenies began to slow down, break apart. The mass began to change color, in small pinpricks and dapples at first. Each spot of color coalesced, came together inside the larger mass, then continued to pass from eenie to eenie. They sprouted spines, grew cornices, their whole appearance changing as the Scale took them over.

The Scale are converting the Far Reaches eenies from the inside.

Holy shit.

The Scale are converting OUR eenies from the inside.

It wasn't until the rush of silver swarmed her that she hit the abort button.

CHAPTER TWENTY-FIVE

"GODDAMNIT!" Helen punched the release button inside the coffin and impatiently waited for the lid to cycle open. The Scale had brought pressure to bear in a way she hadn't expected. Helen was used to recalcitrant waldos, gummed-up joints, glitches in the code. Having a waldo fight back had been painful, like trying to wiggle your fingers and biting your tongue instead.

Her elation had lasted for a half-second when the Scale "talked" to her. Helen had felt, finally, like she had a line on a reason for Ted's death. Then it had all gone pear-shaped, along with her mood.

"Ivester, did you get any of that?" she asked as soon as the lid was clear. Ivester had remembered to shunt her through the buffer this time, so her body was her own again in record time. Helen sat up in the coffin, head still ringing with the sound and fury of the eenie attack.

"Do you ever wake up not angry?" Ivester asked from his spot by the console.

"Not anymore," Helen snapped. "Ivester, these things know we're here." She was still trying to get her head around what the Scale had said.

"Wait, where did you get that idea?"

"It recognized me. It fucking talked to me."

Ivester and Dougal exchanged glances. Helen put a lid on her frustration and took a breath before re-asking her question.

"Did. You. Get. Anything?" she spelled out deliberately.

"Yes. We got everything. And you're right, those are not our eenies. In fact . . ." His grin was one of vindication. "I think we can safely say the Scale are not from around here at all."

"What do you mean, it talked to you?" Dougal fixed on the more immediate point.

"It talked. In English. Like, actual words. Not code or images or any of the other things I've been getting so far. It told me what they're called. It gave me their name," Helen elaborated carefully.

"These things are not intelligent," Ivester pointed out. "From everything we're seeing in the commands, it's all pre-programmed, that's why James has been so quick on the draw. These things are fancy robot-ants, just like our own eenies. Why would it have a name?"

"I was talking out loud, looking for something to use to keep my data collection simple. The Scale, the singular one I was entangled with, not the big mass of Scale as a whole, responded with a name." Helen swung her legs over the lip of the coffin, dropping to the floor in one smooth motion. "How the hell do you pre-program something like that? They'd have to know we, not just our eenies, but WE are on the controlling end of things . . ."

Oh shit.

"Beauchamp." Helen breathed her rival's name as the puzzle pieces clicked into place.

"What about her?" Dougal asked, puzzled. Ivester was a little quicker on the draw; Helen could see the moment the realization hit home.

"They know we're out here because Beauchamp already encountered them on the BrightWinds mission out at Myrian," Helen said. She headed for the office cube in the farthest corner of the lab to change out of her supersuit, mind racing.

"Why would she keep something like this a secret? That's insane," Ivester called after her.

"She also just might not have known. I mean, we didn't really know ourselves until they incorporated that communications particle, right?" Dougal defended the absent OP, but Helen wasn't listening.

She closed the office door behind her and leaned against it for a second, collecting her thoughts.

She knew exactly why Beauchamp wouldn't have mentioned it to anyone. The repeated insinuations that Helen had snapped or was on the way to snapping had been a constant soul-sucking irritant. No OP would put themselves in that constant state of defense willingly.

Even this vindication did nothing to erase the marks of those tiny slings and arrows. As much as she might have given Beauchamp the benefit of the doubt on the outside, on the inside a darker sort of blame was starting to coalesce.

Focus forward, she told herself, drawing her attention away from the bitterness that lay in wait if she slowed down even a little. The stunning image of those brightly colored, urchin-like Scale floating into the air was one that would stick with her. It didn't make Ted or Keller's death worthwhile, but it gave her something to hold up to the light.

Helen stripped quickly, scraping the connective gel off her skin with her hands and toweling off the residue. The blue puddles on the floor shimmered under the lights as the cleanup eenies emerged from the foam mats on the floor to do their job. Ivester had dumped the eenies out of one Far Reaches trashcan on the floor and reprogrammed them to . . . take . . . care . . .

Helen yanked a sweatshirt on over her head and continued staring, mesmerized as the gel puddle was rolled over by a wave of iridescent grey eenies that consumed it all, then vanished back into the matting underfoot. Just as they had rolled over and subsumed the Scale out at the Golfball.

"IVESTER!" She yanked on pants, ignoring the way the legs and arms stuck awkwardly against her still-damp skin, and shoved the office door open. The engineer was in some sort of deep conversation with the analyst when Helen emerged, mind alight with her new revelation. "The Scale and our eenies. They do similar things, they take similar actions. They understand each other."

"On first observation, that seems to be the case." Ivester frowned. "But I caution against jumping to conclusions just yet."

"Of course you do, but is it possible that the Scale targeted our NAV Feed because they *know* the NAV is the one who passes commands to the eenies?" Helen continued. Ted's last act had been to pass instructions to the eenies building the Golfball.

"It's not unreasonable, but again, such a response should have to be pre-programmed," Ivester responded. "It does beg the question as to how they might know which of the quantum entanglement Feeds to target."

"Beauchamp. Her AI NAV shut down the mining operation on Myrian because of catastrophic failures that we couldn't find when we got out there. What do you want to bet they ran into the same sound in the Feed that Ted and Mira did? That's where they figured out our weakness: they broke the BrightWinds AI NAV first."

"We've only just scratched the surface here," Dougal said. He clasped his hands behind his back and paced. "We don't know if these are a naturally occurring life form. We don't know if they're some kind of exploratory force, but wild speculation is going to send us off in the wrong direction. We need proof."

"I don't think it matters," Ivester pointed out. "We're on a clock. The jumpgate is going to be completed in a month, maybe less. Even if they are friendly critters bringing sunshine and champagne, we can't let them through." He cast an apologetic glance at Helen. "The entanglement Feed's sending gibberish again. I think it's safe to say your upgraded Scale has been eaten. How do you feel about trying again if we get a clear signal back?"

"I'm game," Helen replied.

"All right. Dougal and I will keep working on the information you passed back to us. I'll need to bring this to the board's attention. They're not going to be happy Far Reaches is holding the bag on this one. In the meantime, I have an awkward favor to ask," Ivester said.

Oh no.

"You want me to go talk to Beauchamp." Helen gritted her teeth reflexively. It was an obvious next step. If Beauchamp knew about the Scale, they needed to know whatever they could get out of her. "Are you fucking kidding me? If she's directly involved, I've got a list of things as long as my arm she needs to answer for, starting with Ted's death."

"Even if all she can do is tell us what happened out on Myrian23A5, every little bit of information will help me make our case to keep the gate closed," Ivester said. He caught Helen's gaze, grey eyes bright with intent. "If she is responsible for Theodore's death, and for the assault on you, we will make sure she is held to account for it, but for now we need information."

"You can send someone else."

"Look, we know you have a history, but it's not like she's violent," Dougal said, missing the point.

"*I* might be," Helen ground out.

Dougal and Ivester looked at each other nervously. The idea that Helen might be inclined to act out hadn't occurred to either of them.

Dougal implored. "Look, she's an OP, she may have been in communication with the Scale. If anyone can make a connection with her, you can. Please try."

"Set it up at Wade's." Helen's warring desire to confront her rival won out over common sense. "It's public, the place is always crawling with OPs and NAVs from every firm in town."

Helen closed her eyes, counted to five.

Save the planet first. Revenge later.

"I'll see what I can get out of her. She owes me that much at least."

CHAPTER TWENTY-SIX

WADE'S WAS A BREATH OF FRESH AIR after the long hours in the Recovr team's lab in the sub-sub-basement. When not being rented out for a corporate function, Wade's was a favorite hangout for OPs and NAVs from all five competing firms. Walls flickered into and out of existence as diners engaged or dismissed privacy screens depending on their mood.

Helen arrived early and tipped Titus for a table near the center of the space. Anyone wanting to listen in would be blocked by the conversations of the crowd of patrons around her. While people and cameras would be able to confirm they met, Wade's unique layout meant that the actual content of their meeting would be hard to come by.

Outside the glassine shields that reflected the worst of the solar radiation, Helen could see an afternoon sky painted with blues and pinks as the sun started its downward slide towards evening.

"Ms. Vectorovich! Glad to see you back!" Titus circled around and greeted Helen as if he hadn't just pocketed a hefty tip for seating her. With Wade's serving as the de facto hub for OP and NAV after-hours mingling, Titus knew every OP and NAV in the city by name. Helen looked up from the tasting menu into artificial blue eyes that delivered sincerity on demand.

"Hi, Tee. The usual please." Helen folded up the menu and set it aside. She was agitated and by no means hungry, but ordering was another box on the checklist of old habits she could use to stay focused. She had no idea what she was going to say to Beauchamp or how she was going to convince the other OP to reveal what she knew. *Ted would know.* Helen was coming to realize that those gaps were entirely of her own making. Ted had a gift for people, but that didn't mean she couldn't manage without him.

"Of course. Are you here on business or pleasure?"

"Business. Meeting up with Catherine Beauchamp, of all people." Helen allowed herself a tight smile. *Presuming she shows.*

"That's bold. Well, if you've come to bury the hatchet, please remember there's a surcharge for bleeding on the table linens," Titus pointed out with an arch smile.

"I'm here to make a peace offering. No bleeding required, I hope," Helen elaborated carefully. It stung going through those careful social motions without Ted, but she would manage. The side effect of Titus knowing everyone was that Titus talked to everyone. She recognized a few faces, so the meeting would hit the rumor mill within an hour. By getting Titus' ear early, Helen would be remembered in Flight Ops gossip as the party taking the high ground.

Goddamn, people are a lot of work.

"I'll keep the bandages ready," Titus called over his shoulder as he went to fetch her order.

Helen grinned despite herself. Wade's collected a lot of after-hours personnel in various stages of work-related disrepair, with all the hazards that went along with mixing frustrated humans with recreational substances.

She turned her attention back to scanning the entrances. Helen didn't believe that Beauchamp was directly responsible for the poison in her coffin. Actual physical action wasn't the other OP's style. Even at Ted's wake, Cat had a proxy, someone or someones who took the actual action while she stood by and observed. Did she mastermind it? Convince one of the overworked techs to change the mix? As much as Helen might like to take Beauchamp to task for, well, everything, she would have to leave that to the Metro police. Helen's task right now had to be figuring out what Beauchamp knew about the Scale.

You can always kick her ass after you save the planet, right?

Dougal and Ivester had roped in two more members of Analysis to break down the information that Helen had been able to retrieve. Until the Feed out to the Golfball was clear again, Helen was free to work towards tying up the rest of the loose ends.

And here comes the biggest loose end now.

Catherine Beauchamp paused when she stepped in through the restaurant's door, scanning the room. She'd changed her look, gone sleeker and more streamlined. The other OP's signature aqua poof had been slicked back into a tight bun at the nape of her neck and her wardrobe had gone just a bit more tailored. She caught sight of Helen and appraised her for a long moment before approaching.

"Helen, sweetie. I wasn't sure you were serious about meeting." She took a seat without shaking Helen's offered hand. "It is still Operator, right?"

"Until the day I die," Helen said with perfect seriousness.

Beauchamp smiled, the *pulling back your lips without any real humor* kind of smile. It was oddly automatic. She raised a finger to call Titus over. "I heard about Keller. That's horrible news."

Helen managed to keep the frown off her face. Something was off in Beauchamp's responses. The bad attitude was there, but the usual malice behind it was missing somehow, like she was just moving through the motions. It was unsettling.

"I'm sure you're curious as to why I wanted to meet with you, all things considered," Helen said. Titus appeared with Helen's order and Beauchamp's usual, stalling her opponent's response. Neither woman wanted to be overheard.

"Curious is the word. With all the trouble going on over at Far Reaches, I figured you'd have been fired by now." Beauchamp raised an eyebrow. "Looking for a reference letter? I don't suppose being batshit crazy is going to look good on a résumé."

Helen took a sip of her drink to cover her irritation. "No, I've got that part covered." She changed tack before Beauchamp's gloat got a good head of steam on it. "I'm here to talk to you about Myrian23A5."

Beauchamp stopped, glass halfway to her lips. Helen caught a flicker of fear behind her eyes before she set the glass back down and arched an eyebrow. "I've run more than a few missions for Far Reaches, Helen. I don't recall that one in particular."

"I'm surprised, but learning from your failures was never your thing. It was from your time back at BrightWinds. An asteroid mining facility and an artificial intelligence NAV gone a bit wonky?" *Gotcha.*

Catherine's expression darkened, eyebrows drawn into a straight line.

I know what you're afraid of; now let's find out why.

"I'm sure anything done under BrightWinds purview has stayed under BrightWinds purview. And is *none* of your business," Beauchamp said coldly.

"Normally that would be the case," Helen said. "But Far Reaches picked up half of BrightWinds assets out of bankruptcy and Beyond Blue picked up the other half. We found something out there. What I want to know is if you sicced it on the Golfball intentionally."

"If you have all the records, then you know as much as I do. Myrian23A5 was a mess when I got there. The AI NAV declared it a total loss and it was scrapped, end of story."

"And yet I found a perfectly functioning mining waldo and a whole lot of dust."

Beauchamp's lip twisted. "You were on about dust before, after you screwed up the Golfball launch. I think you're seeing things."

"Did they talk to you, Cat?" Helen pushed her line of questioning forward. It didn't matter if Beauchamp thought she was crazy. What mattered was that she get Cat to drop her guard, to let something loose. If nothing else, Catherine Beauchamp had a temper; maybe she'd get mad enough to slip. "Did you talk back to them? They knew they could target the NAV array, that it was a weak point. That's why they went after Ted, he was the NAV. Did you tell them to target him, Cat?" Helen pressed.

"Dr. Hofstaeder needs to redo your psych eval," Beauchamp sneered. "I warned her of the long-term effects of that feedback. Not my fault if she didn't listen."

Snippy? Yes. Insulting? Check. But despite all of their differences, this was a different OP than the one she was used to seeing at Far Reaches Flight Ops. Better controlled, tighter lipped. *More afraid.*

"You knew about the feedback." Helen caught the thread the other OP had left dangling, tugged at it. "When we opened up the Golfball and that sound came through the Feed, you knew exactly what it was because the same sound took out your AI NAV. And you didn't raise a finger."

Not exactly fair, Beauchamp hadn't been on the Golfball team at that point, but Helen was pushing buttons now, looking to play on any latent guilt that might have been keeping the other OP up at night.

"I didn't know anything. The NAV called it, I dumped out, end of story. Everything else, everything that came after, is on you." Beauchamp broke cover and leaned forward, more than a touch of menace in her expression. "It's Ted's own fault he decided to stick with you as his OP. If I'd been there, I could have saved him."

The tacit admission hit home. Beauchamp had been trying to play a long game, and when Ted failed to do as he was told, she'd written him off. Helen rolled over the flash of anger and pressed harder. "And now Beyond Blue's involved. Did BrightWinds run into them more than once, Cat, or were you the only OP to find the *iLlumina*?" Helen deliberately wrapped her tongue around the name the Scale had given her. The look of shock and surprise on Beauchamp's face was priceless.

"You don't know what you're talking about." Cat picked up her cup again. Helen could see her fingers trembling with the movement. The mean girl façade came down for a minute, just long enough for Helen to catch a fresh look of fear and resolve in Beauchamp's eyes.

"They are nothing to be trifled with. They get into your head and you can't shake them loose."

"Cat, the BrightWinds mission was a year ago. They can't still be talking to you."

Beauchamp gave Helen a thin, fatalistic smile. "Like I said, you don't have any idea what you're up against. And as far as anyone's concerned, you're just another OP who cracked under the pressure. And once Beyond Blue secures the Golfball assets, it's not going to matter anymore."

"So you're the one directing the Scale?" Helen latched on. "You made them some kind of deal out there at Myrian and it got Ted killed. So what now, you let them through the gate, walk them right back here?" Helen wasn't sure how deep Beyond Blue was in, but she had some confirmation now. Beauchamp was working to bring the Scale to the gate.

Beauchamp cocked her head as if listening to the wind, then knocked back the rest of her drink and set the cup on the table.

"Ted made his choice. If he'd requested me as his OP for that mission, none of this would matter. Instead he stuck with you," she sneered. "Now you're about to be shut out and what, you think I'm going to tell you anything?"

"You have to know we can't open that gate," Helen implored. "It doesn't matter if the Scale are good guys or bad guys, we can't let an unknown organism into our biosystem."

"The gate has filters for just this kind of eventuality," Beauchamp replied. "We can keep the iLlumina under control."

"The filters are for something simple, like a homegrown virus. They're not going to be able to handle something that plans ahead," Helen said.

Beauchamp gave her a thin smile. "I'd suggest you take the next job offer that comes up and get out, but I'd much rather see you go down with the ship." She stood up in one smooth motion and left the table without another word.

Goddammit.

Helen stared after the other OP, fists clenched. She had her confirmation, if not actual evidence. Beauchamp had met the Scale out
at Myrian, maybe even directed them at the Golfball. Beyond Blue
knew perfectly well what was going on out there. If they managed
to keep control of the Scale, they'd be able to take control of the
jumpgate. It wouldn't matter if Line Drive went forward: all those
resources, all that power, would be held hostage.

"Well, that went poorly," Titus said as he refreshed her glass.
"This one's on the house."

Helen's smile was a wooden and automatic as Beauchamp's had
been.

"Thanks, Titus. The Far Reaches vending machines leave a lot to
be desired."

"Sorry you're left holding the olive branch. That one's been pissing off people left and right lately." He nodded in the direction of
Beauchamp's exit.

"Oh?"

He shrugged. "You're not the only person I've seen meet up with
her over the past couple of weeks, and every one ended with an argument. Rita from BrightWinds, Migos from Animus, even an analyst
from Far Reaches, and they don't usually hang out after work with
the OPs. In fact, your boss Keller was in here with her the night he
got murdered. Horrible stuff." Titus shook his head and moved off
to tend to another customer.

Helen stared after him in shock for a long moment. The revelation that Beauchamp had met up with Keller before his murder
rang in her head like a bell. She clenched and unclenched one fist
at the realization that, even if Beauchamp wasn't the one pulling the
strings, she was almost certainly calling targets for whoever was.

Bitch.

CHAPTER TWENTY-SEVEN

"So they do have a plan. This isn't some aggressive life form we can hold back with an interstellar bug spray," Helen said a little too loudly. The three new people working with James on the touchscreen wall glanced up, one with a smile. Ivester waved a hand at them and they resumed their work. Dougal closed the office door to keep the rest of their conversation private.

Too damn many people.

It felt like there were interlopers in her secret clubhouse. Helen'd taken her time returning, walking through the well-lit areas of downtown on her way back to the Far Reaches campus, burning off the terrified rush from her success at getting confirmation from Beauchamp. Some self-destructive part of her tempted fate, daring Beauchamp or her cohorts to come after her so she'd have a chance to take all her frustrations out on some unsuspecting thug-for-hire. So she'd have a clean, easy way to tie someone, anyone, to the deaths of her friends, rather than this double-handful of theory and half-spoken fact. Some part of her enjoyed the distraction, being a part of the flow again after so many weeks in Far Reaches' basement. The rest of her was mulling over the conversation with Beauchamp, picking it apart in her head.

It had taken her a few blocks of angry footsteps to puzzle it out. The missing entanglement particles from the Myrian23A5 mission were the key. Far Reaches had bought the salvage rights and hired all the OPs. Beyond Blue had acquired the AIs and with them the NAV half of the communication sets. That meant that Beauchamp was using the Beyond Blue particles to talk to the Scale. It also meant that when Keller tried to get access to those assets, he tipped them to what Recovr was up to.

"Well, you were right, this sure sounds like a battle plan," Dougal said, drawing Helen back to the here and now. The three conspirators had retired to Ivester's office to review what James had been able to piece together for them. Ivester's casual relationship with chairs meant he was seated on the desk. Helen had picked the chair farthest from the door, with her back to the corner. The meeting with Beauchamp, as insightful as it was, still had her on edge.

"James was able to put all that together?" she asked.

"James and the analysts Dougal pulled in from upstairs. It wasn't easy, but a program is a program is a program and James can throw a lot of processing cycles at another program," Ivester interjected. "Having your coffin hooked into a Scale meant we were able to match program commands to very specific responses. Even if you or I couldn't catch them, James made short work of it."

"The plan, at least as this—" Ivester waggled his fingers, searching for a word, "—cluster of Scale knows, is to first reclaim the Golfball as raw materials. Once that's completed, they'll move to building out a transport they can control."

Dougal picked up the thread. "It's a form of compartmentalization, very like what we use for our eenies. No cluster is going to know the big picture, they just have their instructions and get a new set when the job's done."

"So the Scale aren't out at the star yet?" Helen asked, surprised. In the back of her mind, the idea that all of deep space was already inhabited by the Scale had begun to take hold.

"We chose Otlyan23 because it's an orphan. No planets, no real interaction with its neighbors, just a spinning ring of asteroids and stellar gas around it that we can mine for materials. I think it's clear that the Scale are trying to find a way to get there and they're piggy-backing on our tech to do it."

"If this is true, why didn't they just jump straight there with the micro-gate from Myrian? Why bother with the Golfball at all?" Dougal asked.

"That's easy enough to answer. Power." Ivester called up a map of Otlyan23's local neighborhood, setting the small white star spinning in the space between them. A bright blue line traced the path from where the Golfball lay, at the outer edge of Otlyan's gravity well, to the orbital position of the planned gate. The path of the payload that Helen had launched over a month before was outlined in pale green and came to a neat stop at the same moment in space. He pulled their point of view farther out to show the Myrian asteroid in frame.

"That's the payload's path into Otlyan's orbit. On the way, it's been collecting material and building an army of our own eenies so that it can build us a great big star-powered gate. When the Golfball gets there, the particles get incorporated and voila, we have our key. Now, Otlyan's too far out for the Myrian gate to reach it, but when the Golfball caught a loop around this moon here for a boost, it passed just within reach."

Myrian lit up, showing a translucent sphere that showed the limits of that asteroid's micro-gate. One of the loops for the Golf-ball's long trajectory just passed within the furthest edge.

"Beauchamp said that Beyond Blue wants to control the gate. Have they made an offer to Far Reaches to acquire any of the Line Drive assets?" Helen asked. She reached out a finger and spun the little glowing ball on its axis.

"Not that I've heard, but since the board retired me, it's been a little harder to keep track." Ivester frowned. "I'll see what I can find out. There are other interested parties involved, so there's no guarantee Beyond Blue's offer would be accepted. But that far out in space, possession is pretty much law. If they make it out there and seize the asset, a court has no way to really stop them. We'd have to go get it back ourselves."

"Do we know anybody else inside Beyond Blue who could get us a copy of their internal timeline?" Dougal asked. "If they've already got an object in orbit, then this might all be moot."

"The announcement was a cover for them taking Otlyan over from our Golfball. They don't have anything of their own even close. If we can keep the Golfball from making its rendezvous, the gate will be safe," Helen replied, thinking back to Beauchamp's reactions during their conversation. "Beauchamp will warn their team that we are on the offensive, if Keller didn't tip them to it already."

The idea that Keller had been killed for asking too many questions about Beyond Blue's side of the Myrian assets didn't sit well with Helen. It just added to the sense of dread that was getting harder to ignore, day by day.

"The Golfball contains the particles we need to control the jumpgate when it comes online. If we send it off course or destroy it, then it's all been for nothing." Dougal got to his feet and started pacing. "So let's tackle the problem we can tackle right now. How do to stop the Scale from taking over the Golfball?"

The analyst caught Ivester's virtual Golfball between his fingertips and expanded it. Windows opened up, displaying information gleaned from all their attempts to connect.

Under his quick-moving fingers, the Golfball came apart. Helen could see holes within the delicate structure, indicating elements that had gone missing: some because the Scale had eaten them away, some because the eenies had been interrupted.

"Hold on a moment." Helen took a closer look. The timeline of events showed holes opening and closing within the structure, like little mouths gasping for breath. "There are repairs being made."

Ivester and Dougal both crowded in to get a better look until Helen zoomed in on the simulated image. "The Scale are eating the Golfball, but it looks like it's being restored almost as quickly as it's being destroyed." She scrubbed back and forth along the timeline, showing the Golfball in various states in sequence.

"You think our eenies are still following their programming?"

"Why wouldn't they be? It fits with what I saw when I was out there," Helen said.

"If our eenies are out there and capable of receiving new instructions," Dougal pointed out. "Maybe we can actively turn them on the Scale, not just chewing them up as if they're space dust, but treat them like an overrun."

"We can't get back out there until the signal clears," Ivester replied. "The coffin can't connect without a waldo and the Scale seem to be onto the fact that we can piggyback onto them."

"What about the NAV's signal?" Helen asked. "We've only been working with the OP signal. What if we can hook my coffin up to the NAV computer?"

Ivester and Dougal exchanged glances. "There's a five-minute time limit on the NAV signal, remember? Now that the Scale know we are here, that limit might be much shorter."

"I think it's worth at least a peek to see if we have a second avenue of communication," Helen replied. "Beauchamp must have told them we're avoiding that channel, so they won't be looking too closely," she continued in earnest. "And the NAV channel can reprogram our eenies. My OP channel doesn't have that capability."

"Our eenies aren't built for battle, they're for construction. They have a very specific set of commands we can work with," Dougal said.

"Did you see the video I was passing back? They have already adapted. The Scale aren't even ahead of them. It's an impasse. There's got to be a way to give our eenies bigger teeth."

The waves of iridescent silver eenies were still fresh in Helen's mind.

"She's right. As far as the eenies are concerned, the Scale are just material to be recycled. The Scale probably feel the same way about the eenies." Ivester grinned, struck by the outrageousness of the idea. "What we've got is two competing armies of builders. The eenies are attempting to build Golfball Phase II and the Scale are trying to build whatever the hell it is they are trying to build."

"They're evenly matched." Dougal took a deep breath, eyes alight with the idea. "So there's a possibility the problem's already been solved," he continued. "If they are really at an impasse, the Scale can't build what they need to take over at Otlyan. We could just leave everything alone."

No. No. No. After all the work they'd done to push forward, sitting back and hoping for the best was the worst idea Helen had heard. Before she could interject, Ivester brought up reality.

"That's not going to last." He scrubbed the sequential images of the Golfball back and forth, eying the changes in the shifting gaps in its frame. "A 'perfect balance' between these two armies will tip, sooner or later, and there's no guarantee it will be in our favor. If the Scale tactics change at all, I don't know how flexible the programming on our eenies will be." He called up the specs for the nano-machines designed for the Golfball. "But I think we need to figure it out pretty quickly."

He turned to Helen. "We'll get the coffin set up to entangle with the NAV computer, but I want your word that you'll drop out at the four-minute mark. We can use that link to give the eenies programming that will target the Scale."

"How do you build a battle plan to fight an army that just rebuilds itself?" Dougal asked.

"You call in a specialist," Ivester said. "Fortunately, a 'Grey Goo' scenario was postulated more than a hundred years before we even developed this technology. Dealing with runaway eenies is something Far Reaches already has experience with. We can adapt those protocols to fit our current situation."

Of course, there's also Beyond Blue to deal with. Helen glanced over at Ivester and Dougal, already digging into Far Reaches' eenie emergency plans, thick as thieves. She felt a quick jab of loneliness. First Ted, then Keller. She felt the loss of both compatriots, but never so much as when she was spinning her wheels waiting for the plotters and planners to finish so she could get back in the coffin.

Dougal's right. Tackle what's in front of our face first. Fix the Golfball, save the world.

CHAPTER TWENTY-EIGHT

THE COFFIN LID SLID CLOSED, blocking out the sounds of the Recovr lab. Helen took a deep breath and settled herself more comfortably against the thick gel padding. On the surface, entanglement was entanglement and the only difference between a NAV and an OP was the depth.

An OP was fully entangled, with the joints and drives on any given waldo mapped to respond to the electrical impulses that drove a living human body. NAVs were much more removed. Their job was to operate the larger hardware. Open the doors, run the software checks, reprogram the eenies, all things that could be done from an integrated console. Much like a radio in your hand or a radio built into a car were the same technology, the quantum entanglement part of the system worked the same in both cases. It was the user interface that carried the differences.

So Helen had no real idea what to expect when she entangled with the NAV particle out at the Golfball.

She took a deep breath as she lost control of her fingers, her arms, resisting the urge to flex those muscles one last time. What lay on the other side was an unknown—even Ivester could only offer her generalities. If NAV communications at the Golfball were still intact, she'd be constrained, limited to usual NAV operations.

She'd be unable to act as a physical body, but able to interface with the computer and reprogram the eenies. If NAV communications had already been consumed by either the Scale or the eenies, then she'd have to adapt on the fly again. All she knew at the moment was that the connection was still open.

"Ready, Operator Vectorovich?" Ivester's voice was the only one on the line. NAV didn't have an emergency channel, so she'd be cut off entirely once she entangled. Ivester had considered aborting the mission when faced with that fact. Helen had talked him into it only by allowing them to program in a kill switch. At four minutes, she'd be disentangled, no matter the circumstances.

"Fire it up," Helen replied. Her vision blurred to black as the entanglement sequence began.

"See you in four minutes." Ivester's admonishment rang in her ears, the last communication she would have.

Keep it short. Keep it simple. Just a test mission to see if the NAV line is still usable, Helen reminded herself as her vision cleared and she found herself inside the Golfball's NAV array. *Oh wow.*

Helen had been expecting a tightly constrained environment, the virtual version of wearing a straitjacket. The NAV computer was an unexpected, completely chaotic joy. Helen stretched and flexed experimentally, but her physical actions went nowhere. It was akin to floating in a large bathtub full of body-temperature water.

Her Insight was flooded with information from the NAV computer. Most of it she chose to ignore, shunting it off to the side. Warnings from various parts of the Golfball, error messages as non-critical systems malfunctioned. Elliot and Zai had successfully triggered the program to break down the Golfball and rebuild it into what would become the heart of the communications frame for the jumpgate. Instead of completing their task, the eenies were running up against the Scale, stuck in an endless loop of destruction and creation. The two tiny armies were very nearly at an impasse.

She dumped everything to a logfile to hand over to Ivester and the techs later. Somewhere in this glittering storm of errors and rapidly decompiling programs lay the eenie development environment. Helen checked the countdown.

Three minutes left.

Helen scrambled to clear as much of the NAV computer as possible, digging in deeper to find what she needed. Ivester had given her the file that should deliver new programming to the eenies. It would free them from the endless reconstruction loop they'd been trapped in and allow them to go solely after the Scale. It didn't guarantee they would be able to destroy all the Scale on the Golfball, but it would give them a better shot.

Helen glanced out over the miniature war zone playing out across the entire interior of the Golfball. A few idiot lights still sputtered here and there, but the majority had been turned into an alien landscape of eenie-driven design and error. Helen could clearly see the outlines of the two armies as they faced off, one brightly colored in patches and moiré patterns, the other like liquid silver. It was a patchwork of opportunistic encounters that ended with one cluster consuming the other. Neither seemed programmed to flee or regroup; they just kept eating and building, eating and building.

Two minutes thirty seconds.

Both sides had long, winding supply chains. The opponents consumed in one skirmish might be carried or floated like spiky puffballs to another location to build more of the same. It was gorgeous, like watching two lichens fight over the same bare patch of rock, except with the speed cranked up 100,000 times.

The regular NAV cameras showed Helen the brightly colored shells of the Scale, but when she switched to the ultraviolet spectrum, it reversed, the Scale turning a dark, matte grey and the Far Reaches eenies exploding in their own fantastic colors.

An internal communication request caught Helen by surprise. The NAV had no backup channel like OPs did, so that meant the call was coming from inside Golfball. Normally that line would be reserved for local radio communications between the waldo and the NAV. Since the waldo had been completely consumed by this point . . .

Helen answered it.

Two minutes.

Without James backing her up, the language of the alien Scale was indecipherable. Her Insight paraded gibberish in front of her eyes as it tried to make sense of the syllables.

"I know at least one of you fuckers speaks English," Helen said.

There was a pause. The voice that followed sent a chill down Helen's spine.

"Now, now, that's hardly the language of the diplomat." The voice belonged to Catherine Beauchamp. It was distorted, filtered, translated and retranslated back, but unmistakable all the same.

"Beauchamp?"

One minute thirty.

"Cat? What the absolute hell?"

"I warned you to put Far Reaches in your rearview mirror. Looks like you were crazy enough to ignore my advice." The other OP's voice came through the Golfball's internal comms, doubtless connected somehow by the Scale.

"Cat, what the hell is going on? How are you even here?"

"Now that I'm back at Beyond Blue, I have a direct line into the iLlumina command structure." There was a long pause, filled with chatters and half syllables. "Everybody's talking. Everybody. All the time. I know exactly what is going on with every single Scale in this cluster at every single moment."

Helen started searching, looking for a difference in the colors, in the quantity of the Scale laid out on the Golfball's surfaces before her. They had to be organized somehow. The patterns on the shells repeated, like clustering together with like. There had to be a central node, a command post from and to which Cat was communicating. It was the kind of problem she'd send back down the line to Ivester, but this time she was cut off, alone.

"So you brought the Scale here from Myrian, fine, we already knew that. But why are you still talking to them? Why are you *helping* them?" Helen tried to keep the other OP talking, keep the communication open as long as possible while she hunted for the source. Pieces of the puzzle continued to fall into place.

"Helping them? Not a chance. They're working *for* me. I know you've been poking around, trying to figure out if there's anything you can do. Let me save you the trouble. The Golfball is mine. The Scale will consume it, rebuild it, and bring it to *our* new gate right on schedule. Beyond Blue will own your very expensive asset and there is nothing you can do about it."

One minute.

"Cat, you can't be serious." Helen continued searching frantically. "Industrial espionage is one thing. Great, you scooped us, you get a cookie. But we can't let these things through that gate. That will bring them right to the edge of our inhabited worlds."

The language of the Scale grew more angry, syllables coming faster, sharper. It was like Cat's words were being echoed by a chorus of minuscule voices.

"You misunderstand, sweetie. I'm the one controlling the Scale. I tell them what to do, where to go. This isn't just espionage, this is now a war. The Scale won't come through the gate unless I tell them to, and if I tell them to, well, that's going to be a very tough time for everybody."

The statement of intent was chilling. The scenario Cat described was way outside the capacity of a semi-disgraced waldo jockey to fix.

"It's a hostage situation, you mean," Helen retorted angrily. "You're going to hold an entire system hostage for what, exactly?" She was only partially aware of the import of what Cat was saying; she didn't have time to parse the seriousness of that information. She just kept talking, feeling around the edges of her counterpart's frustration.

Thirty seconds.

This was a conversation for bigger dogs. Maybe they could entangle Ivester to negotiate, maybe XERMo could pass this on to the government. The list of maybes spiraled out of Helen's control and she had to let them go, refocusing on the one thing she actually had a hand in. *Take back the Golfball.*

"You don't understand, Helen, the Scale don't care. There is no malice, there is only expansion. We encroached on their territory back on the Myrian asteroid, and now they are encroaching back. I can keep them under control for now. That's something worth paying a price for, don't you think?"

"So why the hell are you bringing them straight to us?"

There. She had it.

By flipping back and forth through the spectrums available to the NAV camera, Helen identified a new cluster of Scale. Not centrally located, but tucked way back in the corner, looking more like an idiot light gone dark than a cluster of alien eenies. A single mass that the NAV computer highlighted as quantum-particle dense. It had to be the connection point for Beauchamp. Now, Helen just had to get to it.

If I can cut Beauchamp out of the equation, maybe our eenies can get a leg up.

"Cat, you can talk to them." Helen kept talking. "Help us open a dialog. We can get somebody up here to negotiate, but not if they get through the gate."

"Time's up," Beauchamp said.

The disentangle sequence began.

Not yet. Notyetnotyetnotyet. Helen fought the disentanglement. Ivester might have hard-coded in the kill switch, but an Operator, any Operator, was far from helpless once entangled. As the edges of her consciousness flaked away, Helen dug into her Insight, finding the kill switch and disabling it. It stung, like someone had run sandpaper over her eyelids, but the connection was under her control again, at least until the Almighty Ivester panicked and pulled her back into her own body by force.

One minute past, not a second more, she reminded herself.

If Beauchamp really was in control of the Scale, then why didn't she bump up the timeline, attack Helen the same way she had Ted? Unless that five-minute mark was something hard-coded in, somehow.

Move faster.

"I'm not going anywhere, Cat, so let's see if we can figure this out. You know nobody's going to let you get away with this, right? XERMo or one of the other agencies is simply going to kick in your door and take the NAV particles away from you." As she talked, Helen dug into the eenie software, loading the files she needed to reprogram the eenies. She was out of time, so she had to switch tactics.

"This is a surprise." Beauchamp didn't bother to listen. "Sticking around until the last possible moment? I would have thought Ivester would have pulled you back out by now."

The Scale covering the surfaces of the Golfball began to collect into larger groups, aggressively flanking and surrounding the patches of eenies. Helen could see Beauchamp's influence as the Scale began to attack in earnest and the eenies started to lose ground.

Fifteen seconds past.

"Aw, Cat, you're an OP, you know how stubborn we can be." Helen found the file, sprang it open, and found herself faced with a familiar checklist of items ranging from Panel Reconstruction to Catastrophic Meteorite Strike. Helen began to thumb through the list. *A hundred-plus missions under your goddamn belt and you can't think of the protocol you need.*

A properly entangled NAV would have everything at their fingertips already. Despite her skill as an OP, there were just some things NAVs had a lot more training in. She burned precious time loading up Ivester's "eenie overrun" software and sending it to the remining "builder" eenies. Now she needed a solution that would let her get back out to the Golfball again after her five minutes were up.

Eenies acting out of turn were destroyed and added to the feedstock. Larger, more complex tasks meant that programming instructions had to be streamed to the eenies from the NAV computer. Whatever else happened, Helen had to keep these NAV particles safe, otherwise Beauchamp would be the only one who could control anything.

I hope.

If Ivester got his act together and pulled Helen back to her body, she wasn't sure how quickly they'd send her out again. Better to take the risk and put her own army of eenies on the offense before she had to ditch out.

Thirty seconds past . . .

Helen found what she needed. Designed to fix strikes from micro-asteroids, it would attack a specific section of the Golfball, break it down to its component molecules, and rebuild it to spec.

Helen cast about for the eenie clusters closest to the NAV computer. A fine dust made of eenie shells floated over the battlefield, static forces causing them to clump together and drift where they fetched up against surfaces. The Scale were moving in a hurry now, destroying as they went, leaving the remnants for later.

Helen found the three closest eenie clusters and made a connection to them, delivering their new instructions through the NAV's coded channel. Once they had received everything, she could hit the abort button and get safely back to her own body, a billion miles away.

Five minute mark.

Helen recognized the sound. The same crawling chattering noise, the same incomprehensible squeals. Except here, inside the NAV computer, it was far, far worse than she had experienced before. There was pain, sharp needles in her temples and behind her eyes. Here in the NAV computer, there were no barriers, nothing to dull the pain, nothing to separate her from the knives that seemed to find easy purchase in the space behind her eyelids.

But she had to hold her focus on the connection until the eenies had received their new programming.

"Oh, I see you've reached the five-minute mark." Beauchamp's voice was there, buried in the sound and fury. Helen could not tell if she was hearing Beauchamp over the local channel or whether it was part of the attack that felt like it crawled around the inside of her skull, scrabbling at the bone with glass shards for fingernails.

Helen pulled her focus tighter, allowed the pain to slip past. In her memory, she could see Mira seizing in the NAV's chair.

Constrained as she was inside the coffin, there was a very real risk that nobody would realize Helen was under attack until it was too late. *They can just bury me in it as is, I suppose,* she thought darkly.

Beauchamp continued talking. "The five-minute mark caught my AI NAV too, but by that point BrightWinds was on the downward spiral. They didn't bother to investigate, they just took it offline. Beyond Blue lost two human NAVs before they figured it out and came to me, but you wouldn't have heard about that."

"Two NAVs?" Helen ground out the words between clenched teeth. "You let them kill two NAVs?" Almost there, she just had to hang on a few more seconds. *Keep her talking. Keep her distracted.*

"It was before they came and recruited me. It was before they knew what they really had," Beauchamp said, her voice like acid in Helen's ears. "You can't hang those around my neck."

"And now? Can you call them off or are you going to let me go the way of Ted and the other two NAVs?" A small part of Helen's mind was genuinely curious in that quiet, detached way thoughts got when faced with ongoing pain. The extent of Beauchamp's control would be a puzzle for another day.

"I could, but calling them off is not in the plan. If whatever trick you're trying to pull gets you killed, then Far Reaches will shut down the entire Line Drive project. Beyond Blue is prepared to pay handsomely to take over all the assets. And if not, the PR fallout will be crippling. In fact, it's been suggested that the best possible outcome from my trip all the way out here is that you somehow find yourself unable to disentangle at all."

Lovely, she's gloating. Helen would have rolled her eyes if she'd had any. She'd known Beauchamp was gunning for her, but this, this gun-for-hire aspect, was toxic. *It's fucking crazy.* The sound was coming in waves now, maxing out the data transfer down the entanglement link back to her body a billion miles away.

Oh. That's how it works.

It wasn't interference they were crowding the link with, it was instructions. They were trying to overload her neural pathways, cause a short circuit in the brain itself. *The mother of all grand mal seizures.* But Helen was working with an OP's entanglement rig on a NAV line, not a NAV's brain-only set of wires. Those instructions had a lot more places to go than just the cortex. Helen's OP hardware was distributing the attack to her entire system: brain, body, even the coffin would be picking up the load. It hurt like hell, but it would take longer to kill her.

You have a harder time taking down an OP because of the hardware, Helen realized. *I've got you now, you fuckers.*

The eenies acknowledged their new instructions and moved in her direction. Helen confirmed and turned her attention to another set. She needed as many eenies as possible if she was going to have even a chance at pulling this off.

Helen's NAV sensors were obscured by the scrabbling dust of the Scale as Beauchamp turned her microscopic army against the NAV computer. She felt a shiver in her mind as the feeling of being covered in biting ants overrode her conscious thought processes for a moment, giving Helen an extreme case of the willies. If she dialed the camera down far enough, she could see individual bellies, stubby legs, and stabby manipulators as they started chewing away, destroying the electronics and recording surfaces as they went. She might have been screaming out loud, it was hard to tell with her body so far away. In moments Helen had gone blind and deaf.

Shit. Beauchamp got the drop on me.

In Helen's moment of distraction, Ivester disentangled her before she had a chance to block him again.

CHAPTER TWENTY-NINE

"JUST WHAT THE HELL WAS THAT?"

If Helen had been able to move a muscle she might have flinched. Ivester wasn't shouting, but the force of personality behind the words felt like a physical shake.

"Four minutes, we agreed on FOUR. It's been seven. Why didn't you abort?"

The coffin had been folded open, lid off, sides down, a whole new series of wires and connections added in the time she'd been entangled. Ivester was furious. Dougal similarly so. Helen counted to ten and made sure she could move her lips before responding.

"Beauchamp was out there." She checked the drug delivery on the coffin's screen. Everything hurt. Whatever the Scale had sent down the line to her body had left it feeling sore and aching all over, like every muscle had been tenderized by a thousand tiny mallets. The health monitors were throwing up screaming red warnings about isometric tissue damage and neurotransmitter deficits. She dialed up the painkillers and dialed down the stimulants. *Good thing this coffin's not sending data to Hofstaeder yet or I'd be in even more hot water.*

"Wait, what?" Dougal's expression changed to surprise.

"You heard me. Beauchamp was *out there*. She's Entangling through NAV particles from Myrian. Directing the Scale, giving them an advantage." Helen waited while the feeling was restored to all her limbs. Ivester's anger quickly ran through confusion and emerged at incredulity.

"How the hell did she manage that?"

"You're going to love this. She's in their command chain. As far as the Scale are concerned, she's just a bigger, bossier Scale. Ivester, you've got to send me back out."

"Send you . . . No. Absolutely not."

"Yes. Now. I sicced our eenies on keeping our NAV particles safe. If I did it right, they'll break up the NAV computer and incorporate it just like the Scale were doing. Now I've got to get your overrun software installed and break the communication with Beauchamp. If I can stop her, then we can get the upper hand."

"That's good enough, we can monitor it from here."

"No. We can't." Helen closed her eyes and keyed in the start sequence by touch. "Look, according to Beauchamp, the Scale are not friendly and she is bringing them right to our new gate at Otlyan. If she loses control of them, if they slip the leash, then there's nothing to stop them coming through whenever the hell they want."

"We're a research team. If Beyond Blue is really going to use the gate to try and take over the system, that's got to go right to XERMo," Ivester growled.

"Look, by the time I get back out there, our eenies should have incorporated the Golfball's NAV particles the way the Scale did the OP particles. I can waldo one of those eenies and direct the overrun software take the Myrian NAV particles away from the Scale. We can try to make direct contact with the Scale to see if we can talk them down. If Beauchamp's been doing it, then we've got the same capability."

"Okay, okay, okay," Dougal intervened. "Five minutes, give us five minutes."

"We don't have . . ." Helen started.

"Just let us load you up with a new set of protocols for handling the eenies." Dougal moved back to the touchwall and started transferring files before Helen could object.

"These are from XERMo's containment library." Ivester leaned over the edge of the coffin. "Everything they use to bring an eenie overrun back under control. We're going to give our eenies the biggest teeth we can, just make sure you record the data . . ."

He looked worried. It was a look Helen was getting used to. She didn't like it, not on Ivester.

"And don't die. You're the only OP we've got."

"Not planning on it." Helen closed her eyes, watching the countdown as the files transferred. As soon as the counter reached a hundred percent, she started the entanglement sequence. "Don't pull me out again."

"The hell I won't."

The sequence kicked in and Helen raced back out along the Feed to the stars.

CHAPTER THIRTY

WHEREAS THE INSIDE of the Scale had been full of chatter, and the NAV array had been filled with whispers and knife-sharp signals, the space Helen found herself now entangled with was absolutely, perfectly, serenely quiet.

Something had happened to the NAV computer.

Someone had eaten her NAV computer.

Excellent.

Her Insight connected, bringing up code and information in a language she understood. It was Far Reaches tech, whatever it was. Helen watched as signals were found, one by one, and stitched in to her interface. Beauchamp hadn't been fast enough; the eenies had gotten to the NAV particles first. But Beauchamp didn't know that Helen had already successfully waldoed a Scale once before, so her guard should be down. *Almost successfully.* Just how far down into the eenie food chain her NAV entanglement particles had been absorbed, Helen wasn't sure yet. She hadn't really expected it to work.

Through the information in the Insight, she could see inside of the Golfball as the war zone it had become. Unlike the Scale, which moved in blobs and organic clusters, the eenies were much more regimented, organized. Each eenie connected to six sibs, which in turn connected to six sibs and so on and so forth. It was like being a knot in a three-dimensional net. A net that was strengthening by the moment. The builder-eenies had taken the new instructions with a will and were cranking out new units with a single purpose.

Where the OP particles had been passed back and forth between Scale to Scale depending on who ate whom, the rank of eenies Helen was working with had escaped with the Golfball's NAV particle, following her instructions. It meant she'd have a little time to work out a plan.

Helen rapidly dug into the packets of data that Ivester had uploaded at the last minute, all of them varying degrees of deadly, each designed for a very specific kind of eenie bloom. From her place in the network, she disseminated those new instructions to the rest of the eenies, informing them all the Scale were an overrun and as such had to be brought back under control.

"Oh, so you're back." Helen wasn't sure where the sound was coming from, but she felt Beauchamp talking to her through the strings that connected her to a million sibs. The eenies must have connected to the Golfball comms for some reason, maybe while trying to reconnect the NAV particles to the computer.

"You didn't think this was over, did you?" Helen felt out along the wires, but the source, whatever it was, was out of her reach. Unlike Helen, who had made a direct connection to the eenies, Beauchamp seemed to be one-off. She was communicating through a node somewhere like a NAV, not waldoing like an OP. Helen queried through the network, trying to get a sense of exactly where she had landed in the interior of the Golfball. This eenie didn't have eyes, per se; it was more like a form of echolocation data coming in from her six sisters. Her Insight took that data and mapped out the 3D space, showing she was fetched up on the wall below a little knot of Scale that Beauchamp was communicating through. In real-world terms, it was a matter of millimeters, but now Helen was riding an eenie smaller than an orchid seed. It was going to be a long walk.

"Truth be told, I did. But I'm glad to see you're not giving up just yet."

Helen didn't like the sound of that. Forty-eight hours ago, she would have sworn that Beauchamp, while a complete and utter ass-hole, was not of murderous intent. She had since been disabused of that notion.

I wonder what else she thinks she's got.

The computer mapped out the clusters of Scale, giving Helen a battlefield view of the various skirmishes. From the thousand-meter lens of the NAV computer, Helen had only been able to understand the broad strokes. Now, embedded as she was in the eenie army, she was intimately aware of a thousand smaller skirmishes going on, a war being fought on hundreds of fronts smaller than her fingertip. In some cases, one side was simply rolling over the other, but in other cases, both sides were drawn to a standstill. In all cases, however, the eenies were at a disadvantage.

Let's start by fixing that. The Scale tactics all seemed to involve surrounding and swarming, much like angry clusters of extra-stabby ants. The eenies were still doing their best to consume and rebuild, but not fight back. The software Ivester had sent along would make short work of that.

Good thing they let me back out here.

"Oh look, someone put on their war paint." Beauchamp's voice mocked her. "Do you really think that will help? I have a secret to tell you, my dear. The iLlumina aren't programmed, not the way we do it. They've been evolved up, like a living organism. They can adapt without anyone telling them what to do. They don't even *really* need me."

Next order of business is to shut her the hell up. Helen flexed her fingers, feeling the eenie she was riding respond, gathering its legs under it. It was much more agreeable to her control than the Scale had been, much more like guiding a well-trained dog than riding a waldo. It was eager to please in a way she hadn't expected. Helen checked to see if any of her eenies had made an attempt on Beauchamp's communications node, but came up empty.

Now that she was looking through the "eyes" of an eenie, the bright blooms of color on the Scale made her uncomfortable, suggested they were toxic, indicative of a flaw, of broken code. They were off-pattern and as such had to be remade. Helen's eenie built its spikes out in response to the new programming, long thin probes that were used to find or create weak points in materials. *Or to disable other eenies running off-spec.*

Helen started moving, calling smaller ranks of her sibs to her, setting herself up as the top node in the lattice. They responded, abandoning fights already lost. Many of the eenies were slow to change tack, simply choosing to continue consuming the ground they stood on, continuing their endless mining of the Golfball's inner surfaces now free of the competition. It was the Scale between her and Beauchamp that Helen had to worry about. They started to swarm together, clustering around the edges of the communications node Helen was targeting, forming a barrier of protection.

"You're outnumbered by the millions," Beauchamp taunted.

Helen still didn't respond; she'd blocked out better insults from better OPs in the past. She focused instead on Beauchamp's node, the way the Scale formed an interlocking, organic pattern as they moved into position. Her Insight analyzed the pattern, picking out weak points that replicated across the entire surface. Helen transmitted that information to the rest of her eager cluster and they all surged forward as one, ignoring, even climbing over Scale on their way. She was distantly aware that her little grouping was attracting more and more eenies. They were all sibs, and the top eenie gave the commands, which meant they'd all do as Helen asked.

That was the trick, she realized, *the ask*. The Scale she'd waldoed before had been reacting to her giving commands, rather than making requests. The eenies were designed to do as they were told, but the Scale understood themselves as an independent entity.

Ivester's going to love that idea . . .

Something caught Helen from underneath. She felt one leg held, then another. She issued a command to her sibs and they came together, spikes out. They couldn't defend her against so many Scale at once, but they could make sure the entanglement particles got into another eenie. Helen felt herself being vivisected, split apart. The Insight, everything, went mercifully black.

After a disorienting moment, Helen opened her eyes again. Her rank of eenies had pulled the NAV quantum particle before the Scale could finish her off and plugged it into a new body. The echoes of pain were still there, in her limbs, in her chest where they'd split her open to retrieve the particle. She shrugged it off, knowing she'd pay for it later in nightmares and indecisive moments. She reached out to find her rank still on the move. As they lost members, more of her siblings came to fill in the gaps, making the formation stronger, more resilient.

"Oh, there you are. I thought we'd got you that time." Beauchamp's voice again. "How about this time?" Helen felt herself being caught, pinned. A part of her lattice collapsed around her, pulling in to repeat the process. Searing pain, blackness, and then Helen was awake in another new body, abandoning the previous one to be consumed. She reissued her order, focusing on getting up the wall to Beauchamp, and more eenies answered.

"Go home, Helen. Beyond Blue owns all of this now. You're playing in my playground."

Get stuffed. The thought never materialized into words. More and more of her sibs joined the push as her orders echoed outward. Her new eenies, freshly minted per Ivester's specs with all the hooks and teeth required to bring an overrun back under control, had begun to feed in to her formation. Helen became aware of her rank not as a series of minor entities, but rather extensions of herself. She was no longer waldoing a single eenie; she was a single mind with every thought having a physical body of its own.

Wow.

Helen repeated her order to attack Beauchamp's communications node, and felt it ripple outward, reaching an even greater, even deadlier number of eenies. She was still outnumbered, but now she had specialists.

Helen lost another body, then another, as Beauchamp continued to try to break her rank. As each attack rolled over, Helen's entanglement particles were simply attached to a new body in a staccato of sharp lines of pain and focus. She didn't allow it to slow her down.

Helen leapfrogged, carried forward from eenie to eenie by the surging tide. Ahead of her, Beauchamp's command node lay bare. Beauchamp's Scale had begun to yield, and they pulled back as if to protect themselves, opening the path. It was unexpected, and from her position, Helen couldn't tell if she was winning, or if they were retreating. She couldn't afford to waste a possible advantage. The only way she could see to end this was to cut off Beauchamp's control of the Scale and recover those stolen NAV particles from Myrian23A5.

She surrounded herself with specialist eenies, cautioning them as her own cluster moved forward. Unlike her cohort of eenies, the Scale had a will of their own. They could be bucking Beauchamp's commands, but she had no way to be sure.

Out in the greater universe of the Golfball's interior, the fight was still going on. Helen felt eenies go dark, a prickle of information that burned like an arm fallen asleep. At the same time, she felt new eenies blossom into existence to fill those voids. Since she'd delivered the new programming, they'd managed a nearly one-to-one replacement ratio, but it wasn't going to be enough.

"Helen, wait. . . ." The fear in Beauchamp's voice meant next to nothing.

Helen reached out with a million tiny fingers, sweeping over the communications module and crushing her rival in her palm.

With a pop, Beauchamp's influence vanished. The Scale slowed and a silver tide of eenies swept in.

So it wasn't just *the Scale.*

Inside the perfect quiet of her current eenie, Helen felt a question emerge. Not in words she could understand, but in the commands streaming in from her sibs. It was like listening to someone speaking an unfamiliar language, but their gestures and expressions gave you the highlights. The eenies had remained connected to the Golfball's internal communications; maybe the Scale were trying to use it as well.

Oh, what the hell. Maybe there's a way out of all this.

"I am Operator Helen Vectorovich. I'd like to talk."

Helen held her breath, hoping for a response. She was about to give up and disentangle when her eenie spit forth a stream of fear and information she couldn't quite get her head around. She whipped around in response to find herself faced with a fast-moving river of brightly colored bodies

Then everything went black.

CHAPTER THIRTY-ONE

THE RESPONSE OPTIONS hung in the air ahead of her. It was a simple yes or no on the surface, but Helen unconsciously understood that a dam might burst once she answered it.

Yes/No

Yes or no WHAT? There was no proper question associated with it, just a positive and a negative option. The darkness lessened and Helen realized she was still entangled. The eyes she looked through were not hers. The lungs she breathed with were not hers. The . . .

Lungs? Helen couldn't remember a waldo design that had lungs.

Since when did the Golfball have AIR for breathing?

She was prodded unpleasantly, knocking her out of her line of questioning. A quick turn, a glimpse of translucent silver legs that belonged on an eenie rather than a human, but she was alone in a darkened room.

That's not right, either. She could feel someone else in the space with her, a waiting presence like someone preparing to speak.

Stuck in the buffer maybe? She couldn't remember if she'd tried to cut the connection. After reading Ivester and Dougal the riot act, they'd never once missed running her through the buffer on the way out of a waldo. The buffer felt different than this, though. The space she found herself in was not trying to be something. The buffer pretended to be real, something you could wrap your head around on the way back to the meat of the real world. This was less well formed, like it needed more information. Like it was waiting for a response.

Helen closed her eyes and cast about in her own head for a moment. No Insight, no coffin interfaces, nothing she could get her hooks into to get back to either the eenie she'd been riding or her own body, trapped in the experimental coffin back in the Recovr lab.

One breath.

The last thing she remembered was the stream of information from the Scale. She'd asked them to talk, without any real idea of who or what she was asking the question of.

Oh shit. Did they take me up on it?

Two breaths.

As long as she was breathing, she could act. As long as she could act, she could figure this out. Something . . . Someone prodded her again. She opened her eyes to find the Yes/No still hanging there. She looked away, but the words moved to match, staying directly, stubbornly, in her line of sight.

"Clearly you want me to pick an answer. So what's the question?" she asked aloud.

The space around her winced, some combination of a change in brightness and a shift in perception, like the sound of her voice had startled it. The response prompt flickered and vanished.

Well, I've got to be somewhere. If she were stuck in the buffer, then Dougal or Ivester should be talking to her. That left the probability that she was still entangled with the NAV particle, but no longer riding her eenie. Recent experience had shown her just how the NAV particles could be transferred from nano-machine to nano-machine without her losing her entanglement connection.

They must have picked up on what she was doing and grabbed the NAV particle out of the eenie. It was the most reasonable option.

One breath.

The tension and the horror of that final push to cut off Beauchamp came rushing home. Maybe, just maybe she'd pushed it too far. *Total disassociation?* That didn't feel right. *Dead?* The Scale and the eenies both recycled everything. They wouldn't have destroyed the NAV particles even if they'd finally turned on her. She wasn't sure destroying the NAV particle while she was entangled would result in her actual real-life death. She wasn't even sure a quantum particle could be destroyed, by ordinary physical means anyway.

Two breaths.

The chattering that had plagued her since her very first trip to the Golfball rose up, flowing outward to the walls of the liminal space around her. The room had begun to move. Not big motions, just small jitters in space, like she was seeing every particle of matter in the walls do a little dance.

It's all made of Scale, she realized abruptly. The space that contained her was a bubble comprised entirely of the bodies of living, active Scale. She'd been entrapped, encased. The realization snapped her out of her panicked spiral. She was still here, still entangled out at the Golfball and she was . . . *imprisoned? Captured?* She stretched her limbs out, tried to get them up where she could see just what she was working with. Knowing she was entangled, knowing she was riding a waldo, even though she didn't have the Insight to outline the interface, was strangely comforting. It gave her solid ground to stand on.

They're not attacking, that's good, right? So now what?

The prompt reappeared. Yes/No.

Helen stared at it for a good long minute. It didn't make sense. Why ask for a response to . . . nothing? As far as she knew she hadn't been asked a question. She didn't speak the language of the Scale. But if they couldn't recognize each other's language, why was she being asked to respond?

The Yes/No prompt fuzzed, broke apart and was replaced by 1/0. *Oh.*

Maybe not Yes/No as the response to a question, she realized.

Maybe positive and negative? It was two states: one on, one off. It was the most basic metaphor behind the quantum entanglement used to command a waldo. Arrange the particle one way to get a one, arrange it another to get a zero, and with enough ones and zeros strung together, you had information shuttling back and forth across a billion miles of empty space. It was simplistic but it was a place to start a conversation.

Shit. I'm not qualified for this.

Without access to Insight, Helen was limited to the information in her own head, but an Operator, any Operator, understood something about the science that makes running a waldo possible. *So if they're asking about a language we can both use, simple is good.* Ivester's theory was that if she could waldo a Scale, they might have a similar logic to their programming. If he was right, and they had more similarities than differences, then this might be their suggestion for a common language to use. She reached out an arm and a multi-jointed limb came into view.

The prompt ahead of her fuzzed and returned to Yes/No.

Well, I've rarely regretted a yes. Helen reached out and tapped at the word where it hung in the air. It vibrated, wobbled like jelly. She looked closer, felt the familiar strain as she cranked the focus tighter. To her surprise, she found that the numbers and letters were made up of an even smaller class of Scale, hexagonal forms that reached for one another and clung to form larger shapes. Around the corners of her vision, the blue and orange fairy lights of Insight reemerged, like they'd been shadowed over by something.

Is this how they got to Beauchamp? Helen asked herself. Or was what she seeing now something else entirely? A version of the Scale free from Beauchamp's influence might be something they could actually work with.

"OPERATOR HELENA VECTOROVICH, I can see you're NOT DEAD YET, so you damn well better answer . . ." Ivester's voice erupted from the perfect silence that had encapsulated her. Helen jumped, guiltily, at the note of panic and dialed the volume down. Around her the vaguely colored walls of the bubble pulsed in time, as if the sound waves from Ivester's voice were passing through.

"I'm here. I'm still here," she replied, a little more slowly than she would have liked. Her tongue felt thick, dry, like she'd been sleeping with her mouth open.

Bleedthrough, she realized. The Scale she was riding didn't have lungs, or a tongue, so she was getting bleedthrough from her own body back in the coffin.

"What the hell was that? Did it work?" Ivester's voice again.

"I'm getting bleedthrough on this end," Helen replied. "Can you guys fix that? I might be out here for a bit longer."

"On it. Then tell me what's going on."

Helen now had full control back. She stretched her arms and legs, watching the information come through to be translated by Insight and sent back down the line to the coffin.

"Guys, you need to air-gap the coffin. We don't want James or any of the other house computers hooked up directly right now."

"Why? What the hell is going on out there?" Dougal's voice now, he must have swapped in for Ivester.

"I cut Beauchamp off from the Scale, so they're not attacking our eenies anymore. They've gone back to the same 'eat and rebuild' loop they were on when we first connected with the Golfball. Our eenies are on the offensive for now, but we might want to call them off." Helen asked the Insight to bring up a binary translator. Something that could turn a string of ones and zeroes into something she might be able to use for conversation. "I think we've bought some breathing room."

All around Helen, jelly-like clusters of the tiniest Scale had begun to come together into strings of abstracted ones and zeroes.

"Guys, I can't read that off the cuff, you're going to have to give me a few . . ." Helen said out loud to the room, more for her own benefit than the Scale. She felt back on her game now. The idea that the Scale might be something more than a space-going ant, that Ivester might just be right about a first contact scenario, was exhilarating. She opened the lenses as far as possible, found the gap that suggested the start of the string of numbers, and began sending images back down the line to Ivester and Dougal.

"Can't read what? And what in the hell is THAT?" Ivester was back online again.

"That . . ." Helen fired her tiny maneuvering jets to follow the string as it continued to develop, making sure she caught each number in the sequence as it gelled out of the air. "That may just be the first contact you were hoping for."

"You're talking to them?" This from Dougal again; they were playing hot-mic back in the lab, but this time Helen couldn't care less.

"When I cut off Beauchamp's influence, they got a lot less bitey. It looks like they're suggesting we start with some kind of binary language, so this is what we are getting to work with right now."

"What happened to Beauchamp?" Dougal asked sharply.

"I took back the particle. I don't know what that looked like in her coffin, but I bet she was pretty pissed about it." Helen finished collecting the message. She'd have to wait a bit to be sure all the images made it down the line before jumping out. It meant she could spend some time getting to know the Scale a little bit better.

"Okay, stay there for now, give us everything you can. I'm going to grab Hofstaeder to see if we can fix the feedback problem," Ivester said.

"No problem. The Scale are just waiting on something, maybe a response to whatever that string of numbers says." The eenie she was waldoing remained eager to please. It was delighted that a connection had been made, but she couldn't quite understand why. There was no pushback, no real mind outside of some core programming. Nothing to fight, no siblings to talk to, no sense of being part of a greater whole. It was a little lonely. Helen hadn't noticed sooner because being alone was a much more natural state for her. Now that she noticed, and compared to her earlier time with the Scale and even the eenies, the lack was clear.

"Oh. I've been air-gapped."

The Scale had captured this eenie without destroying it. She'd been cut out from the rest of her network. Without sibs to talk to, to give commands to, she was just a single mote of dust. No influence, not a threat. Her only hope, if she needed to pick up the fight again, was to disentangle and hope the OP particles had ended up somewhere good.

"If they can do this, why didn't they just isolate Beauchamp?" she wondered aloud. "Why let her run the show?"

"Oh, that's simple enough. Cat was always much further up the command chain," Dougal said matter-of-factly in her ear.

"Makes sense, I suppose, but now that we've cut that particle loose, she's going to have a hard time using it from here on out."

"I'm sure she's got a few Scale left. They'll recapture it soon enough."

"Wait . . ." Realization dawned just a little too slowly. "How do you know anything about Beauchamp's Scale?"

"There's a funny story behind that," Dougal said smugly. "Time to come back."

The disentangle caught Helen by surprise and she was yanked, unceremoniously, back though a billion miles of space.

CHAPTER THIRTY-TWO

HELEN OPENED HER EYES, then closed them again, seeking the comfort of the Insight behind her eyelids. The lines and lights failed to materialize. She was alone in her own head. No Scale, no Insight, no NAV particle.

That's not right at all.

"Helen?"

She opened her eyes again, staring at the depths of the Recovr lab ceiling. The sides of the coffin had been folded up, wires removed so she was back inside a self-contained unit. She cast about with her eyes, the only other part she could move, to find Dougal smiling down at her.

"Dougal, what are you up to? Where's Ivester?"

"I sent him to get the doc, which means now I'm on a time limit."

Helen tried to move and found her limbs still restrained by the supersuit. It could take hours for everything to wear off unless she could get to the coffin controls. Dougal hadn't bothered with the buffer. Her brain hurt, her body hurt, phantom pains of being pulled apart again and again. She could feel where every limb had been severed in the push to stop Beauchamp, dozens of phantom arms up and down her ribcage. Somewhere in the back of her head she could hear screaming. She wasn't sure if it was hers.

Damn, if the drugs are still in effect, I shouldn't feel anything. But that didn't count with phantom pain, nerves firing without any actual physical cause. It was distracting, even more so because she knew there was no recourse, just time.

"Why Hofstaeder?" In the corner of her vision, the lights of the Insight began to emerge, a "reboot" icon flashing as the entanglement system tried to right itself.

"Oh, that's easy. The system will show a call went out, I made my best effort, but Doc got here too late to save you."

To save?

"Cat thought you might cause her some trouble out there." Dougal moved closer to the tangle of wires and tubes from the coffin, voice lowered. "And logging in through the NAV particle, that really was a risk, don't you think? I mean, first Ted, then Mira, and now you. There's no way Far Reaches is going to keep this project on the books. Beyond Blue's already putting together the paperwork."

It took a few moments for Helen's brain to catch up.

Oh shit. Dougal's working with Beauchamp.

"Dougal, I don't know what you're thinking, but don't do anything foolish." The phrase sounded stupid as it left her lips. Dougal's eagerness to join the Recovr team, his quiet defense of Beauchamp, his insistence on trying every other theory before recognizing the Scale. Helen had been focusing on just one adversary. She hadn't counted on lingering loyalties. Beauchamp hadn't quite cut all ties at Far Reaches. Helen fought down the rising tide of panic as the understanding that she was alone, paralyzed, and defenseless set in.

"Dougal, you helped me cut off Beauchamp's communications with the Scale. It worked, I made contact." Helen's mind raced. Her only hope was to keep the analyst talking, keep him engaged until . . .

Until what, Ivester gets back? One of the other techs wanders in?

"That was an unfortunate risk. Ivester wouldn't let me touch the programming, so I had to rely on Cat to be a better waldo-jockey than you. That's not a mistake I want to repeat. Beyond Blue will be handling all contact with the Scale from here on out."

"And me?" Helen cast about for questions to ask, anything that would allow her to keep Dougal occupied for just one more minute.

"You? You will suffer a catastrophic equipment failure, simple enough. Experimental setup, known problems with the entanglement Feed. I'm afraid you're going to have to sit there and feel it all while I fry your nervous system."

"Why? What's the point?" Helen asked, as calmly as she could. In the bottom corner of her vision, the Insight reboot icon vanished and the loading sequence began. If she could just keep Dougal from doing anything fatal until she got control of the coffin computer again . . .

"The Scale are coming, Helen. Beyond Blue has a plan to handle them." Dougal unplugged one of the fat ropes of cable from the side of the coffin and checked the contacts before returning it to its socket.

"Dammit, Dougal, we don't even have a handle on what the Scale ARE."

"You don't. We do."

"YOU? You mean Beyond Blue? What, you think you can handle some kind of alien invasion all by your lonesome?" *Keep him talking.* The Insight lit up and Helen tried to connect to the coffin, but whatever Dougal had been doing kept it offline. *Shit. Okay, call for help.* She reached out, found the link to Recovr's communications system and connected, only to find herself blocked.

"Of course we are. Once we control the jumpgate, we control the access. We can choose when and where they come through. We can even dictate when and where they land first. Anyone that wants to escape being overrun will have to cut a deal with us."

Helen's blood ran cold. "Deal with you? That's just evil." Helen cast about inside the Insight, looking for other opportunities: fire alarms and warning systems were cut off, she was blocked from accessing Ivester's touchwall, maintenance systems . . . *MAINTENANCE SYSTEMS.*

Like every room at Far Reaches, things like the maintenance of the surfaces or the trash disposal were all handled by a wide array of eenies. Every one had a direct link to James, who controlled everything in the building from door locks to vending machines. If Helen could get access to the maintenance system, she might be able to get a message out.

"Oh, don't worry, we're not going to let them overrun the planet. We'll keep them pointed at the orbital resource platforms, the lunar bases. Distant Sun's going to be parking a comet in orbit next year, so that goes on the list of things we want."

Helen's fingers and toes began to tingle. The paralytic, the spinal block that kept her body from thumping about in the coffin while her mind was a billion miles away, was starting to wear thin. It wasn't going to be quick enough. Helen reached out to Far Reaches' maintenance eenies through the Insight and kicked in the "Catastrophic Overrun" protocol Ivester had given her to deal with the Scale. She wouldn't be able to waldo them, not without a quantum particle, but she could use them to cause some chaos. The security warnings began to cascade outward through the system, opening up new avenues, unlocking the millions of little nano-machines that lay sleeping in the rafters, under the floors, deep in the trash cans.

An Operator, any Operator, was far from defenseless once they got their coffin connected into a computer system.

The reaction was immediate, starting with a series of sharp *thunks* and a sudden tightness in the air as the Recovr lab sealed itself off from the rest of the building. The fire-suppression robots unlocked from their cubicles in the corners of the room, three child-sized tanks on treads, ready to cover anything too hot in retardant foam. They were programmed to avoid anything that registered as living. Live bodies were a job for the human emergency responders Helen hoped would be on the way.

"What the hell did you do?" Dougal was immediately on the defensive, stepping back from the coffin, which suited Helen just fine. The lights in the room dimmed, shifting from workday yellow to watch-your-ass red. In the shifting colors, the tattoos across his skin seemed to crawl and twist, an eerie callback to the corrupted waveform Helen had first seen laid out in the Analysis lab.

Helen started laughing as she realized that the maintenance robots thought she was the only human in the room. Dougal had done her a favor. He'd made himself invisible to Far Reaches security cameras, showing up as an inanimate object, a piece of lab equipment. It must have been the same trick he and Beauchamp pulled when they'd poisoned Helen's coffin the first time.

It meant that the fire-suppression robots wouldn't have any reason to treat him as anything other than a hazard.

Helen waded into the computer system and took control of the largest of the maintenance robots. It wasn't a waldo; she couldn't simply slide it on like a glove and wiggle her fingers, but she could point it at Dougal and convince it that the analyst really, truly was on fire.

"Waldoing the maintenance robots? I should have killed you faster." Dougal did the math and stepped up, throwing switches on the side of the coffin. Helen hasn't about to correct him. Helen wasn't about to tell him that, by stepping forward toward the coffin, where Helen was still recognized as a living, breathing body, he'd triggered the emergency response. Maintenance saw Dougal as a bit of flaming lab equipment rolling towards an incapacitated human.

The wall of flame-retardant foam that hit Dougal knocked him backwards onto his ass. While Helen directed the largest robot over to the coffin, placing it between Dougal and whatever switches he might start messing with, the other two robots joined in, keeping their streams directed on his thrashing form. Dougal spluttered, shielding his face with one upraised arm as the force of the jets slid him backward on a concrete floor now gone slick. When he hit the edge of the mats, close to Ivester's touchwall, he managed to get his feet under him again. The robots backed off. Now that he was well away from the lab's only "living" occupant, he was no longer an immediate threat. No amount of prodding by Helen could convince them to continue the pursuit.

Shit. Hurry up. Hurryup. Hurryup . . .

Helen's fingers regained some feeling and she worked them frantically, trying to restore muscle control a little bit faster. She was still bound in the supersuit, but if she could reach the manual release, she'd have a chance at actually defending herself.

"Fine." Dougal spat the word. He engaged the touchwall, opening up the software to bring Helen's coffin back online so he could access the computer. "I'll kill you from here."

Helen got control of her fingers and used them to pull her hand, her arm along. The neoprene of her suit, the stickiness of the gel padding in the coffin, meant each motion was in millimeters, the weight of her own nerveless arms holding them in place. It wasn't going to work, she wasn't going to be free in time, and whatever Dougal was planning to do to her through the coffin's interface was going to be the absolute end of her.

Dougal coughed. He'd sucked in a lungful of fire-retardant foam when Helen had blasted him.

Too bad that shit's not poisonous.

Somewhere, down beneath the rising fear and frustration, an idea took hold. The chemicals might not be poisonous, but they were laced with eenies, units to handle the cleanup once the all-clear had been given. They'd resurface and repair anything splashed with the foam. They weren't designed to work on living beings; they were built to clean up concrete floors and transparent aluminum displays.

And Dougal had made himself look just like a piece of lab equipment.

Helen gave the Maintenance system the "all-clear."

A series of thuds told Helen that the lockdown had been released, doors and vents opened to let emergency responders in. The door was kicked open, and Helen could hear the rush of bodies and chatter of commands, but she couldn't see them from her coffin.

"LOCK THIS ROOM DOWN." Helen didn't recognize the voice, but she recognized the tone.

Someone's taking over.

Dougal coughed again, and this time, bright red blood spattered the touchwall. His eyes widened, and he put a hand to his lips, disbelieving.

"What . . ." The paroxysm wracked his frame as the fire-retardant eenies he'd inhaled resurfaced the inside of his lungs like they would a concrete floor, destroying alveoli, turning the sensitive cell membranes into feedstock as they went. Dougal made an attempt to take Helen with him, pawing at the commands on the touchwall to no avail. He collapsed, clutching at his chest, a horrible wheezing sound the only communication he had left.

"Helen? Dougal?" Ivester's voice was full of questions.

"Medic!" Hofstaeder read the room faster. She rushed to Dougal's side, dragging a first responder in her wake. Helen couldn't hear what they were saying, but she could see Dougal's hand pointing a bloody finger in Helen's direction before collapsing back. "Someone get a call into County Medical."

No. That's where Ted died.

CHAPTER THIRTY-THREE

"JUST WHERE THE HELL IS HOFSTAEDER?"

The walls of the hospital room were not painted in Hofstaeder's signature, calming pink. Pale greens and blues dominated the space instead, giving a sense of clinical efficiency. Cold, calculating, the room was strangely empty of the usual collection of medical machines and monitors. It felt more like a quarantine than a recovery room.

Even the Scale-space was warmer than this.

"Doctor Hofstaeder is Far Reaches' private medical personnel. She has no jurisdiction here," the nurse replied tartly.

Helen didn't like her, but she couldn't put her finger on why. Something in the way she looked around Helen, rather than directly at her. She was the first person Helen had seen since waking up from a nightmare filled with angry sand and the unendurable quantum scream of a wind she couldn't feel.

"So I got pushed to County?" Helen asked the next reasonable question.

The nurse smiled, lips pressed into a line, a gesture as clinical as the rest of the room. "All your questions will be answered when the doctor on call comes in." She was a slight woman, pale green scrubs casting her golden skin a couple shades darker than her hair.

"And who's that?" Helen eyed her cautiously as she took a medical tablet out of her scrubs pocket and fished a cable out from the foot of the bed. The gesture was odd, most medical gear was wireless, secure, easy to clean and easy to store. With a quick snap, she plugged the tablet in and started collecting information.

Helen was used to the constant whispers of Far Reaches. Even the public spaces had wireless communications that pinged and passed feedback to her Insight. The silence in the air started to creep in.

Different hospitals, different tech.

But this was County. As a government-owned facility, it worked with bleeding-edge medical technology. This was where they had brought Ted.

This is where Ted died.

"Captain Marshall and Attaché Ravennis will be in to check on you later today."

Shit.

"Attaché" meant XERMo had stepped in, *or stomped in.* Ivester must have finally told the board what they'd been up to. Or perhaps Dougal had leaked something in his attempt to let Beauchamp keep control. Helen took a deep breath, let it out slowly.

"So do you work for County or XERMo?" Helen asked the next logical question. There it was: a flinch, a tightening of the shoulders. *Watch for body language,* Ted used to say. *That tells you what people are really feeling.*

"All questions . . ."

Helen waved off the canned response. "Will be answered later, I got it." Without access to Insight, she was cut off, unable to get a look at where she was from the outside. She had been isolated. Quarantine was looking more and more likely.

Don't panic. Panic never helps.

She needed to figure out what they were thinking. She needed more information if she was going to build a checklist to get herself out of this.

"Can you at least tell me how long I've been here?" Helen shifted in the bed, felt the connections along her spine pinch. Unlike the coffin-kluge Hofstaeder had used to save her before, this hospital had swapped out her neoprene supersuit for the medical variety. It meant they had access to her nutrient drips, the drug delivery ports, all the interfaces she used to connect to a coffin. But without the coffin computers, without her Insight, Helen had no way of taking those back.

"All questions . . ." the nurse began.

"Ugh, you've *got* to be XERMo." It was another bit of information that Helen could work with. XERMo had rules, very specific ways of doing things. She just needed to dial in.

But if XERMo had been called in, things must have gone from bad to worse.

"Can you tell me what happened to Dougal?" Helen didn't want to think about it. Didn't want to think about the damage the eenies had done, of what they would have done to his lungs, his skin.

What you *did*, she reminded herself unkindly. *That's why you're here, right? Not because County has better care, better doctors.*

The fact that it had been self-defense seemed unimportant.

The nurse blanched at the question, golden skin going pale. She popped the cable out of the tablet and let it clatter on the floor, rather than putting it away.

Oh shit. She's nervous.

Helen saw it now. The nurse had been staying well out of arm's reach, keeping the tablet at the full stretch of the data cable, not getting any closer than she needed to.

So what the hell is going on?

"You know the answer to that." The nurse stepped back, pocketing the tablet. "All your questions will be answered when the doctors get here."

"Look . . ." Helen fished around, looking for a name tag or other identifier in order to make a connection. "I'll take anything you can give me. I'm alone in here, there's not even a screen to watch the newscasts. I'm stuck in a bed. I have no idea why Hofstaeder transferred me here or if anyone on my team was hurt."

The nurse paused, considering, one hand on the door handle.

"I'll see what I can do, but no promises, okay? We're on orders to make minimal contact until you get debriefed."

Helen spread her hands in a gesture of acceptance. "I'll take anything. Thank you."

As the nurse slipped out of the room, Helen got a glimpse of someone in a uniform outside. It was uncomfortably familiar.

Except this time there's no Keller to find you.

She tested that thought, turned it around in her head, measured her distance from it. She'd grown used to the painful reminders of Ted's loss, of Keller's murder. The way they stung and then passed on. This was different. There was nothing. The idea fell quietly into empty space.

This was familiar too.

While an Operator, any Operator, was far from helpless when connected to a coffin, Helen had been carefully cut off from anything that might allow her to act, even from her own emotions. That was something even Hofstaeder did lightly.

Helen closed her eyes and walked back through the last of her memories. Dougal's accusing finger, Hofstaeder taking charge. Getting out of the coffin had been a challenge, since Dougal had already fried some of the hardware, so the only solution had been a manual disconnect. Hofstaeder had knocked her out for that, officially because it was safer, but Helen could read the anger in the line of her jaw. Ivester, she hadn't caught a glimpse of, but there had been panic in his voice. The idea that she had simply straight-out murdered her colleague should have been more distressing, but whatever they had her on took the edge off that too.

The knock on the door broke her focus.

That was fast.

The two who entered where both definitely XERMo. A tall, dark-haired man in the lightweight daily-wear uniform Helen had become familiar with in the early days of the Golfball's launch had to be the attaché. The woman Helen recognized. She'd been working with Hofstaeder to upgrade the coffins. The pale green scrubs were new, and her Captain's bars were missing. Oddly enough, uniform guy was the one with the smile: bright white teeth and brownish skin that should have put Helen painfully in mind of Keller. That alone was enough to put Helen on her guard, "no-care" drug cocktail be damned.

"Operator Helena Vectorovich, nice to see you awake." The smiling attaché spoke first. He was new; when Helen had first connected to the Golfball, Dr. Tate had been the liaison between Far Reaches and XERMo. The captain faded back, her eyes on the medical tablet she'd brought in.

"I'm Ani Ravennis, Senior Attaché between XERMo and Far Reaches, and this here is Captain Jira Marshall. She's been assigned to head up your personal care team during your stay here at County. We're looking to get you healthy and back to work just as quickly as we can."

"What happened to Tate?"

The professionalism of the smile never wavered. "He continued on with the rest of Line Drive when the Golfball portion of the mission was decommissioned. I've been assigned to handle this new, and surprising, turn of events."

Helen eyed them both, weighing her next words. There was a process here, a checklist she could execute to get out as quickly and smoothly as possible. The presence of the attaché meant there was something official going on. She just had to get a handle on all the details.

"Nice to meet you both," she said perfunctorily. Helen turned her attention to the captain, who was still paying more attention to the information on her medical tablet than to either Helen or Ravennis. "Excuse me, Captain Marshall, can you give me a quick rundown on what you've dosed me with since I've been in your care?"

The two officers exchanged a glance like they'd been caught at something.

"All in good time." Ravennis redirected the conversation like he did so all the time. "We need to go over just what happened in the Recovr lab while it's still fresh in your mind."

"The lab security cameras and coffin logs should tell you everything you need far more accurately than I can," Helen replied. "Without knowing what Captain Marshall's been giving me, I can't be sure I'll be accurate." With no idea where Ivester or Hofstaeder were or what the status of the connection to the Scale was, Helen chose to play it close to the vest. Holes in an Operator's memory were a well-known problem after a bad drop-out, and she'd had more than her fair share of those recently. She could keep them at arms-length for a little while, at least.

They exchanged another look.

"Whatever you can give us will be just fine, I'm sure." Ravennis pressed on, throwing up more red flags.

"Of course. Once my advocate arrives, we can put something on paper for you." Talking to Hofstaeder, being debriefed by Ivester and the Far Reaches team, those were all par for the course because she *worked* for Far Reaches; there were binding, career-crushing contracts involved. Keller's reminder that she needed to negotiate better, that she needed to make better use of her advocates came to mind.

"Well, Miss Vectorovich, we're just trying to get an overview of events, nothing official, nothing binding."

"I'm under contract. I can't say anything without my union advocate present. You know how it is, I'm sure."

Helen caught the hint of a smirk on Captain Marshall's lips. She knew better, at least. A flash of irritation crossed Ravennis' face, gone as quickly as it appeared.

"Of course. Let me go check on their arrival time. I'll be back in a moment."

Captain Marshall watched him go, then tugged on the door handle to be sure it had closed completely.

"Well, now that's out of the way, let's talk about your after-care," she said briskly.

"After-care? What exactly happened? I had a bad drop-out, that's all."

"What I know, medically, is that something went wrong with your coffin software. You narrowly missed having your nervous system burned out," Marshall explained. "We think it's part and parcel with whatever short caused the maintenance systems to go haywire."

"Haywire?" Helen didn't correct her, didn't offer up any new information. She wasn't sure how to approach what she had done to Dougal, so she kept her mouth shut. "What happened to Dougal?"

Marshall pursed her lips. "I don't have that information. He was transferred to a different medical facility."

"Different? Which one?"

"Sorry, I don't have any of that information. Now, let's talk about your recovery."

CHAPTER THIRTY-FOUR

"SHE'S NOT ALLOWED to talk about that. Terms of contract." Helen's advocate had his nose buried in a checklist of items that XERMo wanted answers to. She'd forgotten his name again. He was an average man in an average suit with an unflappable demeanor that Ravennis seemed genuinely stymied by. Helen got the impression that he had faced down bigger bears than XERMo and that this barely rose to the level of "remarkable" in his career memoir.

XERMo had filled out her tiny room with a table and three folding chairs. They'd been brought in at the beginning of the session and would be folded up and taken out again at the end.

They hadn't allowed her out of the quarantine room without an escort. They had finally allowed her out of the bed after the advocate had argued it was no longer necessary and could be considered unlawful restraint, if it turned out that her recovery was, in fact, progressing quickly. Books and other entertainments had started showing up, but no screens, nothing with an outside connection. Helen remained isolated from outside contact. The doctor should have made the call to release her, but in quiet conversation, Helen had managed to tease out that her recovery was supposed to be as slow and complete as necessary.

They didn't want to let her go.

"XERMo has an ongoing contract with Far Reaches regarding the Line Drive mission and all its offshoots," Ravennis tried to argue in that same reasonable tone he'd been using for days. The man's feathers never got ruffled; he never seemed to get upset or angry. He was an implacable wall of authority and uniform. Helen went out of her way to get under his skin, to no observable effect. Their impasse had stretched on for days now.

"Those rights were signed away when XERMo agreed to allow Far Reaches to scrap the Golfball portion of the mission and prep it for sale."

"That was before this . . ." Ravennis waggled his fingers, searching for a word . . . "glitch turned out to be something bigger. There is an exigent circumstances clause in all our contracts . . ."

"Which you have been unable to prove."

"Because your client refuses to cooperate."

"Because my client refuses to throw away her contract, her seniority, and her career to help you do your job." Helen's advocate barely even glanced up from his tablet. "Once you prove exigent circumstances, we can have a different conversation."

Helen relaxed back in the chair they'd provided, ankles crossed, arms folded across her chest. There was nothing for her to do except glower at Ravennis until she got the go-ahead to answer a question.

"Fine. Let's move this along and start with any questions that aren't restricted," Ravennis conceded gracefully.

Helen was sure he was simply taking another tack, trying to see what he could get her talking about to then pull the conversation sideways. She'd seen the tactic years ago, when she and Ted had been called on the carpet for Ferguson's Asteroid. Ravennis seemed to have graduated from the same school of negotiation. Ted had watched carefully, explained to Helen what he saw. It was surprising how transparent it was once you understood what you were looking at.

"Excellent." The advocate pushed a sheet of paper across the desk to his counterpart. "Ms. Vectorovich has given written responses to the following questions and we have vetted them to be sure the contents are within the guidelines."

Ravennis took the page and pushed his chair back, getting to his feet to pace the room as he read. Her advocate threw her a glance, a warning to stick to the script they'd already discussed.

"So, Ms. Vectorovich. It says here that you joined the team at Recovr after you were taken ill in a coffin-related accident, is that accurate?"

"That is accurate," Helen replied shortly, using as few words as she could.

"And your Doctor Hofstaeder cleared you to return to active duty before you joined Recovr?" Ravennis didn't look up from the page. He seemed to be reading and re-reading the answers, looking for holes, places he could force an opening.

"That is accurate," Helen replied again.

"And at the time you were unaware that there was an existing relationship between Catherine Beauchamp and Dougal Monroe."

Helen hesitated. She knew that Beauchamp had tried to go over Keller's head to get assigned to the Golfball recovery mission, that she had contacted Dougal directly. She didn't know if that counted as an "existing relationship."

Her advocate gave her the nod and she collected her thoughts. "I knew there was a working relationship."

"But nothing further?"

"Nothing that I was aware of."

"This was the incident that prompted the decommission of the Golfball component of Line Drive." It wasn't a question, so Helen gave no reply. "Catherine Beauchamp was believed to be at least partly responsible for that incident, is that correct?"

"As I understand it, yes."

"And now it is understood that Dougal may have assisted her in that task?"

"I don't know." The line of questioning had shifted, Helen saw it. A quick glance at her advocate suggested he saw it too, but he nodded for her to continue on.

"Don't know? But the video and data logs show a very similar set of circumstances taking place before the accident that brought you here."

"I haven't seen either the video or the logs," Helen answered truthfully.

"But you're the one who suggested that those logs held the truth."

"I suggested you check because I had just regained consciousness. I didn't want to give you bad information."

"So you directed us at the logs to keep us on track."

"A bad drop-out can cause memory issues."

"But you didn't have a bad drop-out. The logs clearly show a controlled return."

Shit.

"Would it interest you know that the logs and the recordings had been tampered with?"

Her advocate took notice, shook his head at her ever so slightly. Ravennis continued his uneven pacing. It was starting to wear on her nerves.

"How do you mean?"

"Forensics found software running that kept Dougal from being recognized as a living entity by the maintenance and fire-fighting systems."

"That seems strange." Helen already knew about Dougal's trick; she'd taken advantage of it to unleash the eenies on him. A sick feeling twisted in her gut, but as Ravennis continued to sketch the outlines of a larger industrial espionage theory, she refused to allow herself any sympathy for either Beauchamp or Dougal.

"It is strange. It's also telling that the same software was used to conceal whoever accessed your coffin software in the earlier incident, the one that resulted in the spinning off of the Golfball from Line Drive."

Her advocate got to his feet. "Ms. Vectorovich is hardly qualified to analyze two separate incidents in which she, for all intents and purposes, was the aggrieved party."

"Fair enough," Ravennis conceded. "But that does go towards my next point. If these two incidents are so closely linked, then we are looking at a single case of industrial sabotage that began while the Golfball was still under our jurisdiction on Line Drive and continued through the activities at the Recovr lab."

"So?" Helen couldn't help herself. It seemed a harmless enough response, but it gave Ravennis a springboard from which to drive his point home.

"So. Exigent circumstances. XERMo still has the right to access all of Recovr's information under the terms of the original Line Drive agreement."

Oh shit.

Her advocate shuffled his papers together and swept them into his binder in one swift motion, cutting Ravennis off. "I believe this now requires the opinion of our legal team."

"So, Ms. Vectorovich, do you know if Dougal was after the connection to the alien organism out on the Golfball all along? Or was that just a bonus once they'd pried the Golfball free from Line Drive?"

"How the hell would I know that? Go ask Dougal."

A line of worry sketched itself across Ravennis' forehead, very brief, very fast. *They don't have Dougal.* The realization was like a blow. If Beauchamp and Dougal were still able to act, if Beyond Blue was protecting them, then everything was still at risk.

"That's enough, Ms. Vectorovich," her advocate warned.

"I presume you know *something.* You were the one who turned on the fire suppression system in the first place." Ravennis directed his gaze directly at Helen. Helen met it without blinking, despite the stab of guilt. She wasn't sure why they were keeping her isolated, but she was absolutely sure that she'd done what she had to in order to stay alive. She wasn't about to let anyone get any traction on that point.

"Not another word from either of you." The advocate stepped between Helen and the attaché. "We can start again after legal brings us their assessment."

CHAPTER THIRTY-FIVE

IT WAS JUST OVER TWO WEEKS before Helen finally returned to Re-covr—two weeks of enforced downtime and a series of interviews with XERMo that never seemed to go anywhere but circles. They knew about the Scale, that was clear, but Helen couldn't get a handle on who had told them or what they were planning to do about it. She was unable to contact or connect with Ivester or Hofstaeder, and the feeling of being shut out began to rattle around inside her head, trying to find a place to stick tight. Helen was cut off as completely as they could keep her.

Her union advocate continued to argue that keeping her under quarantine conditions was inhumane, but XERMo just quoted laws and statutes and ignored her advocate. In turn, Helen crushed her guilt about Dougal and allowed them to chase the "industrial accident" line of reasoning. She was under no obligation to compromise herself, employers be damned.

Helen had been assigned a new XERMo doctor after Marshall had been too kind. The new captain was an unsmiling woman with an unsmiling manner who failed, repeatedly, to keep Helen locked out of XERMo's network, thanks to the tablet that Marshall had loaned Helen for personal use. Helen had been able to watch, helplessly, as Catherine Beauchamp vanished into the wind and Beyond Blue closed ranks around her. Both sides committed legal teams to what was shaping up to be an epic fight and XERMo was squarely in the middle, trying to get their hands on every piece of tech that had even come in contact with the Scale.

After completing every list and checking off every one of XER-Mo's boxes, when Helen finally stepped back through Recovr's doors, she found it empty, the coffin completely disassembled and spread in parts across the lab.

"What the hell?" she asked, half to herself, half to the empty room. She opened up her Insight, checked to see if there were any messages, any information. She had gone directly from the hospital at County to the Far Reaches campus simply to reconnect with James, to get her Insight access back. The Far Reaches AI informed her that neither Hofstaeder nor Ivester were available or on the Far Reaches campus at all, so she'd headed to the lab to see what was left.

"We have a problem." Ivester's voice sounded in the air. Helen looked around the room, using the Insight to locate the source.

Office, of course. She nudged the half-open door with a foot, peeked inside. The man himself was seated on the floor, making adjustments to some piece of hardware. The desk surface was covered with a dozen or so of the coffin's drives and other internal parts, all in varying states of disassembly.

"What kind of problem?" Helen asked. "And why does James think you're off-site?" She entered the room slowly, a little suspiciously. Ivester's normally pale skin tone had picked up an undercurrent of grey, the kind that meant not enough sleep and probably not enough anything else, either.

"I'm hiding. So's Hofstaeder, at least for a couple days."

"Isn't this a bit obvious as a hiding place?" Helen closed the door behind her and moved to the desk, shoving the coffin parts out of the way so she'd have a place to sit. "Anyone who knows you is going to look here first."

"James has informed the authorities that I'm out of the country in Tuyen for the next week. They're probably going to try to arrest me when I show up at the airport coming back."

"ARREST? What did I miss while I was out?"

"We managed to extract that communication from the images you sent back. It was, in fact, an offer to open a dialogue."

He paused while he tried to press a circuit board back into place.

"But there was a bit of bad code couched inside." Ivester gave her a rueful grin. "So it seems the question of whether the Scale are friendly or not still remains to be answered."

Helen remained silent, waiting on the rest of the explanation. It was coming. Ivester got to his feet, dropping the part he'd been adjusting onto the desk with its sibs.

"What this means, however, is that I had to let XERMo back in, despite your best efforts. We had to get through to Beyond Blue to get a crack at those missing NAV particles and we have to figure out how the hell we reboot a first contact situation."

"And now they're going to arrest you?" Helen asked, disbelievingly. "That's a bit of an asshole move."

"Well, they're a bit pissed that we did an end run around them in the first place."

"And that's why the coffin's in a thousand pieces?"

"Well, as of now, you are the only person we know of to ever successfully waldo an alien life form. I'm trying to figure out just how that happened."

"Before they arrest you," Helen repeated.

It didn't seem fair. They had done their best, their level best, to manage crazy circumstances. Dougal's betrayal had blindsided them all. Despite surviving his horrific encounter with the maintenance eenies, the rogue analyst was now wanted for poisoning Helen's coffin. Twice. Beyond Blue still had the NAV particle from Myrian but were denying everything. Catherine Beauchamp had been quietly spirited away to some kind of corporate-run recovery program before the authorities could even think about questioning her. The idea that her rival was taking advantage of some cushy corporate getaway set Helen's teeth on edge, but she'd been far too busy to pursue any kind of revenge just yet.

"Well, I may have been exaggerating a bit, or at least I hope I am. The point is, I can't find anything unique in the coffin hardware or software that would let you make a connection like that."

"I'm not sure I follow."

"If I'm right, and forgive me if I hope I'm not, but if I am, then it looks like you might be the only person we have that can talk to the Scale."

"But Cat—"

"Catherine Beauchamp was communicating with the Scale, yes, but that was just delivering commands. I've had James dig through the data you brought back, and she wasn't doing what you were doing. Dougal might know something, but he's under arrest right now and not saying anything to anybody."

"You've been busy." In her mind's eye, Helen went back over the moments when she connected to the Scale, trying to remember if she'd tried anything different, done anything unusual.

"The point is, XERMo's going to need you too. I'm trying to keep the team intact. I want us to be the core of any diplomatic group that XERMo puts together to meet with the Scale. Are you in?"

Helen spent a long minute considering, but really, there was only one answer.

"I'm going to need a raise."